"It's high noon on the high seas!"
                    —Publishers Weekly

GILLESPIE: The submarine's second-in-command—with mutiny and treason only the beginning of his doomsday plan.

SOMMERVILLE: The Secretary of Defense —ready and eager for nuclear war.

ANDERSON: A peace-loving Admiral with wife problems—and the one man who could prevent world destruction.

SWEPT UP IN A SUPERCHARGED CONSPIRACY THAT MELTED THE HOT LINE BETWEEN WASHINGTON AND MOSCOW

"A nail-biter!"—Chicago Daily News
"A hair-raiser!"—The Oakland Tribune
"Breathstopping"—Booklist
"Tense!"—St. Louis Post Dispatch

NORTH STAR CRUSADE

William Katz

A JOVE/HBJ BOOK

NORTH STAR CRUSADE

First Jove/HBJ edition published December 1977

Library of Congress Catalog Card Number: 74-16619

Printed in the United States of America

Jove/HBJ books are published by Jove Publications, Inc.
(Harcourt Brace Jovanovich) 757 Third Avenue, New York,
N.Y. 10017

For Jane, Sharon, and Abigail

Author's Note

The author wishes to express his appreciation to
    Peter Lampack, an extraordinary literary agent,
who guided this book from its inception;
    Clyde C. Taylor of G. P. Putnam's Sons, for his
thoughtful editing, invaluable suggestions, and
splendid cooperation;
    and Jane Katz, for her meticulous review of
each draft of the manuscript and her incisive
editorial comments.

Part I

1

Two days out of Groton and 803 miles into the Atlantic, Captain Alan K. Lansing stared at the depth gauge of his final command, the missile submarine *John Hay*. When the cruise ended, his career would be over.

Butterflies flew around inside his stomach as he slowly gazed around his ship's control room. This was home, and he wondered what would happen to him when he finally left it.

There were the usual concerns, too—perhaps exaggerated because this was his last cruise. The list ran the gamut of a submarine commander's nightmares—radiation leak, explosion in one of the Polaris missiles, collision under the sea, collapse of the ship's hull.

But now he yawned, glanced down at his new Rolex watch, a fortieth-birthday gift from his wife. In ten minutes his executive officer would relieve him.

Lieutenant Commander Richard Gillespie lay in his berth, his blue eyes half open. Unable to sleep, he stretched and then turned toward a ship's clock. In eight minutes he would get up and relieve Captain Lansing. As he lay back on his foam-rubber mattress, Gillespie felt the same pangs in his gut that Lansing felt. For Lansing they signaled an end. For Gillespie a beginning.

Two minutes later he dug under the mattress and fingered the .45-caliber pistol. He swung out of bed and shoved the weapon into his blue Dacron submariner's suit. Then, picking up a thin leather attaché case, he opened the bulkhead and stepped out to the passageway.

Captain Vladimir Sverdlov was disgusted. He was a distant relative of the Soviet Navy's revered Admiral Sverdlov, and that alone should have assured him a better fate. It had not, and so at forty-six he could only try gracefully to accept his minor command, the destroyer *Dostoyny,* now on patrol duty in the western Atlantic. His ship was a recent type, known in the United States as the Krivak class. She carried surface-to-surface and antiaircraft missiles, antisubmarine rockets, torpedoes, and conventional guns.

The *Dostoyny* was assigned to monitor American submarine activity and to test new submarine-detection sonars. A sister ship, the *Svirepy,* cruised five miles away. The most interesting activity during these patrols was the overflights by instrument-crammed American reconnaissance planes. Sverdlov couldn't understand why the Americans took so many pictures of the *Dostoyny* when there were detailed photographs in *Jane's Fighting Ships.* One time he flashed a message to an Orion patrol bomber saying that he would send the Pentagon a full-color set of eight-by-tens if they would send him an Instamatic.

As Gillespie walked slowly past the crew's mess, he glanced in at Chief Petty Officer Cecil Kester, a heavy, bulbous-nosed twenty-six-year veteran. Kester caught the glance and immediately set aside his heavy mug of coffee, grabbed a navy tool bag, and followed.

The officers' wardroom was next door to the crew's mess and directly under the control room. Inside was Lieutenant Edward Lent, a round-faced Southerner. When he saw Gillespie and Kester, he picked up his own attaché case and also followed.

Gillespie, Kester, and Lent scaled the ladder leading to the control room. Gillespie walked vigorously into the room, the other two right behind. Alan Lansing looked up and nodded.

"Evenin', Dick."

Gillespie stepped in front of Lansing but did not return the greeting. He just stared silently into Lansing's eyes.

The captain was baffled. He glanced at Kester and Lent, who had no reason to be there, but before his question could be articulated, Gillespie had pulled his .45.

"Captain Lansing," Gillespie said calmly, "you are no longer in command of this ship."

Gillespie pointed the gun at Lansing's heart while Kester and Lent drew their weapons and covered the six crewmen in the control room. Pencils dropped. Hands froze on controls. Nobody moved.

Lansing looked Gillespie up and down, then did the same to Kester and Lent. His face at first showed no concern. He returned his gaze to Gillespie, looking deeply into his eyes, until he could hold it in no longer and began to break down in laughter.

"Fan*tas*tic!" he shouted. "You scared the hell out of me. Now, who stole the strawberries?" The crewmen looked at one another, amazed, then, one by one, roared with laughter. It was a great joke. *The Caine Mutiny* on Lansing's last cruise.

Gillespie's expression remained unchanged. He waited patiently. Then, louder and more firmly, he repeated, "You are no longer in command of this ship! This is no joke, Captain Lansing."

The smile remained fixed on Alan Lansing's face, though one element of concern was beginning to nudge the back of his mind. The showing of guns was unnecessary dressing for the joke and very much against all regulations. Get it done with, he counseled himself.

"You're all disloyal!" he shouted, a bit of the Bogart lisp seeping through.

Gillespie clicked off the safety of his .45 and raised the gun to the captain's mouth. "Put your hands on your head!"

Lansing's smile melted. "This has gone far enough, Gillespie," he snapped.

"Do it!" Gillespie ordered, and the blood seeped from Lansing's cheeks as the reality of the situation hit him full force.

Suddenly the captain flushed with anger. "What's this all about?" he shouted.

13

"We'll discuss it later," Gillespie responded. "Consider yourself a prisoner."

"Are you *mad?* My God, this is mutiny. You'll spend the rest of your life in jail."

"Now you listen to me carefully, Captain," Gillespie said. "Each of us is carrying a bag with explosives. If you make any attempt to regain command, one or more of these bombs will be set off."

Lansing did not have to ponder the threat. An explosion aboard the *Hay* could rupture her hull and send them all on a violent, agonizing dive to death. Gillespie and his accomplices had already gone too far for him to risk calling a bluff.

"I will do nothing to endanger the lives of my crew," Lansing said evenly.

Gillespie nodded, then walked to the ship's bullhorn and flipped a switch while pivoting with his pistol to cover Lansing.

"Hear this! This is the executive officer speaking. We are now on a highly classified combat exercise, with the executive officer in operational command. Until further notice, no member of the crew is to enter the control room. That is all."

Gillespie checked the *Hay*'s position and ordered the pilot to turn a sharp fifty-three degrees to starboard. Then for more than two hours they waited in stony silence, Gillespie keeping his eyes on the control panel and refusing to answer any questions. The exposed handguns discouraged unnecessary movement. Finally Gillespie gave another order.

"Surface!"

It was unprecedented, and it violated the whole concept of the Polaris submarine system. To hide beneath the seas, never to transmit messages except in distress—these are the sacred rules of the game. Now, a third of the way into the Atlantic, the *Hay*'s klaxon horn pierced every ear and the roar of her ballast tanks blowing water reverberated throughout her hull. Like a dark monster searching for prey, she came to the surface. Alarm spread through

14

the crew. There was instant speculation about mechanical breakdown or radiation leak.

Once on the surface, Gillespie ordered the *Hay* stopped. The radarman reported another vessel nearby. Gillespie handed his pistol to Kester and his explosives to Lent. Moving quickly, he climbed up the superstructure, pausing at the top to catch his breath. He opened the hatch and looked out at the dark Atlantic, inhaling the crisp, salt air. The night was clear, the sky bright with stars.

Off to port, the *Margie I,* a sixty-foot white yacht, blinked a green signal. Crewmen immediately put two small motorboats over the side of the yacht, and six men jumped into each. As Gillespie watched their approach, he thought of the event that had led to this operation. It had occurred on July 20, 1960, three years and one month after his graduation from Annapolis.

The center of the world for the United States Navy that day had been a balmy, sunlit spot off Cape Canaveral. The USS *Observation Island,* an electronics ship, was standing by, its decks top-heavy with military brass, civilian contractors, and invited friends of the Pentagon. Lieutenant (jg) Richard Gillespie was there as well. The atmosphere had been electric.

"Fifteen seconds!" a voice had barked on the bullhorn as everyone on board gazed out to sea. No one dared speak. Besides the voice, the only sound came from curious sea gulls flapping in circles above the ship. In the ocean beyond, the focus of hundreds of riveted eyes, there was only an occasional streak of white foam from a submarine's periscope as it sliced the surface.

"Ten seconds!" announced the voice.

"Five!"

Lieutenant Gillespie felt his heart stop.

"Four . . . three . . . two . . . one. . . .

"Zero."

For a moment nothing happened.

Then, in a scene that would have pleased De Mille himself, there was a great rush of parting water and a *whoosh* that to technicians aboard *Observation Island* was like the sound of a newborn baby's cry. A white twenty-eight-foot missile broke through the surging foam at a fifteen-degree angle. The lungs of every man watching froze with the breath inside. The missile rose, its engine still, then, fifty feet above the sea, there was a burst of searing flame and a thunderous roar. The *Observation Island* erupted in cheers, whistles, and flying confetti.

"Get up there!" men yelled.

And it did. The United States had successfully fired a ballistic missile from a submerged submarine. Gillespie listened as the voice read a message from the skipper of the sub, the *George Washington,* to President Eisenhower and the chief of naval operations: "Polaris—from out of the deep to target. Perfect."

Polaris. The name rolled over and over in Gillespie's mind. It was the scientific name for the heavenly body that most call the North Star.

At the time, Gillespie was assigned to the navy's Special Projects Office, which had developed Polaris. He had only recently become intrigued by politics, and he was, as a friend had said, "slightly to the right of the kaiser." He had a knack for sensing how others felt about "things," a knack he soon employed to form special friendships within the Special Projects group. Gillespie and his friends were kiddingly accused of having political clocks that had stopped with the Rosenberg trial.

When the Polaris development program ended, Gillespie's circle of scientists, engineers, and officers decided to stay in touch and formalized their association into what Gillespie named the North Star Society. The members met periodically to discuss what they considered a virtual catalogue of treachery: the downing of Francis Gary Powers in his U-2 over Russia; the loss of Cuba; the nuclear-test-ban treaty; the "no-win" Vietnam War; the capture by North Korea of the USS *Pueblo;* the Communist victory in America's colleges; the murder of J. Edgar Hoover.

Slowly Gillespie had evolved a program of action to

present to his North Star comrades: It seemed clear that only through all-out war—nuclear war—could a free United States survive and the Marxist disease be exterminated. Millions would die, but the United States, being morally and militarily superior, would win, and the cause justified the extreme sacrifice.

As Gillespie pressed his view in North Star meetings, it began to take hold. There was only one glaring problem: No member believed such a war was likely to take place, for the superpowers didn't want it, and no provocation seemed strong enough to push them over the brink. Unless, of course, as Gillespie pointed out, the men of North Star *made* it happen.

This was the idea that had brought twelve determined men to a rendezvous aboard the USS *John Hay* on a quiet November evening in the western Atlantic. Gillespie had given it a name: the North Star Crusade.

Standing in the open hatch of the *John Hay,* Gillespie watched the motorboats come alongside the sub and the passengers climb one after the other onto the landing ladder. As the last man left each boat, he pulled a rubber plug in the bottom. The boats sank quickly, disappearing beneath popping bubbles. The twelve men quickly descended the ladder to the control room. Gillespie was the last man in.

"Dive!" he ordered.

Of the twelve newcomers, seven were scientists and engineers. Their mission was to unlock the safety devices that prevented unauthorized firing of the Polaris missiles. The other five were technicians, on board to assist the first seven and to police the ship.

The seven senior men were:

Jack Condon, forty-two, associate professor of physics, Stanford University.

Arthur Litauer, also forty-two. A short, earnest student of political philosophy and a weapons expert at the nuclear installation in Hanford, Washington.

Jack Rains, slightly roundish, prematurely bald, thirty-

17

six. An engineer with Cal Tech's Jet Propulsion Laboratory.

Kenneth Mayer, at forty-eight the oldest of the group and the meekest. Professor of aeronautical engineering, MIT.

Elroy Francis Bates, a former college football star. Electrical engineer, Westinghouse Electric.

Charles Bernstein, thirty-nine, a quiet, scholarly navigation expert from Sperry Gyroscope.

Donald McNamara, a black man, professor of chemistry at the University of Illinois.

"Hear this!" Gillespie announced to the ship. "Twelve civilians have just boarded. They are part of our exercise. You will extend them every courtesy." He then ordered the pilot to turn 145 degrees to port and to proceed at thirty knots.

Gillespie spent the remainder of the evening examining intelligence charts showing the patrol stations of the Soviet destroyers *Dostoyny* and *Svirepy*. When he had menorized all he needed to know about the ships, he prepared to get some sleep. He established a security force consisting of Kester, Lent, and the five junior technicians and set them to guard Captain Lansing and the men in the control room. The rest of the crew remained unaware of what was happening aboard their ship.

Gillespie awoke at 0500—5 A.M.—and returned to the control room. As anticipated, the *Hay* was only twenty statute miles from the Soviet position. He ordered the radar antenna raised above the surface and the sonars fully activated. At 5:23 he called battle stations. Surprised members of the *Hay*'s crew, not used to drills at this hour, hurried to their assigned places and awaited further orders. The scuttlebutt began to flow.

"Hear this! This is the executive officer speaking. We are about to engage in a combat drill in which we will fire live torpedoes at an actual target. Captain Lansing expects that each of you will perform as if at war."

Captain Lansing, still under guard in the control room, could say nothing, could only watch in horror as events unfolded. The most awesome weapon of modern times,

18

the nuclear missile submarine, with all its hundreds of safeguards and security measures, had succumbed helplessly through the simple, almost primitive act of hijacking.

Eighty seconds after Gillespie made his announcement, sonar picked up the sounds of a twin-propeller ship of destroyer size. Radar confirmed the contact. Gillespie ordered the radar antenna lowered and the periscope raised. When he sighted the sleek-hulled destroyer with its stubby superstructure, he had no way of knowing whether it was the *Dostoyny* or the *Svirepy*. It did not matter in his plans. Gillespie ordered the *Hay*'s four torpedo tubes loaded.

Four nineteen-foot torpedoes, each one twenty-one inches in diameter and weighing 3,600 pounds, slid into the tubes of the *John Hay*'s bullet-shaped bow. They were Mk 48 Mod 1's, designed for use against surface shipping and submarines. They homed in on an enemy vessel by locking onto the sounds it made. No Mk 48 had ever been used in combat.

Captain Lansing felt a clutching at his throat as he watched Gillespie track his target in the periscope. Gillespie actually looked pleased as he went through the attack sequence.

Aboard the *Dostoyny*, Captain Sverdlov lay in his bunk, dreaming. There was his son, Leonid, only thirty, stepping up to the lectern in Stockholm to accept a Nobel Prize. He had won it for a complex discovery that had led to a cure for coronary-artery disease, which had killed both of Sverdlov's parents. As he dreamed, Sverdlov's sonar room reported the presence of an unidentified submarine with sound characteristics of the Ethan Allen class. The report was correct—the *Hay* was of that type—but there was no cause for concern. Sub contacts were frequent, and the international situation was calm. The captain would be awakened only if something unusual was observed, such as a Polaris submarine traveling on the surface, but in the decade and a half since they began operations, no Polaris sub had ever been seen by a Russian sailor.

No Russian sailor would see one today.

Only the wakes of four torpedoes would be seen, and then only for an instant by a horrified Russian officer.

Leonid walked back from the lectern in Captain Sverdlov's dream. The dignitaries applauded. He bowed.

A torpedo slammed into the side of the *Dostoyny*. A magazine exploded and the captain's cabin was incinerated.

2

Isaac Anderson stood on the podium of the Pentagon auditorium doing what no chief of naval operations had done before—making a speech to the Women's Peace Alliance, a group not known for its love of uniforms. His invitation to them had created a small scandal in the Defense Department. They were an enemy invasion.

Not that he felt comfortable. He knew what they thought of his chestful of ribbons and his Navy Cross. He guessed they would make little jokes about his bulky frame and bullish face, as if looking like a warrior were somehow his fault. When they looked at him, Anderson thought, they saw a grown-up Sea Scout who spent his afternoons playing war games on big boards. Twenty years before, he would have despised them. He surely wouldn't have addressed them. Now he understood them, even sympathized with them. Not all the way, of course, but a good part of the way. He wanted to convince them that his goals and theirs were essentially the same. They didn't believe it. The Pentagon didn't believe it. But Anderson believed it. He saw some connection between a group that favored unilateral disarmament and an admiral who believed the Vietnam War had been the work of armchair strategists who had never seen combat. The highest officer of the United States Navy was becoming a dove.

He stood stiffly, a hand in each pocket of his tailored blue uniform. The one wide stripe and three narrow ones that adorned his sleeves and marked him as an admiral glowed in the spotlights. Some of the women in the audience squirmed. They were self-conscious, guilty over coming, afraid that someone might question their dedication

21

to the cause. Like the military, peace groups have their own kind of loyalty oath.

As Anderson spoke, his pace seemed faster than it actually was. He was a Virginian, and he still had a drawl, but a lifetime in the navy had given him the clipped word endings that make military men sound military. A hurried, urgent effect. And although Anderson knew that jargon would offend the women, he sometimes fell back on such terms as "defense posture" and "operational capability." They were part of him. He couldn't help it. Nor could he help referring to the women, almost all of them the liberated type, as "you very fine ladies." He mentally kicked himself when he descended into Navyese, using "attackted" for "attacked." But he was willing to say other things that other officers were not.

"I know," he said, breaking into a nervous smile, "that you think we military types are war lovers. You think when we say things like 'Peace is our profession,' we say it with a wink, as if it's part of a con game to get more bombs so we can do what we really want to do—have one big war.

"Well, I'm afraid that sometimes you're right. A strategist once said that most people who study war enjoy it. I'm sorry to say that many officers seem to think war is entertainment, that it's fun. Well, it isn't fun. And people who believe it is are dangerous."

The women applauded. A few middle-grade officers hanging around the back of the hall winced. It is the conventional wisdom of the American military never to admit a liking for war. The war-is-hell school of public relations had convinced many Americans that their military leaders wanted only to throw down their arms. For an officer to suggest that some officers enjoy war is the military equivalent of one doctor testifying against another in a malpractice suit. Anderson wasn't only suggesting it, he was stating it.

A marine lieutenant left the back of the room and a handwritten summary of what Anderson had just said would be on the desk of the chairman of the Joint Chiefs of Staff within minutes. Anderson was amused when he saw the man leave. He only hoped he'd gotten it right.

It was Anderson's second flap of the week. Three days earlier he had recommended to the President that funds for a new nuclear-powered aircraft carrier be deleted from the next budget. With the completion of the *Dwight D. Eisenhower*, he pointed out, the United States would have eleven supercarriers and three older but serviceable carriers of the Midway class. Eleven, he believed, were adequate, a word that itself brings chills to a Pentagon elite raised on the idea that "more" is the loveliest word of all. The funds for the carrier, Anderson argued, should go to submarines or be returned for general federal use.

Anderson wore the wings of a naval aviator and combat ribbons marking service aboard the carrier *Yorktown* during the Korean conflict. His recommendation to the President, therefore, had been heresy, and he immediately became the target of vitriolic attacks by the carrier priests inside and outside the navy, including the executives of some shipbuilding firms. Anderson saw the dollar sign behind their American-flag lapel pins.

Another flap was in the making. Earlier that morning Anderson had written a memo to the Bureau of Ships soliciting views on whether the battleships *Iowa* and *Wisconsin* should be scrapped. The two 45,000-ton relics were tied up at the Philadelphia Navy Yard, where everyone expected them to remain forever. They and the *Missouri* and *New Jersey* were the last of an honored breed, and to scrap them would be forever to close the book on the Old Navy. That was precisely what Isaac Anderson had in mind.

The navy for Anderson began in 1941, when he was appointed to the Naval Academy by his local Congressman. He won the appointment by placing first in a competitive exam given to all ninety-one boys who wanted it. His family had no pull, nor had anyone tried to advance his cause though the political clubhouse. He was simply the outstanding candidate and the Congressman happened to be an honest man. Anderson was in his first year at Annapolis when the Japanese bombed Pearl Harbor. Because of the need for young officers, the navy placed him in an accelerated program, and he was graduated in June, 1944.

His entry into combat was late. On April 1, 1945, American forces stormed ashore at Okinawa in the last of the great invasions, code-named Iceberg. Ensign Anderson was assigned to the destroyer USS *Morrison*, captained by Commander J. R. Hansen. The ship was on Radar Picket Station 1, directing fighters against incoming Japanese planes. Anderson compressed more action into the next month than most navy officers saw in a year. It wasn't only the dive bombers and torpedo planes that he had to contend with. He was prepared for those. He wasn't prepared for a new weapon of a desperate enemy—the kamikazes, the suicide pilots who crashed their planes into American ships.

The *Morrison* avoided the kamikazes for a month. Then, in early May, her luck ran out. Four planes roared in through heavy flak, striking Anderson's ship at two-minute intervals. The explosions tore the *Morrison* apart and she went down so quickly that most of the men belowdecks drowned. Of a total complement of 331, only 179 survived. Of those 179, 108 were wounded. Anderson suffered burns over twenty percent of his body and took four pieces of shrapnel in his chest. Despite his injuries, he saved the lives of two other men by pulling them from a burning oil slick, and for this was awarded the Navy Cross. The sinking of the *Morrison* ended his World War II combat career, however, and left a hellish impression that would never fade. From those anxious, screaming minutes in the bloody waters off Okinawa there came a maturity and a sense of reason. Anderson could not easily send men to face the savagery he had seen.

He went to Pensacola after the war and became a pilot, one of the first to fly the new jets. The navy saw him as a comer, a bright young man with the required combat experience and a gift for handling subordinates. Some superiors complained that he overanalyzed problems, that he actually thought too much. At least one admiral felt that attitude might cause problems in wartime, when

24

quick decisions were critical. Another wrote in a fitness report that "Lieutenant Anderson seems to spend a great deal of time making up jokes about senior officers. Sometimes they're funny, and the importance of humor to morale is not herein discounted. But they often border on disrespect."

At Pensacola, Anderson met and married Julia Everts, the daughter of a local pediatrician. They had no children, but the marriage was sufficiently strong to hold up through long separations.

Anderson's advance through the ranks was rapid. He became a favorite of the Pentagon's new generation of thinkers, men who threw around such terms as "systems analysis" and "second-strike capability." Ultimately he was passed over twenty-three unhappy admirals to become chief of naval operations. Like many men who learn to censor their opinions on the way up, Anderson let loose when he reached the top.

"I'm sorry to say," he went on before the peace group, "that some civilians also take a Hollywood view of war. It's easy to talk about 'supporting our boys' when they belong to someone else's family." The women burst into applause.

"Don't get me wrong," he continued. "I believe in a strong national defense. I believe in fighting for my country and in dying for it if need be. But I don't believe that defense is an end in itself, that the military should be a state within a state. I don't believe," he said quietly, measuring each word, "that either peace groups or military men have concerned the market on patriotism."

A young Wave hurried into the hall through the stage entrance. She walked quickly to a commander who was sitting about five yards from Anderson and handed him a folded note. The commander read it, stood, and went immediately to Anderson's side. He slipped the note onto the lectern and jabbed at it, emphasizing its importance. Anderson scanned the note and looked up at his audience, the awkward smile returning.

"I'm afraid I'll have to cut this off," he said. "I'd hoped we could have questions, but I've. . . ." He stopped, worried that there might be reporters in the room. "I've been called to a meeting. Nothing to worry about." He began walking off.

The women groaned; they felt cheated. Sensing this, Anderson returned briefly to the lectern. "We'll do this again," he said. "I promise." By that time, though, the women were getting into their coats, the microphone had been pulled, and only a few heard him.

Anderson rushed down the hall with the side-to-side gait that led his detractors to call him Andy Duck. He knew that Fred Bixby wouldn't call unless something big had happened. Bixby was chief of staff in the White House and the President's closest political adviser. Anderson sized him up as shrewd, even wise, and he liked him.

The admiral entered his blue-carpeted office and walked to the window side of his desk, which was flanked by American and navy flags. An aide handed him a phone connected directly to the White House. In seconds Bixby was on the line.

"Fred? Isaac Anderson. What's up?"

"Plenty," Bixby answered, his high-pitched voice making him sound younger than his forty-six years. "We just got this over the Hot Line from Moscow:

"MR. PRESIDENT:

"AT 0743 HOURS THIS MORNING, WASHINGTON TIME, A UNIT OF THE SOVIET NAVY OPERATING IN PEACEFUL INTERNATIONAL WATERS 900 MILES EAST OF YOUR ATLANTIC COAST, AND WITH NO HOSTILE IN-TENT, WAS RUTHLESSLY ATTACKED BY SUBMARINE. FOUR TORPEDOES WERE FIRED, OF WHICH THREE STRUCK OUR SHIP. DESPITE THE VALIANT EFFORTS OF HER HEROIC CREW, SHE SANK WITHIN A FEW MINUTES. ANOTHER UNIT WENT TO THE AID OF THE SURVIVORS. WE BELIEVE 237 OF OUR SAILORS HAVE DIED.

"THE SOVIET GOVERNMENT CAN ONLY CONCLUDE THAT THIS UNPROVOKED ATTACK WAS LAUNCHED BY AN AMERICAN SUBMARINE FOR SOME REASON THAT WE CANNOT COMPREHEND. THE SOVIET GOVERN-

MENT URGENTLY INSISTS ON AN IMMEDIATE EX-
PLANATION AND LODGES THE STRONGEST POSSIBLE
PROTEST. IN THE MEANTIME, THE SOVIET GOVERN-
MENT IS PLACING ITS ARMED FORCES ON GENERAL
ALERT. IN ACCORDANCE WITH OUR DESIRE TO AVOID
ANY UNNECESSARY STRAINS, WE ARE NOT MAKING
THIS MATTER PUBLIC.

"That's all," Bixby said.

Anderson thought for a moment, then spun a globe
next to his desk until he was looking at the western Atlantic.

"Impossible," he said.

"Says you," Bixby replied. "Says me. But you've heard
the message and we'd better have a solid explanation."

"Has the President responded to the Russians?" Anderson asked.

"Negative," said Bixby. "He's waiting for you to tell
him what happened out there."

"I'll get back to you as soon as I can."

"Sooner," Bixby implored. "We'd hate to see the ther-
mometer go through the top, Andy."

Two receivers clicked down.

Anderson knew that no American ship had torpedoed a
Soviet destroyer. He also knew that explosions had torn
ships to shreds in peacetime before. But any capable Russian officer could certainly tell whether the blast came
from a torpedo or something else. He wondered whether
this was some kind of Russian trick.

He drew on his intelligence sources. What *did* happen
in the Atlantic? The United States maintains a system of
spy-in-the-sky satellites that can photograph minute details, even allowing exact counts of tanks on a battlefield.
But Anderson quickly learned that cloud cover in the Atlantic had made surveillance photographs impossible earlier that morning. He had to rely on aircraft. Routine
patrol flights were under way, and he ordered additional
planes sent to the scene of the "attack."

As he waited for their report, Anderson pondered the
Soviet message. He had the diplomat's ability to read be-

tween the lines. It was a protest, but a remarkably mild one, considering the charge. An attack on a ship at sea is an act of war and is impossible to justify by an explanation of mistaken identity. The same slow, methodical approach that others had criticized now served Anderson well. He sensed that the mild tone of the protest was due to Soviet confusion. After all, there was no reason why the United States would torpedo a Russian ship unless it was part of an all-out assault on the Soviet Union, and such an assault obviously was not under way. Anderson concluded that the Soviet Premier needed more hard information before taking his next step. He also concluded that Russian naval experts might themselves guess that the ship simply had blown up and that a frantic officer with a wild imagination had blamed a submarine.

His mind went back to the possibility of a Russian trick, some bizarre stunt that might signal the beginning of war. Maybe the Russians were trumping up a provocation as an excuse to attack somewhere. If so, a frightening question had to be faced: Was it—could it be—a time for America to strike first?

The thoughts that went through Isaac Anderson's mind were precisely those that Richard Gillespie hoped for. Anderson couldn't know it, but his list of options had already been carefully considered by a lieutenant commander whom he had never met.

Lieutenant Keith Franklin gazed through his binoculars at the churning sea below. The magnification, combined with the vibration of the Neptune patrol bomber, gave the scene a constant shake. He felt like a little boy with his head against the window of his father's car as it bumped along an unpaved road. The microphone extending from his flight helmet was set an inch from his mouth and was on. He was nervous, hoping to make a good impression. He had never had a direct line to the chief of naval operations before.

The Neptune was obsolete. Two piston engines, two vintage jets, a navy standby of the fifties and sixties now

28

used almost exclusively for reserve training. This one was a hanger-on. Lieutenant Franklin had hoped the navy would let him fly something more to his taste, such as a Phantom fighter, but right now patrol pilots were needed for Atlantic duty. Maybe if the CNO liked his work, he would recommend Franklin for a transfer.

The Neptune was within five miles of the spot where the Soviets claimed their ship had been sunk. As the plane approached, the actual flying was transferred to Franklin's copilot, Lieutenant (jg) Michael LeGrance, a reservist on duty for two weeks, who Franklin thought was a rich, arrogant son of a bitch.

"Target!" Franklin suddenly shouted, easing forward slightly to prevent the aircraft frame from obstructing his view. What he observed below reminded him of the reconnaissance films he had seen on endless repeats of *Victory at Sea.* "Soviet destroyer," he reported, "Krivak class. No number. Proceeding west about eight knots. Much debris and an oil slick around her. Estimate slick one hundred and fifty yards in diameter. I see—stand by—yes, I see boats, apparently from the destroyer. They're picking up bits of debris and one is fishing a body out of the water. There's a small piece of debris on fire just outside the oil slick. It may be a mattress or a padding. There are no other ships or aircraft in the area. We have an apparent sinking out here. Stand by."

As the Neptune banked, Franklin turned to his left to get a good view of the Soviet ship.

"There's considerable activity aboard the destroyer. I see men running around. It's difficult to make out, but they seem to be pointing up at us and shaking their fists. I've never seen that before. They usually just wave."

LeGrance peeled off and brought the Neptune in at 400 feet for a run over the *Svirepy.* Now Franklin could see that the ship was at battle stations. As the Neptune buzzed in, its long straight wings casting a sharp shadow on the Atlantic, Franklin suddenly saw a flash from the *Svirepy's* number one three-inch gun. An instant later a shell exploded 175 feet off his right wing. He grabbed the controls from a petrified LeGrance, gunned his engines, and tore upward, rocking the plane back and forth to evade other shells.

"Warning shot!" he yelled.

No Soviet ship had ever fired on an American plane. Moscow had not ordered the shot, but Washington had no way of knowing that. The blast had been fired by a tense Russian commander acting on his own, protecting his ship under the ancient rule of shooting first and asking questions later. He was, after all, sure that an American sub had sunk his sister ship. He took the minimum action, a warning shot. He was ready to turn his guns over to automatic radar control—a death warrant for Franklin and LeGrance—when the Neptune roared away.

Anderson carefully studied Franklin's report. Navy reconnaissance planes had spotted two Soviet destroyers on patrol the night before, and now there was only one. The Soviet Premier's claim that a ship had gone down was confirmed, but how it had gone down remained a mystery.

As Anderson tried to piece together the small bits of data in his possession, the President of the United States sent the following message, on the Hot Line, to the Soviet Premier:

MR. PREMIER:
WE ARE EVALUATING YOUR MESSAGE OF THIS MORNING. WE VIEW THIS MATTER WITH THE UT-MOST CONCERN. AS SOON AS MY ADVISERS CAN GIVE ME THE NECESSARY INFORMATION, I WILL TRANSMIT A FULL REPLY. WE ACT IN A SPIRIT OF PEACE.

Anderson also acted in a spirit of peace. He knew some military men would say that a Russian ship had made an unprovoked attack on an American plane and that a military response was called for. Anderson's technique was different. It had been given a name by think-tank strategists: crisis management. The idea was to control the crisis, to keep it from exploding. He reached for the

White House phone, but saw its red light flash before he touched it. Bixby had gotten on the line first.

"Andy, Fred Bixby. We've been lookin' over Lieutenant Franklin's stuff. Have you a recommendation?"

Anderson paused. He took a cigar from his desk and started lighting up.

"Nothing of a military nature," he finally replied.

"No recommendation at *all?*"

Anderson hated to be asked to suggest political action, but he knew that when Bixby repeated a question, it had only one meaning: The President was doing the asking.

"Well," he answered, taking a long puff on his cigar and blowing the smoke almost straight up, "I think you should tell Moscow just what we know, which isn't much, and couple it with a straight diplomatic denial that we sank their ship. Look, assuming the Russians are serious about this, they'll believe what they want to believe anyway. We can't *prove* we didn't do it, so the next move is up to them."

An hour later the President of the United States sent the following message, again on the Hot Line, to the Soviet Premier:

MR. PREMIER:

ON BEHALF OF THE PEOPLE OF THE UNITED STATES, I EXPRESS MY HEARTFELT SYMPATHY OVER THE LOSS OF YOUR GALLANT SEAMEN. HOWEVER, I MUST TELL YOU THAT THE UNITED STATES WAS IN NO WAY RESPONSIBLE FOR THE INCIDENT THAT LED TO THEIR DEATHS. THERE HAS NOT, I REPEAT NOT, BEEN ANY HOSTILE ACTION BY UNITED STATES FORCES AGAINST ANY FORCES OF THE UNION OF SOVIET SOCIALIST REPUBLICS.

OUR NAVAL EXPERTS IN WASHINGTON RECOMMEND THAT YOU CONSIDER THE POSSIBILITY THAT THE SOVIET SHIP MAY HAVE BEEN THE VICTIM OF AN INTERNAL EXPLOSION OR A COLLISION WITH SOME UNIDENTIFIED VESSEL OR OBJECT. THE UNITED STATES IS FULLY PREPARED TO JOIN YOU IN ANY IN-

VESTIGATION THAT YOUR AUTHORITIES DEEM WORTH-
WHILE.

YOU KNOW FROM OUR PAST MEETINGS THAT I AM
DOING ALL IN MY POWER TO MAINTAIN CORDIAL
RELATIONS BETWEEN OUR TWO GREAT COUNTRIES.
LET US NOT ALLOW THIS MISUNDERSTANDING TO
MAR OUR EFFORTS. WITH THAT IDEAL IN MIND, THE
UNITED STATES WILL ALSO KEEP SECRET OUR
EXCHANGE OF MESSAGES THIS MORNING.

Now the small Washington group that was privy to the
day's events—the President, Bixby, Anderson, the other
Joint Chiefs, key Cabinet members—waited tensely for
the Soviet response. It came in thirty minutes and took
only a few seconds to print out on the White House
teletype. It had that chill of an era that most rational
people hoped had passed:

THE SOVIET GOVERNMENT REJECTS THE AMERICAN
MESSAGE.

3

The Hot Line was silent for six minutes. Then, at 11:41 A.M., the Soviets resumed:

MR. PRESIDENT:
THE SOVIET GOVERNMENT HAS DETERMINED THROUGH TECHNICAL MEANS THAT AN AMERICAN SUBMARINE OF THE ETHAN ALLEN TYPE, FIRING YOUR MK 48 TORPEDOES, WAS RESPONSIBLE FOR THE INCIDENT UNDER REVIEW. WE ARE WELL AWARE, MR. PRESIDENT, THAT AN AMERICAN WARSHIP WOULD FIRE ITS WEAPONS ONLY ON YOUR DIRECT COMMAND. WE THEREFORE MUST COME TO JUST AND REASONABLE CONCLUSIONS. ONLY YOU, MR. PRESIDENT, CAN KNOW THE REASONS FOR YOUR ACTION. BUT YOUR WHOLE NATION WILL BEAR RESPONSIBILITY FOR ITS CONSEQUENCES.

There was a rumbling of chairs and a shuffling of papers as sixteen senior officials rose for the President of the United States. He sauntered into the Cabinet Room of the White House, a lock of gray hair hanging over his forehead. The equally gray suit, a poor fit, was rumpled. Bixby was right behind him. Norman McNamara, his straight-arrow news secretary, was right behind Bixby. The President nodded, and everyone sat down.

Outside, a crisp November wind rustled the stems in the Rose Garden. A truck horn blasted in the distance on Pennsylvania Avenue. Inside, the long and stately room was hushed. A consuming tension filled the space between the portrait of Dwight Eisenhower at one end of the room and the portrait of Woodrow Wilson on the other. The eighteenth-century draperies and chandeliers seemed a ludicrous contrast to the nuclear crisis at hand.

This was a meeting of CRITIC, a group formed to advise the President in just such a crisis. The committee's membership varied with the nature of the problem, but always included the Secretary of Defense, the Joint Chiefs of Staff, Bixby, McNamara, and the UN ambassador. It usually included, as it did now, top-ranking intelligence and technical experts.

Isaac Anderson sat directly opposite the President, in the spot reserved for the person who would give the major briefing. Aside from the Chief Executive himself, he was the center of attention. The crisis was naval, and Anderson's advice would be crucial.

The chief of naval operations was nervous.

The President took off his jacket and loosened his tie. He had never cared much for protocol or pomp, and Anderson liked him for that. There was something Trumanesque about the man. He had a scrappiness and earthiness, combined with a realistic view of his own limitations. He knew that he had to make up in common sense what he lacked in education or intellect.

Anderson didn't know the President well, having been appointed by his predecessor. He knew he was sixty and had been a Senator from Illinois before going to the White House. He was known as a rough campaigner. During one Senate race he announced, "I have no intention of dragging my opponent's poor child into this campaign." Having thus brought illegitimacy to the fore, he went on to an easy victory.

The President cleared his throat.

"You have all read the Soviets' latest message?"

Affirmative nods.

"Then we can get started. I want to begin by. . . ."

He stopped. There was a rhythmic clicking in the room. All eyes turned to one end, to a four-foot by eight-foot screen suspended from the ceiling. It was the receiving end of the CIS, the Combined Intelligence System. It could display, in large print, any message or piece of information received by the U.S. government and could also show television pictures from surveillance satellites or military units. If the Soviets took any action anywhere, CRITIC would probably watch it live and in color.

Some felt that such devices as the CIS were making it impossible for nations to keep military secrets. But the CIS could not see into underground structures, read the minds of opposing strategists, measure the discipline of an army, or peek inside weapons to reveal critical design changes. There were still plenty of secrets left.

Now the CIS started clicking out a message, as a teletype would. Words appeared on the screen, letter by letter:

US EMBASSY MOSCOW—INTENSE ACTIVITY BY MILITARY PERSONNEL COMMENCED HALF AN HOUR AGO AT THE KREMLIN. ADMIRAL GORSHKOV WAS THE FIRST OFFICER TO ARRIVE, AND REMAINS. THE SOVIETS HAVE CANCELLED A TRADE MEETING WITH US SET FOR TODAY. NO EXPLANATION.

GRUENING

John Gruening was the United States ambassador. The tension went up another notch.

But what would the President's reaction be? In the Senate, Anderson recalled, he had argued for the use of atomic weapons in Vietnam. He was known as a virtual private for the Pentagon's generals. A reporter had asserted, "This man would vote for nuclear slingshots if General Taylor wanted them." He had responded, "If nuclear slingshots were needed to defend our nation, I would indeed vote for them." Even his wife was embarrassed.

But Anderson had noticed a change in the man since he became President. He seemed less prone to hawkish speeches and more willing to restrain his gut instincts. He had told an interviewer a few months before, "I don't see any problem anywhere that can't be settled with a talk and a handshake." Anderson thought that the weight of the Presidency was having a maturing effect. A Senator

35

speaks of supporting our boys. A President sends them to die.

The CIS began clicking out another message—this time an advisory from Central Intelligence:

SATELLITE SURVEILLANCE SHOWS TWO SOVIET DIVISIONS APPROX 300 MILES WEST OF MOSCOW COMMENCING MOVEMENT TOWARD THE CAPITAL.

The President seemed disturbed, agitated, and appeared to rub his top teeth nervously across his bottom lip. There were rumors along the Washington cocktail circuit that he had an emotional problem, that he could not function well in an international crisis. Anderson had never seen any evidence to support this, although the President's sudden loss of temper in a meeting with the Chinese Premier had raised eyebrows. Some said his outburst was caused by worry over his wife, who was a known alcoholic and was largely kept from public view.

Now the President slipped on a pair of rectangular glasses. "I haven't got any great ideas on this," he said. "But I've put our people on a quiet alert—no razzmatazz, y'know—and the Reds've done the same. I've also asked Admiral Anderson here to give us his appraisal."

He nodded to the admiral.

Anderson took a long, deep puff on his cigar and he placed it in a copper ashtray bearing a painted Presidential seal. He blew out the smoke, watching it spread across the high gloss of the Cabinet Room's long oval table. He recalled that the table had been purchased by Richard Nixon to be a gift to the White House when he left office. The identity of the donor reminded Anderson that the room had been the scene of great blunders, as well as great decisions.

"Mr. President," he began, "it seems to me that there are two possibilities here. Either the Soviet Union really believes we sank the *Dostoyny,* or this is the most dangerous hoax in modern times."

"What do you mean . . . hoax?" Bixby asked.

"I mean the Russians may have sunk their own ship with some ulterior motive in mind."

"You think they did that?" the President asked.

"Sir," Anderson replied, "I think we should take this step by step. If you don't mind, I'd like to discuss the first possibility—that they really believe we sank the ship."

"Go ahead," the President said.

"In order for the Russians to believe this," Anderson went on, "they'd have to exclude other causes of the sinking. An accident. A collision. Things of that nature. I believe they *would* exclude them. To understand why, I ask you to put yourself in their position. Try to see the sinking from Admiral Gorshkov's point of view. As you know, he's my opposite number and the father of the modern Soviet Navy. In a matter like this his opinions are vital."

Anderson took another puff on his cigar. The CIS screen was blank, which gave him time for uninterrupted analysis.

"Okay," he continued, "it's early today. Gorshkov gets an urgent message that a Soviet ship has been sunk by submarine. The ship has the most modern detection equipment so he must assume the report is accurate. Because he's responsible for naval defense, he must also assume the submarine is American. But he hesitates. 'Why?' he asks. 'To begin a war with a simple ship sinking makes no sense.' He urges that a protest be sent to Washington, but a restrained one."

"Kind of a probe instead of a hot complaint," Bixby said.

"Precisely. Gorshkov sees no other American moves and this increases his sense of wonder."

The CIS came on again with a message from the commander of the U.S. Sixth Fleet in the Mediterranean:

SOV DESTROYERS APPROACHING CARRIER TASK FORCE THREE. EXPECT SERIOUS HARASSMENT IN NEXT HALF HOUR.

COMSIXFLT

Then, without interruption, a message from the commander in chief of the Pacific Fleet at Pearl Harbor:

COMSEVFLT REPORTS 30 SOV TU-95 MARITIME RECONNAISSANCE BOMBERS HEADING SOUTH FROM VLADIVOSTOK. FLIGHT PATH WILL TAKE THEM OVER CARRIER ENTERPRISE IN SEA OF JAPAN.

CINCPAC

"Christ!" mumbled the President. But he nodded for Anderson to continue.

Anderson tried not to show that he was shaken by the advisories. But a strain in his voice revealed his apprehensions.

"Now," he went on, "the Soviets have protested. We deny their charges, but Gorshkov's people still insist that we sank the ship and with Mk forty-eight torpedoes. So Gorshkov urges a more specific protest, reporting what his people are telling him. We see now that he's also starting some harassment of our ships. I stress *harassment*. He won't shoot, not if I know him. He's too smart to back into a war over an incident he doesn't understand."

"He's applying pressure as a precaution," the President said.

"Exactly, Mr. President," Anderson answered. "It's a firm but not overly threatening deterrent, a warning, so to speak. It also gives him time to consult with his experts. He examines possible causes of the sinking besides an American submarine and starts excluding them."

"Wait a sec," Bixby protested, waving his right index finger. "Are you saying that Gorshkov is harassing our ships even while wondering whether something besides our boat sank his people?"

"Yes."

"Isn't that a little extreme for a smart guy like him?"

"Maybe, from *our* point of view. But don't make the mistake of attributing to other nations thought patterns like ours. To the Russians, harassing American ships is a perfectly reasonable act. After all, they've done it in the past with *no* provocation."

38

"True enough," Bixby agreed.

"So let's look at some of the alternative explanations that Gorshkov is considering. First, he might wonder if the report from the *Dostoyny*'s sister ship, the *Svirepy,* was a cover-up. Maybe there *was* an accident out there, and somebody wants to protect his career. You'll remember in 1974 a Soviet destroyer blew up in the Black Sea. I'm sure the man in charge wasn't too happy about reporting it back. If today's sinking was an accident, it could have been a highly embarrassing one."

"For example?" the President asked.

"Well," Anderson said, "consider this. The Russians are developing an antisub canister that can be planted at sea, like a mine. On an electronic command, a torpedo fires from the canister and homes in on a nearby sub. It's possible that in lowering the device, the *Svirepy* could have triggered it, sent the torpedo out, and sunk the *Dostoyny.*"

"And they try to hush it," Bixby said.

"Yes."

"Doesn't wash," the President broke in. "Too many blabbermouths. The story'd come out."

"I agree," Anderson said. "Gorshkov knows that. He'd reject the accident theory as highly improbable. So he goes on to the second possible cause. He wonders whether some third power might have sunk the *Dostoyny.* He's written about this in *Morskoi Sbornik,* the journal of Soviet naval strategy. In one article he theorized that a small country could provoke a war between the superpowers by using a sub to sink one side's ships."

"Who would want to?" Bixby asked.

"Well," Anderson said, "Gorshkov might consider the French. They might see a conflict between us and the Russians as strengthening France. And he would consider the Chinese."

"But the Red sonar reported one of our Polaris subs," Bixby said.

"No problem," Anderson replied. "Submarine sound patterns can be simulated."

"If it was somebody else's sub," the President broke in, "couldn't we find it out there?"

"Theoretically, yes," Anderson answered. "But so what? We couldn't prove it sank the *Dostoyny,* and its owning nation wouldn't admit it. But—"

Suddenly the CIS started operating once again. A simple advisory came across:

STAND BY FOR SIXFLT TRANSMISSION.

The meaning was clear. Soviet ships were coming dangerously near American ships in the Mediterranean.

"Keep going," the President ordered Anderson.

"Yes, sir. Mr. President, I think Gorshkov would reject the third-nation theory, too. A third power would be taking an awful risk of starting a war that could destroy everyone. No nation with submarine capability has a current government that seems so inclined."

"I buy that," the President said.

"Gorshkov's third possible explanation," Anderson continued, "might be a coup against the Soviet regime."

"What?" Bixby shot back.

"Not likely, of course," Anderson acknowledged, "but it's possible that the *Dostoyny* was carrying a high official and was sunk by a Soviet sub participating in the coup. Note the report on the two divisions moving toward Moscow. Why in hell would they be moving *toward* Moscow? If they were part of an alert, they'd be moving toward the NATO front. They might be part of a coup. . . . But I don't believe Gorshkov will think so."

"Why not?" Bixby asked.

"It's an old rule," Anderson replied. "The only coups that come off are the ones you don't hear about. Nobody planning a takeover would move two divisions in the open."

"So Gorshkov is still nailing us for the sinking," the President said. "Would there be other possible causes he'd consider?"

Anderson paused.

Now he had to confront a subject of enormous sensitivity. He had kept it for last, hoping somehow that he wouldn't have to bring it up. He glanced around at each person in the room, wondering what their reaction would be to the blasphemy he was about to speak. He puffed at his cigar, letting the smoke out . . . so slowly.

"Mr. President," he said, "there is one possibility—Gorshkov would have to consider it—that one of our submarines acted without authority and did in fact sink the *Dostoyny*."

"Admiral Anderson!" a voice boomed. "Do you realize the implications of what you're saying?"

"I do," Anderson replied.

All eyes turned toward a massive hulk of a man sitting beneath the Eisenhower portrait. His face was flushed with anger. Harley Somerville had entered the discussion. That his anger was directed at Isaac Anderson surprised no one.

Somerville was Secretary of Defense. He disapproved of Anderson because the admiral did not fit his image of a tough-talking, hell-for-leather sailor. He wanted Anderson out, and everyone in Washington knew it. Now he drew an initialed silver pen from his breast pocket and started tapping it against the air for emphasis. His eyes closed halfway, making him look forbidding.

"In all the years of the U.S. military capability," Somerville went on, "that has never happened. It has never happened in the navy. It has never happened in the army. It has never happened in the air force. Our deterrent is based on the concept of absolute control from Washington."

"Of course," Anderson said, "but Gorshkov must consider the possibility that something went wrong this time."

Somerville looked disgusted. Nothing went wrong in his defense establishment.

Harley Somerville was an Oklahoman. He had been an aircraft manufacturer whose business skill turned a small factory into a string of eight plants across the United States and two more in Canada. Somerville believed that success in America was easy if only a man worked at it. He cited himself as primary proof, always pointing out that between the years 1946 and 1951 he worked at least six days a week and never left his office before 9 P.M.

He was an unyielding hawk, a man who thought that the competitive free-enterprise system could be applied to international affairs. Crushing the competition, for example, was a reasonable, even a noble objective. "Toughness" was a word to which Somerville had a religious devotion. American "toughness" was the keeper of the peace. If American "toughness" were questioned, the Soviet Union would quickly attack. "Toughness" was the mark of a man, the foundation of a nation's greatness.

Anderson knew the real reason for Somerville's obsession with toughness. Somerville had not been in combat in World War II. Like many of his kind, Anderson thought, he lived down his guilt by aligning himself with those who bravely faced what he had not.

At sixty-three Somerville had achieved an ambition of three decades—respectability in the American military. He was the head of the entire defense establishment, and men with ribbons on their chests made no moves without his consent. They saluted him. They rose when he entered a meeting, and they deferred to him.

"This morning," he said, "the President gave the Soviet Premier our Bible-sworn assurance that no U.S. sub did this thing. You advised us—"

"Mr. Secretary," Anderson replied, "understand how Gorshkov interprets our assurance. We're saying that we didn't order an attack. He knows we couldn't give an unconditional guarantee that no attack took place."

"That's crazy," Somerville said. "What kind of credibility do we have?"

"Sir, Gorshkov is a sophisticated man."

"I don't care what he is. I think it's very dangerous even to talk this way. You're off on one of your intellectual Sunday drives, Admiral. We must never allow it to be inferred that something can interfere with our control of our submarines."

"We've hardly any control over what Gorshkov infers, Mr. Secretary."

The President realized that the acrimony was serving

42

no purpose. "Well, now, wait a minute," he said to Anderson. "What would Gorshkov think the odds were of something screwy happening on our sub?"

"He'd look at it this way," Anderson replied. "First he'd think of the *Liberty* example. You'll remember that during the Six-Day War in 1967 the Israelis shot up our USS *Liberty*. She was off their coast collecting electronic intelligence. We had alerted all our ships to clear the war zone, then told Israel that they had done so. Unfortunately the *Liberty* never got her order. The Israelis thought she was an Arab ship flying our flag as a disguise."

"What in hell does that have to do with now?" Somerville asked.

"One of our routine commands to a sub could've been garbled and turned into an attack order. But it's a chance in a million and Gorshkov won't take it seriously. He'll go on to the more probable reason for a ship to attack without authorization."

"The madman thing," Bixby said.

"Yes," Anderson replied.

As Anderson prepared to discuss the possibility that a madman had seized an American submarine, Richard Gillespie flipped a radio switch in the *Hay*'s control room. The crackle and whistle of military transmissions began pouring from a small speaker. Gillespie wanted to measure the response to the *Dostoyny* sinking by the increase in the amount and urgency of this military traffic. He expected that there would be an alert of American forces. Earlier in the morning he had heard the increase in patrol-plane activity over the *Dostoyny*'s last location.

He was pleased.

The scientists of the North Star Crusade had begun work on the safety interlocks that kept the *Hay*'s missiles under proper control. There were eight interlocks in all. Under the system in operation at the time of Gillespie's takeover, firing the missiles first required a signal from Washington. It contained a code that released four of the eight interlocks. To release the other four required that both the missile officer and the captain perform a complex set of procedures. The captain did not know the missile officer's role; the missile officer did not know the captain's.

The system was considered foolproof. The possibility that missile experts could board a submarine and simply dismantle the safety devices had never been considered.

Gillespie and his scientists estimated that all eight interlocks could be released in time for a firing at midnight the next day.

The time was 12:33 P.M. Fourteen hours and six minutes from the moment of the takeover. The first safety interlock was partially dismantled. The United States government had thirty-five hours and twenty-seven minutes to prevent the hell that Richard Gillespie planned for the world.

"A few years ago," Anderson said, "I talked with Admiral Gorshkov at a disarmament conference. He mentioned the possibility that a crackpot might take over a Polaris submarine. It worried him. I'm sure that in that room in the Kremlin, he's brought it up."

"Could one fella do this thing?" Bixby asked.

"It's highly unlikely that a man could take over a sub alone," Anderson replied, "and the chances of getting a group together on one ship seem ridiculous. Gorshkov knows that."

"Another thing," said the President. "Some nut like that would probably use the missiles, not the torpedoes."

"Right," Anderson said. "Of course, a crackpot might be unable to arm and fire the missiles or to force the necessary cooperation from others in the ship. But I'd also add that such screwballs usually like publicity. They like to advertise what they've done. We'd have heard from him by now."

"So Gorshkov would likely toss this one away, too," the President said.

Anderson pondered that one for a moment.

"Yes," he answered, "but it would give him the most trouble."

"Why?"

"Because it's the one on everybody's mind—ever since atomic weapons came into being."

"Well, it worries me," the President said. "There're a lot of kooks running around in uniforms."

The President's remark stunned Anderson. Although he agreed with it in part, he was still emotionally involved with the military. He resented such words as "kooks." The remark was all the more shocking because he had never heard the President say anything negative about the military.

"There must be some way we can check out the madman thing," Bixby said. "I mean, it's our sub."

Anderson grimaced, then flicked some ashes into the ashtray. An ironic look floated across his face. He was like the man who had to admit that the perfect bank vault had been broken into.

"That's the problem," he replied. "We cannot check it out. At least not without compromising our deterrent force."

The President's usually animated face seemed to freeze. He immediately understood that there was a flaw in the Polaris system that he didn't know about.

"Explain," he ordered.

"Polaris subs maintain total radio silence on patrol. To respond to naval operations contact would require them to break silence and reveal their locations. And no renegade sub is going to admit what it's doing anyway. True, we might get some information. One of the subs might fail to respond, or if one was far enough off course to have torpedoed the *Dostoyny,* we'd know by its transmission. But the whole fleet would be exposed."

"That may be precisely what the Soviets want," Somerville blared. "It's possible this whole thing is a stunt to get us to contact our subs in a panic so the Russians could sink them."

"That's a realistic possibility," Anderson said.

"I won't have it," the President insisted. "I have an

45

oath to defend this country. I'll go along with your notion, Andy, that Gorshkov understands the odds against a crackpot."

The CIS started clicking:

SIXFLT TRANSMISSION IN APPROX 80 SECONDS.

"Are there any other possible causes of the *Dostoyny* sinking that Gorshkov might be considering?" the President asked.

"I don't think so," Anderson replied. "I've listed them all, and each is extremely improbable. There is no evidence of any of them in the current situation."

"So Gorshkov goes back to his original premise, that we sank their ship," the President said.

"Unless this whole thing is a Russian trick, Mr. President, Gorshkov *must* come back to that premise."

"And we could give quotes from Lenin and he wouldn't take our word for it," the President said.

"No. *We* know we didn't sink the ship, but we all realize that what's true doesn't matter. What people think is true is where the danger lies. Gorshkov will see no logic in our sinking the ship, but he may be impressed by the lack of logic itself. Illogic is part of the element of surprise."

"Is it possible he might ultimately write off the sinking in the interests of peace?" Bixby asked.

"Admiral Gorshkov is a military man," Anderson answered. "There is a mentality there, a way of thinking."

Again he surveyed the room before going on. The words sounded like those he had used before the Women's Peace Alliance.

"Military men," he said, looking directly at the President, "tend to think in terms of fighting wars, not avoiding them."

There was a long pause.

"What a hell of a fix," the President finally said.

"I could think of better ways to spend a day," Anderson replied.

"All right," the President asked, "if we come to the

conclusion that Gorshkov believes we sank his ship, what would you recommend we do?"

"Nothing," Anderson replied.

"Nothing?" Somerville asked.

"It's always possible," Anderson answered, "that the Russians might respond vigorously to our supposed attack. But so far they haven't. If we refrain from any provocation, it would be the best proof that our intentions are peaceful."

"That could be a colossal risk," Somerville said.

"Yes," Anderson replied. "But think of the alternative."

The CIS came on again.

TRANSMISSION BEGINS.

The Russian destroyers had closed on the American fleet in the Mediterranean. The talk stopped. All eyes turned toward the screen. Admiral Gorshkov was making his move.

4

The USS *Little Rock* was obsolete. She was a light cruiser, a relic of a war fought before most of her crewmen were born. She had been modernized, and modernized again, and modernized still once more. But now, after more than three decades, she was approaching the end of her useful life. Anderson looked up at the CIS screen and saw three modern Soviet destroyers bearing down on her. It reminded him of a gang of adolescents attacking an old lady in a bad neighborhood.

As Sixth Fleet flagship the *Little Rock* was the symbol of American naval power in the Mediterranean. That thought went through Anderson's mind, and it embarrassed him. The ship's ancient silhouette embarrassed him. The steel plates on her bridge, buckled from the repeated shock waves of her forward turrets, embarrassed him. Even with her new Talos antiaircraft missiles, which gave her the right to be called guided missile light cruiser, she still represented the decline of the United States Navy.

The Soviet fleet, a pitiful coastal force at the end of World War II, was now challenging the United States for supremacy at sea. Automatically the balance of forces clicked through Anderson's mind: America—125 submarines, Russia—315. America—8 cruisers, Russia—28. America—zero missile boats, Russia—135. Only the American carriers preserved the balance.

CRITIC looked at the screen in fascinated silence, as though watching a tennis match or a prizefight. The Russian destroyers closed hard on *Little Rock,* their forward gun barrels pointed directly at her. F-4 Phantom fighters from the carrier *Constellation* thundered by, but they had standing orders not to attack unless an American unit was fired on.

Suddenly the Russian formation broke. Two of the destroyers turned to straddle the *Little Rock*. They were smaller than the cruiser, but much newer and faster. As the two destroyers maneuvered to keep the *Little Rock* between them, the third jumped ahead and cut in forty-five yards in front of the cruiser's bow. This ship slowed, forcing *Little Rock* to do the same, forcing the American ships around her to slow as well.

"Doesn't that slow speed make those ships vulnerable?" Somerville asked.

"Yes," Anderson replied.

"So?" Somerville asked, a look of baffled urgency coming across his face.

"Not much we can do without shooting," Anderson said.

Both men instinctively glanced at the President, seeking some hint of his response to their exchange. The President ignored it and kept his eyes firmly fixed on the screen.

The distance between the *Little Rock* and the straddling destroyers began to narrow. The ship on *Little Rock*'s bow slowed even more, forcing the Americans to slow down to six knots. Soon only twenty yards separated the cruiser from the Red destroyers. Then, fifteen yards.

The picture in the Cabinet Room was now fed by a helicopter from the *Constellation*. Anderson could clearly see the Soviet captains watching from their bridges. Despite the close distances, they used binoculars. They were studying details and observing the demeanor of the American officers. The Soviet crews were in battle gear. They were poised and ready. The Americans were also at battle stations, but had been ordered to appear relaxed and to make no provocative gestures. Some waved at the Russians, and a few Soviet sailors waved back. For one irrational moment the scene reminded Anderson of the meeting of American and Soviet forces at the Elbe in World War II.

The Soviet ships lurched closer. Some of the smiles disappeared. Hands grabbed railings or anything else that could help a man in a collision. A footage scale was now superimposed on the CIS screen. It showed the distance between *Little Rock* and the straddling destroyers as less than eight feet.

In the Cabinet Room no one moved. Cigarettes burned in ashtrays. Pencils lay on pads. A steward entered to fill water glasses, but saw the time was wrong and silently slipped away.

Anderson looked again toward the President, hoping the chief could put this incident in perspective. The President was staring intently at the screen, but his inner thoughts were not revealed.

Somerville's lips were tight. There was a touch of defiance in his eyes. Anderson realized that Somerville saw the challenge as a personal insult.

The Soviet captains inched their ships even closer. Both eyed the narrowing air between themselves and the armored sides of the *Little Rock*.

Anderson heard new jet noises and the television camera turned upward to show a 747 making an approach run to Rome. Anderson wondered whether the passengers had any inkling of what was happening down below.

The climax came suddenly: a coordinated sharp turn inward by both destroyers.

A thump.

Then another. Then a grinding crunch as the *Little Rock* was squeezed between the destroyers and forced to a complete halt. Another crunch as *Little Rock*'s captain ordered more power, even at the risk of slamming the third Soviet destroyer ahead.

Anderson pushed his chest tightly against the Nixon table as he saw streams of sparks fly from the ships as they ground together. He felt a sudden urge to give maneuvering orders to the *Little Rock* himself, but he knew the officers on the scene were in a far better position to judge distances, speeds, and damage levels than he was. Only the most extreme circumstances would force him to intervene.

The destroyers separated, then moved in again. The speed of all four ships was faster now. *Little Rock* was so close to the third destroyer ahead that spray from the Russian was soaking her bow.

Again the cruiser was bumped from each side. She seemed to vibrate. Her superstructure swayed left, then right. The destroyer ahead slowed almost to a halt. *Little Rock* slowed a bit, but refused to stop.

In previous incidents, Anderson knew, a harassing ship traveling ahead would maintain enough speed to avoid being hit. This time it didn't. Whether it was planned or a tactical blunder, Anderson couldn't know. But suddenly, as CRITIC watched in stilled horror, the *Little Rock* struck the stern of the Soviet destroyer, cutting the Russian's plates both above and below the waterline.

CRITIC could hear the whistles of the Soviet damage-control system and saw Russian sailors run toward the stern. Rapid orders bellowed from the destroyer's bullhorn. Anderson saw a sudden flash of flame, then smoke started to pour from the cut in the stern. Oil was afire. The destroyer momentarily gained speed, then slowed. She appeared crippled.

There was sudden activity on the *Little Rock*'s bridge. Her captain had to move to starboard to avoid striking the forward destroyer again. But another destroyer was still locked on his starboard side. That ship had to be pushed out of the way.

Little Rock lurched, violently slamming the Red destroyer. The Russian officers were startled. They made no attempt to lurch back—the cruiser's heavier plates would inevitably win—but stayed close enough to *Little Rock* to make it impossible for her to maneuver.

Burning oil flowed from the destroyer ahead. The fire came close to *Little Rock*'s bow. She could not stop, and Anderson knew she would have to make it through the burning slick. The *Little Rock*'s captain ordered the ship "zippered up"—the crew sealed inside and the water spray system activated. As the nozzles shot their streams of water in circles, it appeared from above that the ship was taking a violent bath. The system was designed to wash radioactivity off the decks after a nuclear attack. Now it was used to keep the ship free of burning oil.

The *Little Rock* and her 1,700 men surged through the blazing slick, escaping from the straddling destroyers, whose captains chose not to risk their thin plates against the flame. For a moment the American cruiser disappeared into thick black smoke. Then she emerged, her sprinklers still churning.

The Cabinet Room erupted in cheers. Even Anderson joined in.

Men ran onto *Little Rock*'s deck and her senior officers peered out from the bridge. The ship was relatively undamaged. The only sign of her ordeal was the blackened armor on her sides and the disappearance of the name *Little Rock* from her stern.

The crippled Soviet destroyer was listing. Anderson saw several crew members jump overboard, a sign that they were trapped by the fire. The other two destroyers now veered to come alongside, and their crews turned fire hoses on the stricken ship. They also poured foam onto the sea to keep the traveling slick at a safe distance. In a few minutes the fire aboard the Soviet destroyer was out and the other two ships prepared to take her in tow.

The Russian harassment was over.

The CIS screen went blank.

"Christ almighty!" the President groaned. "They have *never* gone that far! Right, Andy?"

"That's correct," Anderson replied. He looked around and saw that about half the men in the room, including the President, were sweating.

"What do you make of it?" the President asked.

Anderson hesitated.

"It was a very intense harassment," Anderson replied. "Anything beyond that would be theory. I—"

"Mr. President," a cultured voice called out from the same end of the room where Somerville sat. Eyes turned. They focused on General Rufus Combs, the chairman of the Joint Chiefs of Staff.

"I think we all appreciate Admiral Anderson's caution," Combs went on, a scholarly, civilized accent to his

52

words. "But we would be remiss if we didn't consider this a highly dangerous, willfully provocative action by the Soviets."

Beautifully stated, as Anderson expected it to be. For Rufus Combs knew how.

Next to Somerville—*always* next to Somerville—sat this elegant general. Anderson knew that Combs and the Secretary would work in tandem for the remainder of the meeting. They were known in Washington as the Siamese Twins of the right wing.

Like many officers who entered the army in World War II, Rufus Combs acquired combat experience as a junior officer. But now his qualifications were as much technical as military. He followed every fashion, including the requirement in the 1960's that an officer know as much about international relations as about fighting a war. In Combs' case that meant earning a PhD from Georgetown in political science. By the time he put on his first star he was as qualified to be Henry Kissinger's assistant as to run a division.

"I would be as reluctant as any man here to consider the use of force in this situation," Combs said. "The thought of nuclear war is horrifying, repugnant. But we cannot wish reality away."

Combs was a graceful and handsome man, with black hair that was slightly longer than the military norm. He was diplomatic to a fault, a quality that had helped his career considerably. But, like Somerville, he was an unremitting hawk. Unlike Somerville, Combs was subtle. He knew how to turn on the agony and pain when arguing for a devastating military solution. He had learned well the lingo of foreign policy, just as he had learned to look pensive, concerned, statesmanlike. Combs was a hawk with a sense of public relations, and so, Anderson believed, he was dangerous.

Seeing Somerville and Combs together at the end of the room, Anderson recalled another member of the CRITIC group, whose chair was empty. Charles Safrin, the Secretary of State, had been the President's closest confidant, a wise old counselor. He had been a moderate, a balance to

53

Somerville and Combs. But Safrin had died of a stroke two weeks before. There was no one to take his place, and the absence of his advice worried Anderson. The admiral felt very much alone.

"Are you suggesting," the President asked Combs, "some form of preemptive action?"

"I'm not suggesting it, Mr. President," Combs replied. "I'm suggesting that it be weighed, considered."

Anderson knew Combs was suggesting it.

"We'll consider it," the President said. "But I want to go back to Admiral Anderson for a bit. He was just going to tell us about this whole business maybe being a Russian trick. I want to hear that before we decide anything."

Eyes shifted back from the President to Anderson, and the admiral felt a sudden tension within him. He was beginning to believe that of all the possibilities, a Russian trick was the most probable.

"Mr. President," he said, "I mentioned earlier that the Russians might have sunk their own ship, perhaps to provide an excuse for some military action. The scenario might go like this: They sink the ship and charge us with the sinking. We naturally deny it. With our written denials in hand, they break the news of the sinking to the Russian people. We get the blame. It's the Reichstag fire all over. Then we have war."

"Because of a ship?" Bixby asked. "If they wanted war, why not hit us with their missiles?"

"Because nobody would win," Anderson replied. "Remember that nobody used gas in the Second World War, and it's possible that nobody will use superweapons in the next war. In fact, there's a theory that the Third World War will be fought largely at sea. Admiral Gorshkov has built up the most powerful submarine force in history. Many of our people doubt that we could maintain control of the oceans against it.

"So it's possible that Russians may now want to fight us in a naval war," Anderson continued, "but they'd want us to be blamed for starting it."

"Could they really restrict a war to the sea?" Somerville asked.

"Nobody knows," Anderson replied, "but they'd try. That would mean we would be the ones who would have to expand the action, either into nuclear war or a ground war in Europe. Gorshkov would count on us to reject a nuclear war, which might end the world, and our European allies might reject a ground war on their soil. Under Gorshkov's thesis, the Russians would win at sea and become the dominant power."

"My God!" Bixby groaned. "And they could do that?"

"Their people have discussed it," Anderson said.

The room fell still.

"Of all the possibilities we've talked about," the President said gravely, "this is the one that fits their military thinking." The age lines in his face, which were often vague, now seemed more prominent. "Right, Andy?"

"That is right," Anderson replied.

Again the CIS began printing out an advisory:

STAND BY. SIXFLT TRANSMISSION II.

The Soviets would now attempt another harassing maneuver in the Mediterranean.

The President, intent on pursuing Anderson's point, ignored the advisory. "Would we," he asked, "would this nation seriously restrict itself to naval fighting in a war with Russia?"

"Mr. President," General Combs quietly replied, "obviously only you can make that decision. But I think the answer is clear. It would be folly to accommodate the Soviet Union's naval strategy. They have more steel and more men. We would have to employ nuclear weapons. We would have to attack on land."

"The general is correct," Somerville agreed. "We must consider nuclear weapons as weapons to be used when they're needed."

The President turned to Anderson.

"Andy?"

"Sir," Anderson responded, "we are only speaking theoretically. Even if this *is* a Soviet trick, we're not sure where it's leading. Until we know, I again urge restraint. We can't risk a holocaust on the basis of what we *think*."

"I disagree," Combs said. "We cannot rule out a preemptive strike against the Soviet Union."

"Mr. President," Anderson broke in, "that would be wildly irresponsible!"

The room tensed, surprised at the sharpness of Anderson's rebuke. But Combs was unimpressed.

"Admiral Anderson," he replied, not sacrificing an ounce of dignity, "we are both sworn to protect the United States. I fully agree with your judgment that we don't know precisely what the situation is. But that very uncertainty poses dangers. Either the Soviets think they've been attacked—in which case they may strike *us* within hours—or they're already in the first stages of war. I submit that action by us is fully justified."

All eyes shifted again to Anderson, but Anderson looked only at the President. He knew that the man was agonized. There was no cut-and-dried Pearl Harbor to shape his course. He was being asked to decide nuclear policy in a vacuum.

"Mr. President," Anderson said, "our forces are on alert. We are ready. I recommend that if we now take a risk, that it be a risk for peace."

The President sat motionless. Anderson noticed that he was gripping the right side of his chair so tightly that his knuckles were white.

The CIS:

SIXFLT TRANSMISSION II BEGINS.

CRITIC turned toward the screen. Again the move was Moscow's.

It was the carrier *Constellation*'s turn to feel the Soviet harassment. The *Constellation* was one of the navy's largest carriers—81,000 tons, more than 1,000 feet long. She carried eighty-five planes, but she also carried a curse. During her construction at the Brooklyn Navy

Yard a fire had broken out inside her and forty-six workers had died. She was heavily damaged, and since that day many navy men felt she was a marked ship.

Her four catapults were now launching Phantoms and the newer F-14 Tomcats. They would be ready to strike if the Soviet Navy extended its harassment to actual combat.

Only 120 yards away was the Soviet helicopter cruiser *Moskva*. She was slightly more than half the length of the *Constellation* and, at 18,000 tons, less than a quarter the displacement. Her design was odd. Forward of her beam, her midsection, was a tall superstructure and an array of missile launchers, guns, and torpedo tubes, whereas aft of the beam she was nothing more than a flat helicopter platform. In silhouette she looked like a ship that had been half completed above the deck line.

From her bridge Soviet Admiral Nikolai Tarsis watched the *Constellation*'s launchings through German binoculars. He turned to issue a quick order to the *Moskva*'s captain. Immediately the cruiser veered to port, closing on the carrier.

The American destroyer *Parsons*, protecting *Constellation*, raced forward to block the *Moskva*, but she was too late. The Russian cruiser had passed thirty yards ahead of her and now had a clear path to the carrier's starboard side. She swerved and started running parallel with the *Constellation*, inching closer.

It seemed ludicrous—the small cruiser taking on the giant carrier—but Anderson knew that it was intended as a dramatic show of Russian determination and courage, and he was impressed by the Soviet audacity. Still, he knew the *Moskva*'s steel plates were strong and modern, that she could handle herself in this kind of harassing operation.

In a few moments she was no more than fifteen yards from the *Constellation*. The carrier, under orders, continued launching her planes. There would be no deference to the Soviets.

The *Constellation*'s captain tried to turn away from the *Moskva*, but the big ship maneuvered slowly and the

Moskva could easily follow her. The Russian squeezed the carrier, suddenly smashing against her flight deck.

She moved off, then smashed again. The grinding and crunching reverberated throughout the Cabinet Room.

Another smash. Both ships were taking damage. *Constellation* had to abandon use of two starboard elevators bringing planes from the hangar deck below, but she continued to launch.

Now, however, the *Moskva* forged ahead, moving up to the *Constellation*'s starboard bow. Anderson watched grimly, and he knew the inevitable had to come: The carrier's captain ordered launchings suspended from the starboard catapult. They were now too dangerous. Although three other catapults continued to launch, it was an American humiliation. For the first time a Soviet ship had slashed the combat power of a United States Navy carrier.

Even the pragmatic Bixby was red-faced.

"Can't we fire across her bow?" he asked.

"Of course," Anderson replied.

"Why don't we?"

"They'd ignore it. What do we do for an encore?"

Bixby fell silent.

The *Moskva* still squeezed the *Constellation*. The carrier's captain, concerned over casualties in a collision, ordered the starboard launch crew to abandon its station, but as one man jumped from a gangway onto the flight deck, he suddenly lost his footing and fell backward. CRITIC watched in horror as he dropped overboard between the *Moskva* and the *Constellation*.

The American captain quickly flashed a signal to the *Moskva* that a man was in the water. But the warning came as the cruiser was again slipping toward the carrier. Desperately American sailors threw their comrade a line. He couldn't grasp it.

The *Moskva* slammed the *Constellation* again. As she backed off, the blood of the crushed sailor stained the sides of the two ships.

In the Cabinet Room, no one moved. But it was a room alive with unspoken rage. Isaac Anderson felt the instinct for combat well up within him for the first time in years. He also felt a streak of guilt. Had he advised a stronger response to the harassment, would that boy still be alive? But he quickly realized he was falling into the same trap as those who argued for an expanded war in Vietnam "until they return our POW's." Thousands had died for the excuse that it was the only way five hundred could come back.

Suddenly the silence in the Cabinet Room was broken.

"That boy," said Combs, "may be the first American casualty of the Third World War."

Anderson desperately hoped not. But he had no rational argument to counter Combs, and anything he said would seem an affront to the boy who had just died. He looked around at the others and finally at the President.

The President sat forlornly, gazing up at the screen. His shirt was completely drenched. Drops of sweat were falling from his chin. Anderson could not forget that this was the man who had lost his temper with the Chinese Premier. The question in Anderson's mind was how far he could now be pushed.

5

The Soviet Premier watched the American sailor die on the Russian version of the CIS. He was not sweating. He had seen too much during World War II, and the sight of blood could not move him.

What could move him—and did—was the thought of the Soviet Union as a nuclear battleground. Death affected him only in the abstract. He had once seen the corpse of a man mistakenly shot by the KGB and had laughed at the mistake, but the mention of thirty million Russians killed in World War II could bring him to tears.

Premier Zorin sat in his own meeting room, looking his seventy-three years. The lines were deep, the skin worn and speckled with age marks. But there was no unsteadiness, and the eyes were completely clear. He watched carefully as the *Moskva* now backed away from the *Constellation*. He had to squint to see details since the Russian CIS was little more than a television console with a twenty-five-inch black-and-white screen. The computers that fed it were made possible by American technology, supplied in the trade deals of the early 1970's.

Although the Premier was emotionally unaffected by the sailor's death, it did not please him. It was the kind of accident, he knew, that could enrage the Americans. Yet he couldn't send his condolences to Washington without appearing to take the blame, and that, he knew, would weaken the impact of the harassment.

The Premier's meeting room looked like the boardroom of an American corporation. There was a long glass-topped table, indirect lighting, plush red carpeting. The appearance was not surprising, for Zorin had conceived the decoration for the room while on a visit to New York. He was, as some CIA analysts put it, a Yankeephile. The idea that America had escaped damage in World War II—and was so rich—impressed him. He admired American resourcefulness, ingenuity, and drive. He was convinced that a country that had accomplished so much had discovered some secret to life. Although he was still a Marxist, Zorin secretly liked to picture himself as an American corporate magnate, and that partially accounted for his decorating tastes. He saw himself as a pragmatist, "a man with hard knuckles," as he once told an interviewer. He read the *Wall Street Journal*.

And yet those reporters who kept calling him "the American Premier" misunderstood him. For beneath the fascination with America was the soul of a Russian and the thinking of a Bolshevik. Behind the devilish jokes that charmed foreign audiences was a deep suspicion of everyone outside the Soviet Union. It was Zorin, Americans preferred to forget, who had personally seen to it that sixteen dissident writers went to Siberian labor camps. Eleven of them had died.

Zorin had once been married, and there had been four playful children. His entire family, except for one daughter, perished at Nazi hands. The surviving daughter died in 1967 of influenza. So Zorin was a lonely man who often took long walks in the Moscow night. Sometimes he stopped in at a restaurant, just to talk and laugh with people. Because of his age, there was no serious discussion of remarriage, although Zorin, perhaps fighting time, kept open the possibility.

He had worked his way up through the party structure, specializing in factory planning. His talent was first recognized when Soviet intelligence reported one of his industrial complexes had made the American target list. He had an uncanny knack for avoiding controversy and keeping in the graces of most factions. In his personal collection were pictures taken with Stalin, as well as with those who eventually denounced Stalin—and with those who ultimately denounced the denouncers.

Yet he became Premier largely by default. The party

leadership wanted an economic expert, and he had outlived the others.

"I still have trouble believing this," Zorin said now to Admiral Gorshkov as they watched events in the Mediterranean. "The President is a rational man. Why would he torpedo our ship?"

"Rationality is an illusion," Gorshkov replied. "What is a rational man but someone who hasn't made his first mistake?" He stared blankly at the screen, letting the remark sink in.

"And you're certain it can't be anything but an attack?" the Premier asked. "This idea of some American submarine acting on its own worries me."

"That's another illusion—certainty," Gorshkov said. "Whoever tells you he is certain in a matter like this is an idiot. Certainty is impossible. All I've told you is the probabilities. The Americans are very good at controlling their submarine crewmen. They have psychiatrists for keeping out the strange ones, the sick ones. Besides, the taking over of a submarine is complex. There are too many people. No."

"You've rechecked the sonar data, Gorshkov?"

"Personally. The analysis is sound. A Polaris submarine."

"But why?" the Premier asked.

Gorshkov then turned sternly to the man who had been his friend for twenty years.

"You keep asking me that. We can only guess at reasons. Once war begins, nobody remembers them anyway. Economic, maybe."

"What?"

"We could make a theory that it's economic," Gorshkov replied. "The situation in America is bad. Marx talked about the need for capitalist societies to have war."

Zorin opened his eyes wide. A slight grin crossed his face. He shrugged his shoulders in a broad, exaggerated motion.

"Marx?" he asked. "Who's he?"

He chuckled at his own question, being well aware of the decline of ideology in the Soviet Union. There had been a campaign a few years before to encourage school-children to read their Communist primers, but it had failed miserably. The young now were more interested in underground copies of American pornographic novels. Marx was becoming in Russia what Jefferson had become in America—revered, although few recalled why.

"Marx was right," Gorshkov said. "The only sure way for the United States to solve its economic problems is war. Look at 1941. Roosevelt never cured their Depression. The Japanese cured it. They attacked Pearl Harbor and the Depression went away."

"That is not the way Americans think," Zorin replied. "They weigh practicalities, not theories. War is practical because it helps their business, but it's impractical because the business could get blown up. Since getting blown up is worse than starving, they don't like war. Look at their free enterprise. They talk about it like God and Christ, but if Lockheed needs money, it runs to the government, just like here. In Moscow we call it socialism. In Washington it's national security."

Besides Zorin and Gorshkov there were only two other people in the room. Gorshkov sat to the Premier's left. The Soviet air and army chiefs were opposite him. If Zorin hadn't respected the power of the other chiefs, only Gorshkov would have been invited to the meeting. Although Zorin often disagreed with him, he respected Gorshkov. The others were technocrats, experts in macines and weapons. Gorshkov was a strategist, a global planner. In an international crisis he was the only military man who had anything important to say.

Admiral of the Fleet of the Soviet Union Sergei Georgiyevich Gorshkov was sixty-five and a graduate of the Frunze Naval Academy in Leningrad. Since 1956 he had been commander in chief of the Soviet Navy and First Deputy Minister of Defense. Among his decorations were Hero of the Soviet Union, three Orders of Lenin, and four Orders of the Red Banner. Gorshkov considered himself an intellectual and was known for his ability to quote from philosophers in six languages. His building of the Soviet Navy was generally regarded as a work of genius.

His soft facial features, receding hairline, and frameless glasses made Gorshkov look more like a kindly grandfather than an admiral. But the appearance was deceptive, for S. G. Gorshkov was a humorless man whose dour expression rarely changed.

The navy was his hobby as well as his profession. Even when he played chess with Zorin, which he did two or three times a week, he thought of the opposing sides as battle fleets, even renaming the pieces to conform to naval nomenclature. The king was the admiral, the queen his chief of staff. The knights were fleet commanders and the pawns ordinary sailors. Gorshkov felt secure enough to beat the Premier repeatedly. Only once did Zorin win. Gorshkov spent a week analyzing the game until he discovered his mistake.

Gorshkov knew the American, Isaac Anderson, and he liked him. But he thought him rather an old lady, wringing his hands over war instead of preparing for it. He saw Anderson as adequate intellectually, but lacking in the special dash required of great commanders. He had, Gorshkov thought, lost something since his heroic days at Okinawa.

Having built the Soviet Navy, Gorshkov had an underlying wish to lead it in action against the United States. His feeling was understandable. The navy to which he had devoted his life had never been tested, and his frustration ran deep. He was a trained musician with a magnificent instrument and no opportunity to play. Gorshkov was certain he could defeat the United States at sea if the chance came. But he had a foreboding that his own death was near, and his yearning for combat had taken on an extra urgency.

Just as Anderson would lean toward peace in his advice to politicians, Gorshkov would lean toward war. But he was too patriotic and self-respecting to allow himself to go too far, and he certainly would never advocate military action when it was not justified. His yearning for battle was partially offset by the desire not to be labeled a warmonger. And he had little regard for military men who liked to appear "tough."

War, to Gorshkov, was an intellectual proposition.

"It is conceivable," Gorshkov said to Zorin, "that the American motive in sinking our ship is purely military."

"What do you mean?" Zorin asked.

"Our navy is growing stronger in comparison to theirs. They could easily believe that it's better to fight us at sea now than in the future. They may be starting a naval war."

"That's a practical argument," Zorin said. "But I wonder whether they'd carry it through. After Vietnam, war would be emotionally difficult for them."

"You can't rule it out," Gorshkov insisted. "Events speak for themselves."

Zorin turned to Gorshkov. There was a sadness in the Premier's eyes.

"I know," he said. "I would like to think that war will not happen. It's wishful thinking."

An aide entered and slipped a piece of paper in front of Zorin. It showed the status of Soviet units on military alert. Among the units listed were two army divisions that Zorin had ordered on maneuvers to demonstrate his resolve. But he had ordered them to move toward Moscow, rather than toward Western Europe, to avoid antagonizing the NATO countries.

Other units reporting included the flight of Tu-95 bombers heading toward the carrier *Enterprise* in the Sea of Japan. Their progress caught Zorin's attention. He picked up a phone that connected him to the technician who controlled his television screen.

"Switch to the Far East!"

Instantly the picture changed. Now Zorin and his chiefs could see the four-turboprop bombers approaching the carrier and her accompanying ships.

The picture changed again.

Zorin saw the carrier, and he knew immediately that it was the *Enterprise*. She was nuclear-powered, and there was no smokestack. Her island—her control tower—looked like a solid square of steel. Above it was a new radar mast that reminded Zorin of the gradually narrowing swirl of whipped cream atop an American ice cream sundae. The *Enterprise* was the most powerful ship in the United States Navy. Zorin knew she was named for the most famous carrier of World War II.

"What do you recommend out there?" he asked Gorshkov.

"Pure harassment," Gorshkov replied. "We must show our resolve all over the globe."

"But nothing further?"

"Not yet. You do not respond violently to an incident. You respond to a strategy. If the Americans do nothing else, we can assume they started something, then changed their minds."

"Because of our harassment?"

"Yes. They got the signal."

"And if they do something else, Gorshkov?"

"Then we assume they're starting a war at sea. Either we strike back at one target of great value—"

"Like the *Enterprise?*"

"Yes. Her fifty-five hundred men would vanish in one nuclear blow. That might make Washington reconsider."

"Or?"

"We counterstrike by a massive submarine assault against the American fleet."

The Premier rose slowly from his chair, revealing a substantial stomach that stretched his black one-button suit. He walked slowly over to a teakwood cabinet, opened a sliding door, and removed a bottle of Jack Daniel's that he had bought on a visit to Washington. Lost in his own somber thoughts of war, he neglected to offer a drink to the others. He poured a glass for himself, drank it in two gulps, then slapped the glass down on the cabinet and returned to his chair.

He sat quietly for a few moments, looking at no one, as though trying to avoid the inevitable question. But then he gradually turned to Gorshkov. He looked deeply into the admiral's eyes, seeking the special wisdom that he thought he possessed.

"They will go further," he said, "won't they?"

There was a slight shrug of Gorshkov's shoulders.

"I told you," he said, "I can only guess why—"

"I'm not asking that!" Zorin roared, a red flush coming to his face. "I'm asking what they'll do next!" The tension was clearly affecting him.

Gorshkov fidgeted with a wooden pencil, finally putting it down. Then he placed his hands on his cheeks, a well-known gesture that told everyone he was weighing his answer with great care. He was conscious of wanting to avoid anything that would later make him sound like a fool, but as he studied the Premier's insistent face, he knew he had to be forthright or be discredited.

"The Americans have never attacked a Soviet naval unit before. The risk is very great, so they would make such an attack only as part of a war plan. That is my opinion."

"Go on, Gorshkov."

"I believe it is likely that within forty-eight hours the Americans will take some new action. We will be at war and the existence of our nation will be at stake. That is also my opinion."

Zorin slumped back in his chair. His head gradually began to hang down to his chest as the graves of Russians killed in a distant war flashed through his mind. Graves of his family, of his friends. But what also flashed was Russian humiliation in the morning of that war. The millions who should have been defended. The soldiers who died for lack of equipment.

He knew more about war than did the American President. He had felt it. He had lived it. He had suffered in ways he could never express. Both he and the President wanted desperately to avoid another conflict, yet both were now considering options that would send their forces into battle. No matter how different their own lives, both men approached war in precisely the same way. Their courses were chosen not by their own feelings, but by the ritual of history.

"You have always dreamed of fighting the American Navy, haven't you, Gorshkov?" the Premier asked.

Gorshkov showed no feeling.

"Only if the time came," he said.

Zorin turned his head and looked out a window, as if making a solemn pledge to Russia herself.

"The time may soon come," he said. "I will not be the first Premier in Soviet history to lose a war."

Richard Gillespie sensed what was happening in Washington and Moscow.

The *John Hay* was able to pick up news broadcasts from the United States. Roger Mudd, hardly a sensationalist, was reporting sudden meetings at the White House. He described the grim faces, the tight lips. The atmosphere, Mudd said, was similar to that surrounding the Cuban missile crisis of 1962. But the press wasn't being told a thing.

Gillespie also picked up increased Soviet military traffic. It was coded, of course, but he could imagine what it contained: orders for submarines to proceed to new stations, for aircraft to fly to secret rendezvous points, for whole armies to move, for missilemen to man their weapons. Even the code seemed to have an urgency about it, a sense of tension and expectation.

As the hours passed, Gillespie's scientists continued working on the missiles' safety systems. Their work went smoothly. The first interlock had been completely dismantled at 1:47 P.M., and the event was celebrated by coffee and cupcakes in the control room. Modest. Subdued. The great celebrations were yet to come.

Even while the scientists worked, life aboard the *Hay* went on with remarkable normalcy. The first familygrams began to arrive. These were up to fifteen-word messages sent through navy communications to members of Polaris crews. They announced births, marriages, deaths. Each crew member was allowed three or four during a sixty-day mission, and although the men could not answer because radio silence was always maintained, at least they knew what was happening at home.

> TO: TM3(SU) GARY F. MC CLOREY
> LINDA GAVE BIRTH EIGHT-POUND BOY. HEALTHY. NAME EDWARD ANDREW. WISH YOU COULD SEE HIM.

> TO: CWO2 DAVID S. RIKE
> DON ENGAGED TO MARRY ELIZABETH NOBLE. WEDDING JANUARY. CAN'T WAIT TO SEE YOU.

> TO: MM1 (SS) WALTER MUNDY
> REGRET TELL YOU FATHER IN CRITICAL CONDITION AFTER SURGERY. MOTHER HOLDING UP. WILL INFORM YOU.

Richard Gillespie took a ship's roster from a cabinet in the control room. He began studying the names and duties of the *Hay*'s enlisted men, putting checks next to some names, question marks next to others. He planned to reduce these choices to two men who would play a critical role in the North Star Crusade. They would, Gillespie knew, have a sainted place in American history.

At 3:14 P.M. Jack Rains of Cal Tech told Gillespie that the second safety interlock had been bypassed. It was sixteen hours and forty-seven minutes from the time of the takeover. Thirty-two hours and forty-six minutes remained to the moment of launch.

6

The President announced only two decisions to the CRITIC group:

"We'll take no major action until we get a better picture of what Moscow is up to. At the same time, I want McNamara to put out a cover story to explain an alert. You know how the papers and the television behave on these things. You get people too scared or whipped up and the chance for peace goes down the drain.

"Everybody knows there's been some new Red guerrilla stuff in Malaysia. So have the cover read, 'U.S. forces were put on low-level alert today, showing our concern over Southeast Asia,' et cetera. Something like that."

The meeting ended. Anderson felt a hollowness. Things were getting out of control, he feared, and the progress in building peace with the Soviet Union was unraveling. But the uncertainty bothered him more than facts would have. He felt like a father looking for a missing son. A corpse would be better than no news at all.

He walked down the corridor just as McNamara was giving the cover story to reporters. Anderson wondered how the press secretary felt, for he knew McNamara had serious problems with secrecy that stemmed from a checkered past as a newsman. He had been Washington correspondent for a conservative Southern paper when Watergate broke in 1972, and at first he had downgraded evidence of Presidential involvement. He even took a few editorial swings at Bob Woodward and Carl Bernstein of the Washington *Post*, who uncovered the scandal. Later he became convinced that the President was involved and started to probe until his paper's management objected and he knuckled under. While other reporters pursued Richard Nixon, he devoted himself to mechanical reports of court hearings and official pronouncements. He became a hero to local rightists, who saw him as a symbol of virtue in contrast to the snakes of the Eastern press.

But he became disgusted with his own performance. His curly hair gave rise to a nickname—other reporters called him "Nixon's poodle." He left his paper, hoping to get a new start on another, but no major daily would have him, and neither would the news magazines or the networks. He took a job on a small money-losing weekly in Pennsylvania for $160 a week. He went into debt. Then his wife divorced him and took their eight-year-old son to live in California.

McNamara was determined to rebuild his name and his self-respect. He became a vigorous, uncompromising reporter of local news. He got a major break when a tipster told him of corruption in the county courthouse. McNamara investigated, and as a result of his work, three judges were removed, five lawyers disbarred, and four men, improperly jailed, were released. McNamara was awarded the Pulitzer Prize for local reporting. He was hired by the Los Angeles *Times* and given another chance in Washington.

This time he made good. He quickly became known as a new Jack Anderson, breaking story after story of official laxity, incompetence, and dishonesty. His reputation grew and he was given a national column. When the new President took office, McNamara was the outstanding candidate for the job of news secretary. His credentials were impeccable.

"Does this alert mean the United States will intervene in Malaysia?" Anderson heard a reporter ask.

"There are no current plans to do so," McNamara replied.

"Mac, is this gonna be one of those Vietnam things, where the story changes every day?"

"I see no reason to believe that," McNamara said.

"Are we ready to fight another jungle war?"

McNamara paused.

71

"I'm not really equipped to say," he replied. "That's one for the Pentagon."

"Are they telling you everything, Mac?"

"Yes."

McNamara's reputation, his greatest asset, was nonetheless a problem for the President. McNamara, the President knew, had to understand that virgin purity was not possible on the inside. Working in the White House meant compromise, withholding of news, and occasional censorship. There would be moments of personal moral crisis. The President constantly worried that McNamara would "pull a Horst," a reference to the resignation of J. F. ter Horst, Gerald Ford's first news secretary, in protest over the Nixon pardon.

Now McNamara was telling lies. He knew they were important lies, necessary lies. Telling them might help preserve the peace. But as Anderson watched, he realized what the lying must have meant to McNamara. He knew that it reminded him of a disgraceful performance in Watergate. The admiral hoped that McNamara understood the difference.

Anderson walked out of the White House and waited a few moments. A gray navy staff car pulled up and came to an abrupt stop. Above its front bumper four polished stars glittered in the morning sun. A sailor jumped out and opened the rear door. His heels clicked; his right hand sliced upward against his temple like a karate chop.

"Afternoon, sir."

Anderson returned the salute with the ease of experience.

"Afternoon."

He started to get into the car, but a female voice interrupted.

"Mind if I ride with you, Admiral?"

Anderson paused and looked back.

Doris Moffitt, a particularly irritating reporter for the Associated Press, had broken off from the White House wolf pack and followed Anderson outside.

"Hello, Doris," Anderson said. "Are you going to the Pentagon?"

"If you are."

"Well, come along. We'll be an item."

They got in the car.

The reporter's request for the ride was nervy, but it fit her reputation. Doris Moffitt was relentless. She was forty but looked older. Her weather-beaten features reflected years of covering the jungle side of the Vietnam War and the Sinai front in the Middle East. She spoke with that knife-edged voice and cold bluntness that characterized some leading female reporters of her generation. Although her ability won her the jealousy of her male colleagues, it also won her the right to be the butt of gossip. It was said, correctly, that she had blessed several four-star generals in Vietnam with personal favors in exchange for news.

As the admiral's car pulled out of the White House grounds, Moffitt flipped a page on her pad and pushed the top button on a ball-point pen.

"I trust you're having a nice day, Admiral," she said, making her usual attempt to disarm her target by small talk.

"Just fine," Anderson replied. A small smile came to his lips. He and Moffitt were beginning a kind of journalistic hide-and-seek. He had been through these probes before, and his Department of the Navy answers were ready.

"Admiral," Moffitt asked, "what is this all about?"

"Well, Doris," Anderson replied, "I'm sure McNamara gave you all the details—"

"All the garbage, you mean. What's really going on?"

Anderson laughed uneasily. He had the usual stiffness of military men in fast civilian company. He didn't know what to do with his hands, first placing them at his sides, then in his lap. He placed the right hand over the left, then went to the reverse.

"Mac gave you the correct information," he told Moffitt.

"It's a naval crisis, isn't it?"

Anderson stiffened slightly. Moffitt knew more than she was supposed to.

"What makes you think so?" he asked.

"Fred Bixby's telephone log."

"What?"

"It shows he made a number of calls this morning, but most of them to you."

"Well—"

"There's something else," Moffitt pushed on. "I dropped into the Cabinet Room after you broke. There were remains of a cigar in an ashtray opposite the President. That's where the man who gives the key briefing sits. The cigar was your brand, Admiral."

"I admire your energy, Doris, but the problem is in Southeast Asia, just as Mac—"

"Bull."

"Come on, now."

Moffitt paused for a moment. She looked out the window at the Washington Monument and began to hum a nondescript tune. She hoped to bug Anderson enough to make him talk.

"Who sank the Russian destroyer?" she suddenly asked.

Anderson burned. But he tried not to show it. He knew there had been a massive leak, that there was no point in denying what Moffitt obviously knew.

"What do you know about that?" he asked.

"A bit," Moffitt replied.

"May I ask who told you?"

"No."

Anderson took a cigar from his briefcase. With surgical care, he tore the top of the cellophane wrapper and took the cigar out. He lit it and flipped the match onto the floor, something he did only when agitated.

"Doris, let me be straight with you," he said. "If you use what you know, it could be dangerous."

"Embarrassing to the navy?" Moffitt asked, needling Anderson.

"No. Dangerous to the nation. A Russian ship did go

down in the Atlantic. It's very delicate. We're involved with Moscow."

"That's news, Admiral."

Anderson turned to Moffitt. His face was cold, almost as if he were about to dress down a seaman for a sloppy uniform.

"Don't pull any of that First Amendment crap on me!"

"Admiral," Moffit replied, "I have more common sense than to use something that could start a war. I thought you knew me better."

Anderson looked Moffitt up and down, then leaned back in his seat. He turned his eyes to the road ahead. He knew instinctively that he could trust Moffitt. To the best of his knowledge, she had never broken a pledge, and he really wasn't worried that she would reveal anything important. He was more concerned about the leak itself. Leaks were common in Washington, but this one outraged him. Clearly it had come from someone who wanted to aggravate tensions. Somerville? Combs? Somebody in the Pentagon who looked forward to a nice little war? Any one of the CRITIC group could have spoken to Moffitt before the meeting or afterward.

Was it possible that McNamara, in a fit of integrity . . . ?

No. He had character. He would have just resigned.

Leaks had a strange history, Anderson knew. Most Americans thought they came largely from the left, a view Richard Nixon tried to encourage. But Anderson knew that many leaks came from the military. Officers regularly divulged secrets to friendly reporters to help push a cause—a new plane, a new ship, an extra infantry division. Daniel Ellsberg was prosecuted for releasing the Pentagon Papers while far more sensitive information was being leaked daily by "patriots." Anderson recalled how a liberal Congressman was hounded by the House for divulging news of CIA operations in Chile, but the chronic drunkenness of a conservative Congressman who handled the most secret military information was ignored. If that alcoholic had applied for a job in the Defense Department, Anderson mused, he would have been rejected as a security risk.

"I assume," Moffitt continued, "that the Russians think we're responsible for the sinking?"

"Yes," Anderson answered.

"And some people expect war and think we should take the initiative. . . ."

"Correct."

"What's your position, Admiral?"

"For your background only," Anderson insisted.

"Of course."

"My position is . . . but you already know. Your source told you."

"My source has a very low opinion of you, Admiral."

Anderson felt the needle. The source was most likely Somerville. Combs shared Somerville's opinion of him, but Combs was too discreet to backbite with a reporter.

"We must act with restraint," Anderson said, a touch of defiance in his voice.

"Is that fair to the American people?" Moffitt asked.

"Yes," Anderson replied sarcastically, "it's fair to them. It may keep them alive."

There was another long, deadly pause as the car passed the Lincoln Memorial and turned onto the bridge that would take Anderson back to the Pentagon. Moffitt made some notes. Anderson puffed at his cigar. He wondered what he had done to deserve Harley Somerville. Most other Secretaries of Defense he could have understood. Almost all he could have tolerated. But Somerville was impossible.

"Admiral," Moffitt resumed, "may I ask you a personal question?"

Anderson was surprised since Moffitt had never asked permission to field a question. Anderson took it as a compliment, a sign that Moffitt might have some regard for him. He was correct. Moffitt privately regarded Anderson as the most impressive man in the administration. But the feeling never affected her questions.

"Ask," Anderson said.

"Do you feel yourself emotionally qualified to lead the United States Navy in war?"

Anderson knew then that a personal attack was under

way against him in this crisis. He assumed it had begun the moment the crisis had. It was aimed at reducing his influence, if not at getting rid of him altogether.

"Completely," he replied.

"Some would suggest that you lack the zeal."

Anderson thought for a moment.

"I lack the zeal for stupid wars," he answered. "I hope other officers feel the same way."

"Do they?" Moffitt asked.

Anderson reached into his briefcase.

"You can read my speech," he said. He took from his briefcase a copy of the talk he had only partly deliverd to the Women's Peace Alliance and handed it to Moffitt.

As soon as the car reached the Pentagon, Moffitt asked to be let out. She hurried off quickly in search of a taxi. Anderson knew he would have to face her again. In a dispute over policy, leaks from one side immediately provoked leaks from the other. Anderson himself had just participated in the process. He didn't like it, and it was technically against the law since CRITIC meetings were classified. But the leakcounterleak system had become the established method of guaranteeing that reporters got both points of view. The battle of the leaks, Anderson knew, would go on as long as the crisis. He also knew that some in Washington had been involved in these battles for years without once being exposed.

Anderson wanted to touch base with the White House on the Moffitt leak, so he asked his driver to ring up Norman McNamara on the car phone. Because the phone was easily intercepted by electronic intelligence, Anderson was prepared for a cryptic conversation. Men who dealt with classified information had a language of their own.

The connection was made quickly.

"Mac," Anderson said, "I was just invaded by Moffitt. She knows about the morning item."

"We're aware," McNamara replied. He was standing amid a clutter of wire stories hanging from hooks in his office. "We got a call from the AP bureau."

"Will they play ball?"

77

"I think so. The boss'll call personally if there's a problem. It's the others we're worried about."

"Has it spread?" Anderson asked.

"Probably. We're concerned about the right-wing sheets running something like 'President appeases. . . .' You know. We've got a bigmouth here."

"Who?" Anderson asked. "Our war hero?" It was an obvious reference to Somerville.

McNamara laughed, the laugh of a man who'd been burned before. "I don't know," he said. "They won't let me re-call the Plumbers."

Anderson laughed, too. But he understood that the name Plumbers brought back memories that McNamara would have liked to forget.

"I'll keep guessing," Anderson said.

The conversation ended. Anderson was worried. If the story broke in detail, he knew, the Russians would be furious. After all, they had kept their promise of secrecy. The idea of requesting the President to impose wartime censorship quickly crossed his mind, but it faded. He didn't even know if it was legal. He did know that the sickness of leaks might now help produce the ultimate catastrophe. He saw McNamara as a cook trying to hold the top on a sizzling kettle of steam.

Richard Gillespie circled two names on the *Hay's* personnel roster. One was a seaman in the Supply Department, the other a machinist's mate in the Machinery Division. He ordered that the two be brought to him. Gillespie informed the sailors that they had been selected for a special mission. It was dangerous, he said, but it was a mission of glory. He told them to go to the torpedo room and wait.

Gillespie ordered the *Hay* south in order to get back on her original course for the next part of his operation. He also kept monitoring the radio circuits, hearing on the Armed Forces Radio that a problem in Southeast Asia had been responsible for the worldwide American alert.

He laughed. He knew that he was the problem in Southeast Asia.

The time was 4:10, seventeen hours and forty-three minutes from the time of the takeover, thirty-one hours and fifty minutes to the moment of launch.

7

Anderson entered the Pentagon and took a drink at one of the building's 685 water fountains. Then he went to the National Military Command Center.

The NMCC was the heart and pulse of the Pentagon. Through its elaborate electronic equipment, the Joint Chiefs of Staff directed the armed forces of the United States. It was near the river entrance of the building, one floor below the office of the Secretary of Defense. It consisted of a series of rooms. Some were mundane—rows of desks, telephones, manual typewriters. Others were exotic. They looked like the control rooms of television stations, with long instrument consoles and TV screens. Both military men and civilians manned the center, keeping it in operation twenty-four hours a day. A general or admiral was always present.

The center linked the Pentagon with the White House Situation Room, the State Department, the CIA, and the National Security Agency. Its computerized information banks contained vast amounts of data that might be needed in a crisis. It could—and did during the Arab-Israeli war of 1973—place all American forces around the world on alert in less than three minutes.

The center was a prime target, a prize for an enemy attack, so there were two backup centers. The Alternate National Military Command Center was deep in a Maryland mountain. The National Emergency Airborne Command Post was an aircraft kept at Andrews Air Force Base, also in Maryland. Anderson sometimes wondered whether there was a fourth center that even he didn't know about. He wondered, perhaps foolishly, he thought, whether the President had some command center he could go to if he felt his own military was threatening constitutional government.

Anderson walked through the center, ignored. That was standard procedure. Those who worked in NMCC were used to brass and were under orders to carry on with their work regardless of who was visiting. An exception was made for the President.

Anderson made his way to the NMCC's most famous gadget, the Hot Line.

Considering its intended role in preventing the end of the world, the Hot Line was peculiarly unimpressive. It looked like the teletype printer of a wire service and was located in a room paneled in plain acoustic tile. Above the printer were two white-faced clocks, each calibrated in twenty-four-hour military time. One gave the time in Washington, the other in Moscow. Anderson watched as a graying WAC major completed one of the daily tests between the two capitals.

After completing her test, the WAC signaled Moscow to stand by for an actual transmission. She began sending a new message that had just arrived from the White House:

MR. PREMIER:

I HAVE JUST MET WITH MY ADVISERS AT THE WHITE HOUSE. I ASSURE YOU THAT WE REMAIN BAFFLED AS TO THE CAUSE OF YOUR LOSS AT SEA. BUT I EMPHASIZE AGAIN THAT NO AMERICAN FORCES WERE INVOLVED. WE CANNOT UNDERSTAND HOW YOU CONCLUDED THAT AN AMERICAN SUBMARINE WAS AT FAULT, AND WE ASK YOU TO REEVALUATE YOUR DATA.

AS YOU KNOW, I HAVE PLACED AMERICAN FORCES ON ALERT THROUGHOUT THE WORLD. THIS IS A ROUTINE PRECAUTION THAT I AM SURE YOU UNDERSTAND. IT IS THE ONLY ACTION I AM TAKING IN RESPONSE TO YOUR OWN ALERT. AS THE HOURS PASS, YOU WILL SEE THAT OUR INTENTIONS ARE NOT HOSTILE.

Anderson went to the Action Center, which looked like the city room of a metropolitan newspaper. He stayed more than half an hour, getting filled in on the status of the American alert. He was particularly interested in learning how closely the Soviets were watching American forces. He learned that Russian reconnaissance flights had been tripled and that their communications networks were four to five times more active than they usually were.

As he was about to leave the Action Center, Anderson saw a green light go on next to a small television monitor, indicating that a live transmission was about to begin. He quickly learned that it would originate in the Far East. The thirty Soviet bombers above the Sea of Japan had been endlessly circling the carrier *Enterprise,* presumably to wear down American nerves. Now they seemed to be readying some direct harassment.

In a few seconds Anderson saw the *Enterprise.* He watched as the Soviet bombers peeled off and began low passes over the nuclear carrier. They were large sweptwing planes, powered by four turbine engines driving propellers. Although they were obsolete by American standards, their sheer size and bulk made them ideal for harassment.

Automatically Anderson tensed. The sight of hostile planes roaring toward an American ship brought back instant memories of Okinawa. Instinctively he wanted to check his helmet, and he almost felt the rims of binoculars against his eye sockets. He remembered the call to battle stations aboard the *Morrison.* The men tramping to their quarters. The whirring of the gun turrets as they turned to assault the incoming Japanese. The firing of the ack-ack. The insistent roar of the kamikazes as they flew their relentless path to death. The futile shouting of men about to be struck down.

Reality overtook him when he looked closely at the *Enterprise* and realized that the ship, like all modern carriers, had no guns. She was defended by missiles and by her own planes. The task-force commander, however, was under strict orders not to fire unless his ships were in danger.

The first plane came in at 350 land miles an hour. It ran parallel to the *Enterprise*'s flight deck and about 500 feet off the water. It was a simple flyby—no unusual maneuvers and nothing menacing. The second, third, and fourth planes did the same. The harassment appeared milder than that practiced against the Sixth Fleet earlier.

Anderson could see from the activity that the men aboard *Enterprise* were generally unconcerned. They were used to low passes by reconnaissance planes. It was something to write home about, to exaggerate in letters to girlfriends and brothers. Tales of harassment were the war stories of the peacetime navy.

The fifth and sixth planes flew by together, still at 500 feet.

Then came the seventh plane.

Not at 500 feet, but at 200.

Then the eighth.

Maybe 150 feet.

Progressive harassment. Still there was no cause for alarm. Soviet planes had flown that low over American ships to take pictures or test targeting equipment. It was annoying and not preventable. And it was perfectly legal.

Number nine, ten, eleven.

Each one lower.

Number twelve came in at right angles to the flight deck and just off the stern—fifty feet off the water.

Now Anderson got a little edgy. Those planes were too close. A sudden wind or downdraft could slam them into the *Enterprise*. The irresponsibility was surprising, frightening. Poor leadership.

Number thirteen buzzed in. Low. Extremely low. Heading right for the carrier's bridge. Men on the flight deck started running, as they had aboard the old carriers of World War II when the kamikazes started their runs. Some hit the deck and covered their heads. A few instinctively clapped hands over ears to keep out the roar of the Red plane's engines. But the Tu-95 veered away.

Plane fourteen.

The same pattern. The men around Anderson moved closer to the monitor. The plane kept coming. Again men on the flight deck turned to run. The plane passed the point where number thirteen had veered.

Anderson could see the officers on the carrier's bridge dive for cover. The Soviet plane kept coming.

A civilian code clerk near Anderson slapped his hands to his face.

Then the pilot veered sharply. Too sharply. The plane literally skidded through the air and for an instant the pilot lost control.

A wing tip grazed a radio antenna. Parts of both the wing and the antenna hurtled wildly through the air. Fragments hit the flight deck.

The plane wobbled and quickly lost altitude. But the pilot was able to recover. Gradually he brought the Tu-95 up and rejoined his formation.

But number fifteen was coming in. And it was obvious that the Russians had learned nothing.

Vice Admiral Richard Simmons, commander of the Seventh Fleet, watched from his flagship, the guided-missile light cruiser *Oklahoma City*. Simmons was fifty-one and considered certain to win his fourth star. He wanted Anderson's job. He wanted it so badly that he sometimes drew sketches showing how he would decorate his Pentagon office once he got it. Even those who disliked him personally granted that he was a superb officer. If war ever came, many in the navy felt, he would be a modern-day Nimitz or Halsey.

Now he faced the crisis of his life, and he had to resolve it in seconds. Soviet aircraft number fifteen was heading straight for the *Enterprise*. Number fourteen had almost crashed. The ship was in danger.

Probably in danger. The remaining planes might fly by safely, but one might strike the ship, crashing on the flight deck and igniting the jet fuel. The *Enterprise* could become an inferno.

Simmons could order number fifteen shot out of the sky. And he could become a national hero or an impetuous monster.

Number fifteen kept coming.

Anderson watched, horrified at the Russian arrogance.

He knew what was going through Simmons' mind. But to Anderson the choice was clear, and Simmons was waiting too long. He turned to a navy captain manning a console that put Washington in instant contact with the Seventh Fleet.

"Order Simmons to shoot down that plane!"

Eyes bolted toward Anderson. Everyone in the Action Center knew the implications of what he had done.

In seconds the National Military Command Center transmitted the order. Anderson watched the screen intently as number fifteen roared forward.

Suddenly a Sea Sparrow surface-to-air missile tore from a launcher aboard *Enterprise* and, moments later, a second. The first one detonated in a ball of flame about thirty yards from the right wing tip of the onrushing Tu-95.

The second exploded eight yards from its fuselage and threw shrapnel into the plane. One piece punctured a wing tank, igniting the fuel.

The Tu-95 veered to the left, then down, and a thundering explosion ripped the blazing wing from the body. The plane crashed into the Sea of Japan.

There was silence in the Action Center. Nobody moved. No expression changed. Then, automatically, thoughtlessly, the room burst into spontaneous applause. One enlisted man threw his hat in the air. There were cheers, anti-Communist epithets, anti-Russian ethnic slurs.

It was the kind of savage reaction Anderson despised in Americans.

"Stop that!" he ordered, and everyone in the room fell silent, as though stunned by the authority of the command and embarrassed by his own lapse of professionalism.

But Anderson continued looking at the screen, watching as plane number sixteen began its run toward the *Enterprise,* then veered away, obviously under a change of orders. The Russians, Anderson knew, were concerned that the carrier would fire again. But Anderson was worried about what the Russians would now do. How would they react to the downing of their aircraft? The answer, he realized, was being decided in Moscow.

Number sixteen rejoined the formation of Tu-95's. Then, as if they were just out for a routine patrol flight, the planes flew off, back toward Vladivostok.

The Russians had decided to break off.

Anderson expected that the Hot Line from Moscow would be sizzling in a few moments, and he started walking toward the room where the receiver was kept. He got about halfway out the Action Center.

"Admiral. . . ."

He looked back. A civilian gestured toward the television screen. Anderson quickly returned.

"Seventh Fleet reports two of those Tu-ninety-fives have turned around," the civilian said.

Anderson positioned himself in front of the screen again, a look of deep concern on his face. He had been premature in his judgment of the Russians. He studied the two breakaway Russian planes via a television pickup from a navy reconnaissance plane that trailed them. They started flying toward the *Enterprise* at a level 8,000 feet. Their speed was low, and they did not look menacing.

Maybe, Anderson thought, they were just returning to take some propaganda pictures. Part of the wreckage of the downed Tu-95 still floated in the water. For an instant the admiral relaxed.

Then, suddenly, he saw a burst of flame under the right wing of one of the bombers. The flame shot back, and a tiny, tubular object lurched forward, trailing a stream of smoke.

Anderson froze. He jammed against a desk to get closer to the screen. His heart hammered in his chest. He now had the Russian answer to their shattered plane.

The Soviet bomber had fired an AS-3 Kangaroo air-to-surface missile, which now streaked toward the *Enterprise*. The Americans were caught off guard. Men who a few minutes before had been tense and ready were now at relative ease, certain that the Russians had retreated. They lost precious seconds returning to switches and controls and priming themselves, and in those seconds the So-

86

viet missile traveled half its distance to the exposed carrier.

Its course was zigzagged, plotted to evade American defenses.

Aboard destroyers, aboard frigates, aboard *Enterprise* herself, radars homed in on the incoming killer. Five-inch guns pounded away.

The Red missile was too close to allow use of a nuclear antiaircraft warhead. An atomic blast amid the fleet would flip smaller ships on end or tear them apart.

Conventional shells burst near the Soviet rocket, but not near enough. Sea Sparrow and Talos missiles strained to follow the Russian zigzag and exploded close to the streaking weapon. But not close enough.

Helplessly Anderson watched the inevitable coming.

The missile suddenly dived toward the sea, then leveled off only 300 feet above water. Now American shells were bursting dangerously close to American ships, pelting them with shrapnel, sending sailors diving for cover.

The *Enterprise* fired one last desperate volley of Sea Sparrow missiles, and the frigate *Coontz* followed with a barrage of twenty-millimeter shells from her six-barrel Vulcan Phalanx Gatling gun, designed for last-ditch defense. But the superbly erratic path of the Soviet missile evaded everything the Americans sent up.

The rocket suddenly dropped, like a fastball finishing its course. Its engine cut out. It slammed into the carrier's flight deck amid a squadron of parked Phantoms.

The explosion of aircraft fuel and ammunition was so bright that it "burned" into a television camera, leaving the image permanently etched.

The stricken *Enterprise* filled the screen as flames shot 200 feet into the air. Deckmen in brightly colored coveralls ran for hoses and foam dispensers.

Close in to the fire, damage-control experts in asbestos suits pushed eight-million-dollar Phantoms over the side to prevent them from exploding. The captain ordered quick turns to spill burning oil off the deck. Seasprite helicopters took off from the bow to rescue sailors forced overboard by the heat.

Carriers had always been known as floating coffins. Everything about them—their open, windy hangar decks, the jet fuel, the bombs, the rockets—seemed designed for disaster. As Anderson watched in frustration and horror, he thought of the fire aboard the USS *Bennington* in 1954, in which 103 men died.

As the fire aboard the *Enterprise* burned out of control, a civilian in the Action Center handed Anderson the first report from the ship's captain. At least forty, perhaps as many as sixty, American sailors had already died.

As soon as Anderson reached his office he grabbed the phone and called the White House.

"Fred Bixby," announced the voice on the other end.

"Fred, Isaac Anderson. I wanted to call to—"

"Andy," Bixby broke in excitedly, "there's hell to pay. Those boys on that ship. Christ, the boss is up the walls!"

That is what Anderson feared. The action in the Mediterranean. The boy overboard. This new calamity. The President could revert, become what he was in the Senate. Rash. Intemperate. Willing to fight with the lives of others.

"Look, Fred, I hope he doesn't do anything—"

"He already has."

"Christ!"

"Look, he didn't drop the bomb or anything," Bixby explained. "He zapped 'em on the Hot Line. Listen to this:

"MR. PREMIER:

"I PROTEST IN THE STRONGEST POSSIBLE TERMS THE CALLOUS, IRRESPONSIBLE, AND BRUTAL ACT BY YOUR NAVAL AIR FORCE IN THE SEA OF JAPAN. THIS ACT, WHICH WE ALL WITNESSED, HAS COST THE LIVES OF MANY AMERICANS. NO MATTER HOW YOU MAY TRY TO EXPLAIN YOUR BEHAVIOR, YOU MUST BEAR FULL RESPONSIBILITY FOR THE OUTCOME.

"I ALSO PROTEST THE EARLIER HARASSMENT OF

OUR FLEET, TO WHICH WE RESPONDED WITH A FULLY JUSTIFIED ACT OF SELF-DEFENSE.

"ALTHOUGH THE INTERESTS OF WORLD PEACE REQUIRE THAT WE KEEP THESE MATTERS TEMPORARILY SECRET, WE WILL ULTIMATELY BE REQUIRED TO GIVE A FULL ACCOUNTING TO THE FAMILIES OF OUR DEAD.

"THIS LATEST OUTRAGE OF YOURS, IN ADDITION TO THE EARLIER BEHAVIOR OF YOUR FORCES IN THE MEDITERRANEAN, LEADS US TO CONCLUDE THAT YOU ARE PURSUING AN AGGRESSIVE COURSE. THE UNITED STATES REGRETS THIS, BUT THE UNITED STATES STANDS READY TO CARRY OUT HER OBLIGATIONS."

Anderson paused for a moment to absorb the message.

"Well, I can't disagree with anything there," he said, "but I want the President to know that the downing of that Russian plane was my decision. I ordered it."

"Their plane deserved it, Andy. The men on our carrier didn't!"

"Fred, it may have been a calculated response. They might not have realized the damage they'd do."

"Fine. Tell it to the widows."

"I'd like to tell it to the President."

"I wouldn't, Andy. His ears are shut."

Anderson was firm.

"I'll take my chances. I want to talk to the President. I've got a duty to advise him on this matter, and there is advice I feel I must offer."

Bixby sighed, sensing Anderson's resolve.

"Just a second," he said.

It was more than a second. It was more like two or three minutes before Anderson was put through.

"Admiral, this is the President."

"Good afternoon, sir. I know how you feel."

"How *I* feel?" the President roared. "Those're your boys. How do *you* feel?"

"Rotten."

"God damn it, Andy, those SOB's are pushing us too far. Admiral, we can't go to the wall!"

"I know, sir. But I—"

"Hold on," the President said. "Somerville is on the other line. I'll put us on conference."

"Christ," Anderson mumbled. He had lost exclusive access to the President.

There was some hurried conversation and a series of clicks.

"Somerville here. Hello, Admiral."

The ice traveled the line and sliced through Anderson's eardrum.

"Hello, Mr. Secretary."

"I'm sick to death," Somerville said. "The way our men died there. I think you'll both agree that we must now take a military option, at all costs."

So spoke the man who had never seen combat firsthand, thought Anderson.

"Wait a minute," the admiral replied. "Let's put this in perspective. It was a *particular* incident."

"Come on!" Somerville shot back.

"We knocked down their plane," Anderson said. "Their reply—"

"Admiral Simmons decided correctly," Somerville insisted. "He oughtta get a medal."

"*I* decided to down that plane. And I don't want your medal. Admiral Simmons will be relieved for his indecisiveness."

There was a long, awkward pause.

"I can't figure you," Somerville said. "You get us into this—"

"Harley, that's not fair!" the President snapped.

"No, I accept it," Anderson said. "I got us into this. I gave the order. Go on."

"Now," Somerville complained, "you don't want to fight back."

"What do you say to that, Andy?" the President asked.

It struck Anderson that he was dealing with a classic crisis mentality. Like Gorshkov, he realized that as crises progressed, men often forgot what they were originally about. The President and Somerville, angered by the attack on the *Enterprise,* no longer even mentioned the

90

source of the problem—the strange sinking of the *Dostoyny*. The latest incident in the crisis became the crisis itself.

"Mr. President," Anderson began his answer, "let's understand what's happened. The Russians chose to harass us. We don't know why because we don't understand the *Dostoyny* sinking. I agree that their harassment was irresponsible, outrageous. But you must remember that the Russians are almost always heavy-handed. It showed in the harassment. But you don't go to war over that."

"Attacks have been made on Americans!" Somerville roared.

"Only in response to our downing an aircraft," Anderson replied. "There have been no attacks on bases or on our country."

"Mr. President," Somerville said, "I appreciate the admiral's position. He's a man of peace and so am I . . ."

Anderson winced.

" . . . but the Russians understand the hard line. If we let these so-called incidents go by, they'll feel free to repeat them. I recommend some form of punishment. A warning. I'd even ask the admiral to suggest one."

"I'll suggest nothing of the kind," Anderson replied, annoyed by the attempt to trap him. "Our objective should be to contain the crisis."

"How?" the President asked.

The question caught Anderson by surprise. He had been so concerned about heading off wild action that he neglected to conceive an alternative.

He stalled, letting the question hang while pondering it.

"Mr. President," he said, buying time, "what is needed is a magnanimous gesture."

"By them, I hope," Somerville said.

"No, sir, by us."

"I won't go for appeasement," the President said immediately.

"Neither will I," Anderson answered. "Appeasement is when you cave in to a willful act of aggression. We're not caving in and we don't even know if the Red strategy is willfully aggressive."

"Go on," the President said.

"They feel," Anderson continued, "that we've done nothing to show that we didn't sink their ship—"

"Neither have they done anything to prove that we did," Somerville argued.

"Mr. Secretary," Anderson went on, "the basic fact remains that a Russian ship has been sunk, and subsequent actions and reactions on both sides threaten to escalate into global war. We have to defuse this thing. I may have a way."

"Shoot," the President ordered.

His thoughts hurried, his idea not carefully weighed, Anderson paused. Then he let fly.

"The *Dostoyny*'s sister ship, the *Svirepy*, is still out there."

"So?" asked the President.

"Let me go aboard."

The air was suddenly dead. Nothing. Zero. Except, Anderson thought, a slight quickening of the President's breathing.

"What?" Somerville asked, barely disguising his seething rage.

"I would ask the Russians' permission to let me board. I'd go to express our personal condolences over the loss of their seamen. We wouldn't take responsibility, and it would not resolve the mystery of their sunken ship, but it would be a firm and unprecedented gesture of goodwill and peacekeeping."

"That," said Somerville, "is the most harebrained scheme I ever heard."

"Mr. President," Anderson continued, ignoring Somerville, "the presence of the American Navy chief on a Soviet ship has symbolic value. They know you would never send me if our intentions were hostile. This could cool things down."

"And what if this whole thing is your Russian trick?" the President asked.

"Then anything we do would be futile."

"You might be captured."

"That's a chance I'd have to take."

"You've got all that classified information," Somerville said.

"Cyanide tablets," Anderson bluntly replied.

"Well," the President said, "I think it's a little harebrained myself, frankly. Look, Andy, you're a valuable man. If I wanted to send a messenger boy, I'd send the UN ambassador. I couldn't give a crap if they captured him, although they probably wouldn't bother."

"That's the point," Anderson said. "You've got to send someone with rank."

"Mr. President," Somerville cut in, "Admiral Anderson is very heroic. But he hasn't considered the effect on the country if he's captured. It would come out. There'd be a loss of confidence in the navy . . . in *you*, sir."

"True," the President said. "Andy, I appreciate your valor. But . . . I don't know. . . ."

"I wish you'd think about it," Anderson said.

"All right, I'll think about it."

The conversation ended.

It was normal procedure for Fred Bixby to monitor Presidential calls. When the President hung up, Bixby charged into the Oval Office.

"Damn!" he said. "I thought Anderson's idea was great!"

The President was startled. "Why?"

"Because it's got spark, it's got impact."

The President rubbed his chin and brushed his hair back. He stared at a casualty report from the *Enterprise*. Fifty-eight dead and the number likely to grow.

"Somerville had a point," he said. "If our top admiral is captured, people'd think we were a bunch of clowns."

"I don't want to argue with you, boss, but I think you're wrong," Bixby said. "If they take Anderson, it's a betrayal. People'll see that we went all out for peace and that the Russians wrecked it. We're the clean ones."

"You think so?" the President asked.

"Absolutely," Bixby replied. "Look, Mr. President, I admit that this whole business could be some kind of Russian trick. But it could also be the screw-up of the century. Christ, it could be the last screw-up on earth. We've got to try to ease things. If Andy went on their boat . . . like I said, it's got impact."

The President walked over to a couch opposite his desk and slumped down.

"Damn, I'm no warmonger!" he said. "But those animals, with their stuff today. I've never trusted 'em, Fred."

"Neither have I," Bixby answered. "But you never trusted Congress either. You eat from the same dinner pail, though."

"Somerville will never forgive me," the President groaned, "and the opposition'll have a carnival if this doesn't work out."

Bixby was an astute adviser and he recognized the moment as one best observed in silence. His point had already been made.

Finally the President clapped his hands together, indicating a decision had been reached.

"Okay. We'll give it a whirl. Get Anderson over here."

Anderson was reading the latest dispatch from the Associated Press. As he expected, Doris Moffitt had scored a beat on the rest of the world, but had used exquisite discretion:

> WASHINGTON, NOV. 23 (AP)—THE UNITED STATES SUDDENLY PLACED ITS ARMED FORCES ON ALERT TODAY AS KEY OFFICIALS MET IN SECRECY AT THE WHITE HOUSE.
>
> PRESIDENTIAL NEWS SECRETARY NORMAN MCNAMARA SAID THE ALERT WAS TRIGGERED BY AN UPSURGE OF COMMUNIST GUERRILLA ACTIVITY IN MALAYSIA.
>
> AN INFORMED ADMINISTRATION SOURCE, THOUGH, CLAIMED THAT THE REAL REASON FOR THE ALERT WAS AN UNEXPECTED INCREASE IN TENSION BETWEEN THE UNITED STATES AND THE SOVIET UNION. THE SOURCE ASSERTED THAT MOSCOW MIGHT MAKE SOME MAJOR MOVE IN THE NEXT 48 HOURS.
>
> A QUALIFIED OBSERVER, WHILE CONFIRMING THE

Anderson knew that he was the qualified observer and that Somerville was the informed source. Bixby's call interrupted.

"Andy, the President wants you—now."

8

MR. PREMIER:

THE UNITED STATES IS DEEPLY CONCERNED OVER THE NEW TENSIONS BETWEEN OUR GREAT COUNTRIES. WE FIRMLY BELIEVE THAT SOME CLEAR GESTURE IS NEEDED TO SHOW OUR GOOD FAITH. THEREFORE WE ASK YOUR PERMISSION TO ALLOW OUR CHIEF OF NAVAL OPERATIONS, ADMIRAL ISAAC ANDERSON, TO BOARD YOUR HEROIC NAVAL VESSEL, THE SVIREPY. ADMIRAL ANDERSON WISHES PERSONALLY TO EXPRESS OUR GOVERNMENT'S CONDOLENCES OVER THIS MORNING'S LOSS OF YOUR SEAMEN. HIS VISIT WILL SHOW OUR PEACEFUL INTENT. WE AWAIT YOUR REPLY.

Zorin was delighted.

To the Premier the American note was an admission that the United States had sunk the *Dostoyny*. And it was a concession that the Soviet response had deterred Washington from further adventures. His policy had worked.

Gorshkov also saw the note as an admission of guilt over the *Dostoyny,* and he was pleased that the strong harassment had brought results, but as the opportunity to prove Russia's naval superiority began to fade, he was aware of a sense of personal disappointment.

MR. PRESIDENT:

THE SOVIET GOVERNMENT GRANTS PERMISSION FOR A TEN-MINUTE VISIT BY YOUR COMMANDING ADMIRAL TO THE SOVIET SHIP SVIREPY DURING THE EVENING HOURS. THE ADMIRAL IS TO BE DELIVERED

Gorshkov was concerned that aides might be used for spying.

There was a strange, sentimental feeling in Anderson's gut as his jet came in for a perfect landing aboard the USS *Lexington*. She was, after all, one of the most famous of American warships. Anderson had served aboard her in 1946, and he had later commanded her. Now he would use the *Lexington* as a launching point for his mission to the *Svirepy,* cruising 160 miles away.

She had fought well in World War II, honoring the name of the first carrier *Lexington,* sunk at the Battle of the Coral Sea. But now she was in the evening of her years, and her designation had been changed from CVA—attack aircraft carrier—to CVT—training carrier. Anderson knew that modern jets had made the *Lexington* obsolete, but he felt the classification was a humiliation, that she was entitled to retire in dignity, perhaps to the reserve fleet. He also felt the passing of his own years.

The *Lexington*'s captain, Archibald Thomas, had been instructed to prepare no special welcome for Anderson. Indeed, many of the deckhands didn't even recognize the admiral when he stepped out of his plane.

A few minutes after Anderson arrived, a second plane landed. It carried a helicopter pilot. The *Lexington* had her own pilots, of course, but Anderson preferred a man who would return to Washington on completing the trip to the *Svirepy.* Security reasons.

Anderson had intended simply to sip coffee, smoke a cigar, and relax while waiting for his helicopter to be given a last-minute check. But he could not resist the temptation to look around, revisit his old quarters, stand out on the flight deck and imagine the Hellcats and Corsairs taking off to strike Japanese targets in the western Pacific. He took a look at the ship's plaque, which recounted her glorious history. He knew that the mission he flew this night, however peaceful or symbolic, might be the most important ever flown from the *Lexington*'s decks.

As Anderson prepared to fly to the *Svirepy,* Richard Gillespie prepared to destroy any chance of peace.

The two sailors he had selected for a "mission of glory" remained in the torpedo room, now guarded by a Crusade member. Part of their mission was being prepared by other members.

It was a strange form of preparation.

The Crusade members had assembled parts of the *Hay*'s fittings and equipment. They went at them with axes—tearing, ripping, chopping. They made sure that many of the fractured pieces bore the name USS *John Hay*.

Most of the scientists, though, continued to work on the safety interlocks in the missile system. At 8:20 P.M. Gillespie was notified that the third and fourth had been bypassed. Four remained.

It was twenty-one hours and fifty-three minutes from the time of the takeover, twenty-seven hours and forty minutes to the moment of launch.

Anderson took off from the *Lexington* at 8:24 P.M. in a Kaman UH-2C Seasprite helicopter. In the right hip pocket of his jacket he carried a cyanide capsule. Not even the *Lexington*'s Captain Thomas knew where he was going. Julia Anderson had been told by a Pentagon aide that her husband was called to important meetings and would be late.

The trip in the Atlantic darkness took just over an hour. At 9:26 the *Svirepy* came into view—or at least part of her did. In typically Russian fashion, the ship was blacked out except for the helicopter platform. She was moving at twenty knots, making the approach difficult.

The Russians were posturing, Anderson knew. They wanted to show that their patrol would go on as usual during his visit.

The pilot touched down, and Anderson glanced out. He was startled. An honor guard, carrying both the American and Soviet flags, was standing at attention. Anderson wondered where they got the American flag, but then noticed that it had only forty-eight stars. It was, apparently, a captain's souvenir.

As he looked out, Anderson felt a weird sensation. He had suggested this mission, yet there was something sinful about it. He was, after all, coming to a ship of an adversary. He was paying respects to *them*. For some reason he thought of General Jonathan Wainwright's humiliation in surrendering the Philippines to the Japanese in 1942. It was irrational, of course, but the idea of presenting himself to the enemy touched his nerves.

A sailor ran up to open Anderson's door, and the admiral stepped out. At first he didn't know what to do. More important, he didn't know what his face should show. He wanted to smile, but was it right to smile on the ship bearing the bodies of the *Dostoyny*'s crew? He noticed that the sailor who opened the door was smiling, and he assumed that the man had been well briefed, so *he* smiled, too. It was a mistake. When he saw the senior Soviet officers, they were not smiling.

The smile melted from Anderson's face, and he took on a proper, blank expression. He stepped down from his helicopter and saluted the Soviet flag on the stern. Again a feeling of sin.

The Soviet admiral, N. I. Kudelkin, approached Anderson with a crisp, but not rigid stride. With him was a young officer, a translator. Kudelkin was three inches shorter than Anderson and much thinner. He looked more Nordic than Russian. At fifty-six he was not considered one of the comers of the Soviet Navy.

"Good evening, Admiral Anderson," he said through the translator. "Welcome to the *Svirepy*."

There was no salute.

Anderson nodded, but his face remained bland.

"Good evening. It's an honor to be aboard."

Kudelkin gestured toward the honor guard. Anderson stepped over to the two rows of sailors, nine men in each row. But as he stood ready to inspect them, he was startled to hear the "Internationale" start blaring from the ship's bullhorn. He snapped to attention and saluted, as did the Russian officers.

The anthem ended, and again Anderson was ready to inspect. But then the "Star-Spangled Banner" began. Another snap. Another salute. But this time Anderson glanced around and saw that one Soviet officer had the slightest smile. He would later find out why. A few minutes before his helicopter landed, the National Security Agency had picked up a satellite sound transmission from Moscow to the *Svirepy*. It contained recordings of both anthems and uncoded orders for a *Svirepy* officer to tape the songs. Premier Zorin wanted to do it up right.

Quickly Anderson inspected the sailors.

"Very fine," he said afterward. "Very impressive."

Admiral Kudelkin then escorted Anderson to his living quarters. They were sparse and cramped, consisting only of a tiny office and a bedroom. His accommodations were far more modest than those given Americans of similar rank, and Anderson wondered whether this didn't make for a better officer.

Kudelkin offered Anderson some vodka. Anderson accepted, and the Russian then proposed a toast.

"To your health, Admiral."

The toast disappointed Anderson. He had hoped it would contain a signal—something like, "To peace and friendship."

"And to yours," he replied.

They drank. Kudelkin gestured for Anderson to sit. They both relaxed on plain metal chairs.

"I understand," Kudelkin said, "that you have come in regard to this morning's incident."

"That is correct," Anderson answered. "I wish to express my government's sincere condolences on your loss. I assure you that we will assist an investigation in any way we can."

Kudelkin looked directly into Anderson's eyes. His bland expression did not change.

100

"Your comments are acknowledged," he said. "Now I would like to show you something."

He rose and directed Anderson to a nearby storage area. There, on temporary wood racks, were the covered bodies of twenty-seven of the *Dostoyny*'s crewmen.

"We want you to see proof of our loss," Kudelkin said. "Of course, you may inspect the bodies if you wish."

Anderson was offended by what he saw as an undignified use of dead sailors, but he hid his feelings.

"An inspection won't be necessary," he said. "We don't dispute the death of your courageous seamen."

"I personally observed the sonar data," Kudelkin replied. Then he suddenly shrugged his shoulders. "But that is not for me to discuss. Nations have their reasons, and one can imagine unknown technical faults."

Anderson didn't even hear the rest of Kudelkin's statement. *That* was the signal. The Russians weren't going to pursue the question of American culpability. For whatever reason, Moscow was willing to ease tensions. Anderson could see that Kudelkin's remark had been dictated by higher authority, since the man seemed pained to let it pass from his lips.

Kudelkin and Anderson walked back to the Russian's quarters, neither saying a word, each lost in his own thoughts. Anderson now felt elated, Kudelkin humiliated. To the American the crisis was nearing an end. To the Russian the Americans had literally gotten away with murder.

Kudelkin removed a paper from his metal desk.

"Premier Zorin has sent this personal message to you on the occasion of your visit," he said. He handed the note to Anderson, who read it twice, carefully:

ADMIRAL ANDERSON:
    YOUR VISIT TO OUR SHIP THE SVIREPY IS AN ACT OF GREAT IMPORTANCE. THE SOVIET UNION TAKES NOTE OF YOUR GESTURE AND IS PREPARED TO CARRY OUT ITS POLICIES ACCORDINGLY. I TRUST THAT YOUR STAY ABOARD OUR SHIP IS A PLEASANT ONE.

Another clear signal. Anderson could feel himself relax still more. In the back of his mind, of course, there was still the suggestion of a Russian trick, but the possibility that the *Dostoyny* went down because of some technological catastrophe appeared greater than ever.

"Shall we drink again?" Kudelkin asked through the translator.

"Certainly," Anderson replied.

Kudelkin poured, and again the two men lifted glasses.

"To a positive future," Kudelkin declared.

"To a positive future," Anderson responded.

He was now even more aware that Kudelkin's every word was programmed in Moscow. He wondered if the translator was a functionary of Soviet naval intelligence, there to see that Kudelkin carried out his orders.

The two men drank. Anderson could hear the chopping of his helicopter as it warmed up, signaling the end of the ten-minute visit. When he and Kudelkin finished, they returned quickly to the helicopter platform, where the honor guard was again lined up. It snapped to attention as Anderson approached, the young lieutenant at its front clicking his heels.

There was more bounce in Anderson's ducklike walk than there had been when he arrived. Few words had been exchanged between him and Kudelkin, but they were words of enormous impact. He saluted Kudelkin, then saluted the Soviet flag on the stern. He felt no guilt this time. Then he boarded his helicopter and flew off in the darkness toward the *Lexington*. He looked back at the *Svirepy* and saw that a few crew members were waving to him.

"Good one," he told his pilot.

9

Julia Anderson was worried.

It was routine to get a phone call saying her husband would be late. But was he really at a sudden meeting, or had something happened to him? Was the Pentagon withholding information? Maybe she should call Bethesda Naval Hospital.

She knew it was childish. She had, after all, lived through Isaac Anderson's combat days in Korea. Like all navy wives, she had learned to accept the hazards of war, and she had understood them when she took her vows. There was no accommodation, though, to a medical problem. When wondering about it, she was no different from anyone else.

Julia Anderson was fifty-three, but, silver hair and all, looked ten years younger. It was not surprising. She rode an English bike six miles each day and had discovered health foods long before they were chic. She had a smallish build, helped along by slim lines and a quick, exuberant walk. The silver hair was cut short and straight. There was a ready smile and a graciousness that reflected both a Southern upbringing and the needs of navy politics.

She tucked herself into bed with a copy of David Halberstam's *The Best and the Brightest*. It was the story of good men getting the United States into a bad war in Vietnam, and she wondered, having heard reports of the military alert, whether a similar disaster was in progress. Julia Everts Anderson was a convert to her husband's passion for peace, and like many converts, she was more fanatical than the man who had converted her. She did not trust the American military.

She wanted the admiral to leave the navy and take a teaching post at a college. It would be a free, contemplative life, and he could spread his ideas without reprisal or pressure. He could have a new kind of influence. "Isaac," she kept telling him, "you could push the Pentagon back where it belongs."

The views were strange for a Pensacola girl whose father thought Franklin Roosevelt was a Communist. Father was still alive and he still wrote letters to "baby Julia," but the letters were bitter. What happened to the Isaac Anderson, the rugged young officer whom he had personally approved for his daughter? What kind of strange things was he saying?

Julia heard a car pull up to the front door of the house. Then slow, heavy footsteps to the large oak door. A navy steward opened it.

"Good evening, Admiral Anderson."

Relief.

"Evening, Jones," Anderson replied, now showing the day's strain.

The steward closed the door.

"May I get you anything, sir?"

"No, thank you, Jones. I just want to get upstairs."

"Yes, sir."

The steward took Anderson's coat and hung it in a hall closet.

Anderson started up the long staircase leading to the bedroom, but as he reached the fifth step, the telephone rang and he paused to hear Jones answer it.

"Sir, it's the White House calling."

Anderson's heart sank. Something had gone wrong. He rushed to the phone. Julia, hearing the words "White House," sat up sharply in bed.

"Stand by for the President," the operator said to Anderson. There were some clicks, and then Anderson heard the familiar, gruff Midwestern voice.

"Andy?"

"Yes, sir."

"Andy, you did a hell of a job."

Anderson relaxed.

"Thank you, sir. I tried to do my best."

"Well, you did more than that. You did your best and a half. Premier Zorin sent me a message and it was soft. I think we're in good shape."

"Sir, is there anything more I can do?"

"No. Hell, no! I think you oughtta take some hot soup. Y'know, that's good after a tough day. Tomato soup. Then you hit the sack."

"Yes, sir. I consider that an order."

"And look, Andy. . . ."

"Yes, sir?"

"Make sure to flush down that poison pill." The President laughed.

Anderson felt in his pocket for the cyanide capsule. "I'll give it a Presidential flush," he said.

"Good night, Admiral."

"Good night, sir."

As soon as he hung up, Anderson went to a nearby guest bathroom and flushed the capsule down.

"Jones!" he called out.

"Yes, Admiral?"

"Jones, I assume you heard all those radio reports about some big doings at the White House."

"Yes, sir."

"Well, I want you to know it all turned out peacefully. So relax."

"Thank you, Admiral. Thank you, sir."

Anderson turned and continued up the stairs.

But what would he be like when he reached the top? It was a question Julia Anderson would never have asked three decades before it. In 1946 Lieutenant Isaac Anderson was the picture of spirit. Every day was a whirlwind, every night a honeymoon.

But the years had brought changes. Now, even on "good" days, Anderson's mood could not be predicted. He could be warm and gregarious one minute, kidding Julia about her father and cracking the latest joke from the Pentagon grapevine. And the next minute he might be

105

in total withdrawal, a face of stone, eyes distant, mumbling answers to questions, if answering them at all, a man brooding over personal conflict with his own profession.

His occasional uncommunicativeness was not directed at Julia, and she knew it. Yet the effect was the same. The sudden dropping away, the long periods of silence, the refusal to be bothered even by important details of the household—only Julia saw these things, for they were part of the private world that Anderson scrupulously kept from his comrades. Only Julia bore the brunt of the tensions within that world. They marred a marriage that was otherwise warm, successful, civilized.

Anderson reached the top of the stairs and walked into the bedroom. Julia looked up and smiled.

"Well, Admiral," she said with a wink and a humorously exaggerated Southern accent, "they gonna pay y'all for this overtime?"

Anderson smiled ironically. He walked over and kissed her, then rubbed her ear in a gesture that had become a habit.

"It's not in the budget," he said.

They both laughed a little, then Anderson quickly took off his shoes.

"You look a mess," Julia said. "They must've put you through hell."

"Yeah, we had some problems. But you must've heard me talking to the President downstairs. Things are okay now."

"Well, I want you to get some sleep."

"Oh, I intend to. I'm under orders from the Commander in Chief."

Another small laugh.

"What actually happened?" Julia asked.

"There was some friction with the Russians. I'm sure you'll read it in a book someday."

"One of the television people talked about the chance of military action. . . ."

"That was possible. But look, I'd rather forget my day. How was yours?"

"Oh, passable. I had to give that talk to the American Legion Auxiliary."

"Some treat," the admiral said.

"Isaac," Julia replied, exasperated, "they're as bad as their husbands. They worship the military as if—"

"I know. You can't change them."

"One of the women asked about you."

"Oh?"

"You know. 'Isn't your husband going a little far?' That kind of thing."

"You should've told her I'm a Commie."

"Believe me, I'd have liked to see her expression. She looked like the type who carries little lists."

Julia looked carefully at her husband, noticing the slight, unusual stooping of his shoulders, the small bags under his eyes.

"You know," she said seriously, "I think you overdid it. Why don't you go in late tomorrow?"

"No, I've got a meeting at ten, another at—"

"So send your deputy. That's what he's for."

"I'd better be there."

"The way you look now, Isaac, tomorrow is going to take a lot out of you."

"Look, Julia, I've got to stay on top of things."

Julia shrugged. "I just hope you stay on top of the ground."

She let that sink in as Anderson started to put away his uniform.

"Isaac," she finally said, as diplomatically as possible, "maybe you should give some thought to what we talked about . . . you know."

"Teaching?"

"There'd be less pressure."

Anderson walked to a closet to hang up his tie. There was a long, awkward pause. He had resisted Julia's wish for him to enter teaching. He knew he could be useful in the classroom and influential with a college as his base, but he still had the military man's suspicion of the open, casual atmosphere of the campus. He couldn't see himself with a bunch of blue-jeaned, cynical students. They were

107

civilians and undisciplined. Besides, they'd never accept him. He'd slip into service jargon and they'd laugh behind his back. Isaac Anderson, the man who raised serious questions about the military, still felt at home only in his uniform. It was his security blanket.

"I don't know," he half replied. "I . . . just don't know."

Julia could see it happening. The vacant eyes. The shying away. The preoccupation. Maybe it was the talk about resigning, although Isaac had always been open when that was discussed. Whatever it was, he now moved more quickly, as if trying to get away, to escape into himself. In a few seconds it was as if he hardly knew Julia Anderson.

"I'd better shower," he said, barely audibly.

He walked into the bathroom and turned on the water. Then he stood for a moment, looking in the mirror and hating himself. He was fully conscious of these episodes of withdrawal, and he knew how cruel they were to Julia. He desperately didn't want to hurt her, but he couldn't help himself. He had an emotional need suddenly to crawl into a cocoon, and there seemed no way to resist. He knew the problem had begun when he first started questioning the assumptions of the military. He thought about getting psychiatric help, and at times he was on the brink. But he was afraid someone in the navy would find out.

He took his shower. Then he and Julia went right to bed, hardly exchanging a word.

But while Julia slept soundly, Anderson tossed. He was keyed up, his system still churning from the day's events. At 3:20 A.M. he got up and went down to the kitchen. He made a cup of cocoa, took a piece of raisin bread, and tried to relax by reading Art Buchwald's column in the newspaper. It dealt with the latest foul-up in the U.S. Postal Service, a subject sufficiently removed from world affairs to serve Anderson's needs.

An aide awakened Richard Gillespie at 4:08 A.M. He had slept five hours.

The *Hay* was now "rigged for red"—bathed in a red light that submarines used at night. It made men look like ghosts, but it also made everything seem more military, more urgent.

Gillespie dressed, then walked to the torpedo room in the bow of the ship. Inside were the two sailors he had selected earlier. They stared at him apprehensively. A Crusade member, who had a crowbar hooked to his belt, kept watch on them with a .45-caliber pistol.

The furniture and equipment hacked from the *Hay* were now stored in the torpedo room, and Gillespie examined them. He smiled as he picked up part of a galley bench. On its underside was stenciled USS JOHN HAY.

Gillespie spoke briefly with the chosen sailors, praising them for their patience, apologizing for inconveniencing them. One was a boy of nineteen who came from Waco, Texas. His father had been in the navy, as had his grandfather. He was of medium height and thin, with searching blue eyes. Gillespie had observed his work in the Supply Department, and he liked him. The second boy was twenty-two, more robust than the first. He had grown up in a foster home in Chicago and was popular for his sense of humor. Gillespie recalled that he had once helped the boy with some mathematics in a navy correspondence course. He seemed bright and eager.

Gillespie walked behind the two sailors. He nodded to the guard, who removed the crowbar from his belt. He handed it to Gillespie, who gripped it firmly. Then he raised it high, took a deep breath, and struck the nineteen-year-old on the back of the head. Before the second boy could react, he struck him, too.

Both sailors fell. The nineteen-year-old was already dead. The boy from Chicago was still breathing, but had a gaping wound above the left ear. Gillespie looked down at the men on the floor, the color of their flowing blood neutralized by the red lights. Then he gestured toward the torpedo tubes.

Anderson still could not sleep. He drifted into the living room, picking up a copy of William McNeill's *The Rise of the West*. He read a few pages, then put it down.

He didn't care much for reading. Despite his emergence as a "thoughtful" admiral, he was not an intellectual man. He felt out of place with intellectuals, inferior to them. They always seemed to quote, to drop names of authors he had never heard of. He avoided them at cocktail parties. He felt that they saw men in uniform as freaks, woodenheads unworthy of their attention. None of them ever wanted to read his book on aircraft carriers.

Anderson saw himself as essentially narrow—a man who knew his place. His hero was George Marshall, a soldier who devoted his later years to peace, but he never hoped to equal Marshall's breadth or influence. Marshall, after all, was a wartime commander, a renowned strategist who had acquired the credentials to help form the postwar world. Isaac Anderson had become an obscure nuclear-age technician.

As he often did when he couldn't sleep, he sat down at a large dining-room table, took out a yellow pad, and started working on plans for the navy. It was during these quiet hours, with memos on radiation levels and blast effects before his eyes, that he felt most sharply the deep conflicts within him. His greatest fear was that other military men, working on similar documents in Washington, Peking, and Moscow, had no such conflicts. The work eventually tired him, and at last he went upstairs, got back into bed, and fell asleep.

Gillespie and the guard swiftly, carefully, lifted the body of the nineteen-year-old into the number one torpedo tube. Then they returned and lifted the second man, now barely alive, into the number two tube.

They rested for a moment, then started placing the broken parts of the *Hay* into the remaining two tubes.

After their work was finished, Gillespie got on the intercom and alerted Crusade members who were manning the torpedo fire-control consoles in the control room.

"Fire one!" he ordered.

The *Hay* shuddered as a column of compressed air shot the stilled body of the first sailor into the icy ocean depths. Immediately his dead lungs filled with water and his work suit bulged with air pockets.

Crewmen working the early shift lifted their eyes. Foreheads wrinkled. Shoulders shrugged. The feel of a torpedo tube spitting its fill was unmistakable, but so complete was the sailors' faith in their officers that they still did not question the action.

"Fire two!" Gillespie ordered.

The second sailor died instantly as his blood-soaked body was jettisoned into the sea.

Again the curious reaction of the crew. Some light sleepers awoke. One noticed that a bunk, usually filled by a guy who told good jokes, was empty. The man was probably in the head. Better get back to sleep. It must be some kind of secret exercise.

"Fire three!"

Amid a torrent of bubbles, parts of the USS *John Hay* surged into the Atlantic and started their drift to the surface.

"Fire four!"

The last tube. More debris.

Gillespie walked quickly to the control room. "Activate SECT," he ordered a Crusade technician. Then he took a piece of yellow paper from his pocket. It contained a single scrawled line. He handed it to the radioman.

"Send this to Norfolk."

He sat down at a console, took some stationery from a drawer, and wrote letters to the families of the two men he had murdered. The first eulogized the sailor who had died when he hit him.

"Your boy was a martyr," Gillespie wrote, "equal to those who fell at Bunker Hill and Valley Forge."

Not knowing of the man who had slipped from the *Constellation* or of those who had perished aboard the *Enterprise*, he gave the highest accolade of all: "He was," he wrote, "the first American casualty of the Third World War."

The time was 4:18 A.M., thirty hours and twenty-one

minutes from the time of the takeover, nineteen hours and twelve minutes to the moment of launch.

Anderson's sleep was peaceful now. There was a mild wheezing from a slight cold caught on the *Svirepy*, but otherwise he was not bothered.

Next to his bed, on a small night table, was the red phone connecting him with the National Military Command Center. Next to the phone was an electric clock shaped like a ship's wheel and set into a case of sterling silver. It had been a gift to Anderson from the British naval attaché. Anderson was especially fond of it because engraved on its back were the names of all the ships in which he had served. It was one of the few gifts he displayed.

Just as the clock showed 4:56, the red phone rang. Anderson stirred, then awakened sharply. He went for the receiver.

"Admiral Anderson."

"Admiral," said a voice on the other end, "this is Major Burns."

"Yes, Major?"

"Sir, the Russians have attacked the USS *John Hay*."

10

The words hit Anderson like a steel pipe across the base of the neck. The salute to the *Svirepy*'s flag flashed before him.

Betrayal.

"What do you mean?" he snapped to Major Burns, as if blaming the messenger for the message.

"Sir," the major said, "we received the following from the *Hay*: Quote—We are under attack by Soviet sub—unquote."

"Did you try to raise her?"

"We have a SECT contact, sir."

"I see." Anderson knew that SECT stood for Submarine Emergency Communications Transmitter—a radio-equipped buoy that floated to the surface and sent out signals if a submarine was in distress.

"Admiral Halaban has ordered antisub forces into the area," the major went on. "The submarine rescue vessel *Ortolan* has put to sea."

"Good," Anderson said halfheartedly. "Very good."

"And, sir, you are ordered to report to the White House at once. Your car is on the way."

"Of course," Anderson said. "Thank you, Major."

He reached over to return the phone, but his hands were shaking and he missed the cradle. The phone smashed against his prized clock, tipping it and causing a loud, metallic clunk. Anderson replaced the phone, ignoring the clock.

Julia stirred, but did not awaken.

Quickly Anderson dressed. Despite the crisis, he automatically checked each item as he put it on. Appearance. Correctness. They were still part of him.

His emotions flowed.

Annapolis, 1941. Midshipman Anderson was at study when a classmate burst into his room.

"The Japs have attacked Pearl Harbor!"

Before Anderson could turn around, the man had disappeared, running down the hall, knocking on door after door.

Betrayal.

Now the *Svirepy*. A Soviet admiral. Cordial words. Anderson was sure that he was clinking glasses with Kudelkin the very moment that a Red submarine was tracking the *John Hay*. The Russian notes signaling an end to the crisis were shams, decoys, and Kudelkin's toast was a mockery.

Again the United States had been humiliated, and he had been part of it. For a moment he thought of resigning, but the thought, competing with stronger feelings of rage, duty, and revenge, melted away.

He scribbled a note for Julia: "Problem. White House. I'll call."

He raced downstairs and out the door. Sentries, there to ensure his safety, snapped to attention. Flattened hands went up in salute. Anderson returned the salutes, but they seemed silly trivialities at 5:19 on the morning of an enemy attack.

The staff car screeched into the driveway. Anderson got in. The dry autumn leaves crackled beneath the tires as the car sped through Washington. The streets were empty except for a few newsboys making early deliveries of the *Post*. The admiral lit a cigar and tried to relax, to think out the meaning of this latest blow.

Why?

Why had the Russians done this?

That was the only question, and the answer would determine what the United States would do in response. Now there welled up in Anderson a war between his gut and his brain. The gut said it had all been a trick, a plot. The brain said, "Maybe," but there might be another explanation. If it was a trick, why the elaborate deception beginning with the *Dostoyny*? It had no logic.

The gut said, "Strike back!" The brain wanted to wait, to get things straight. The gut said this was the beginning of something massive, something springing from the mind of Admiral Gorshkov. The brain said the Russians were behaving in peculiarly un-Russian ways. These people were not subtle. If this was a Russian operation, it was the most subtle thing they'd done in the Cold War.

Some of the things going on in his gut bothered Anderson. There was a sudden cockiness, an arrogance, the lurking feeling of a man getting a chance to prove himself. He realized that he felt *military*. For the first time in years the idea of a fight seemed to please him. The brain fought the feeling, but it remained. Maybe, he thought, Isaac Anderson was really more like Patton than Marshall. Maybe he had been deluding himself, pampering his ego. He had once heard the President remark that the only great Presidents were war Presidents. Surely the same was true of admirals and generals. Maybe, at base, Anderson was no different from the others who privately yearned for glory and victory. As he sped toward the White House, he felt no different. And it worried him.

The car swung into the White House grounds.

"Morning, sir," Commander Hokanson said as Anderson got out. Hokanson was the navy representative in the White House Situation Room. He walked quickly with Anderson toward the mansion.

"Sir," he said, "I've been asked to fill you in. There's been no Soviet military activity since the attack on the *Hay*. As for the sub herself, we still can't raise her."

"When is sunrise?" Anderson asked.

"In a few minutes, sir. We'll search for debris around the area of the SECT signal."

"Any contact with the attacking unit?"

"None whatsoever."

They entered the White House. Anderson had never been there at that hour. It was not the regal place he knew. Janitors, caught off guard by the sudden crisis, hurried to scrub floors and wax door handles. The calendars

115

still hadn't been changed. Older men and women, part of the nighttime cleaning force, looked apprehensive. To them the White House was empty rooms and crushed cigarettes, darkened hallways and scuffed tiles. Some had worked there thirty years and had rarely seen a President or even a Secretary of Defense.

Anderson entered the Cabinet Room. It was grim and taut. The President, in shirt sleeves, seemed fidgety and nervous as he examined a map of the Atlantic. Bixby, as if in shock, hardly acknowledged the admiral as he walked in. Somerville and Combs, looking tense yet confident, sat silently, waiting for the meeting to begin. Their warnings about Moscow had been ignored. Anderson knew their influence was suddenly on the rise.

There had, of course, been other moments of high tension with the Russians, but there was something symbolic in the attack on a ship that every man in the room understood. Historically it had marked the beginning of war or the slide toward war. The *John Hay* suddenly was the *Lusitania*. She was the *Maine*. She was the *Greer,* attacked by the Nazis just before America entered World War II. She was the *Maddox,* attacked by North Vietnamese patrol boats in the Tonkin Gulf, leading to American action in Vietnam. The shooting down of an airliner could kill more people than an attack on a submarine. But the submarine had the force of history behind it.

Anderson read the atmosphere in the room. It was a war atmosphere.

There was no war atmosphere in Moscow. It was afternoon, and Premier Zorin was happy. He saw himself as a world statesman, a man of peace.

An aide knocked at the door, then entered and placed a piece of paper on Zorin's desk. It was green, the code for "urgent."

"What is this?" Zorin asked.

"Washington," the aide answered.

The Premier snapped it up. It was from the Soviet Embassy in Washington and told of a sudden CRITIC meeting at the White House. A few moments later Zorin's emergency phone buzzed. He put it to his ear and heard Admiral Gorshkov tell him that the United States had just begun a massive antisubmarine operation in the Atlantic. Zorin ordered Gorshkov to come to his office at once.

The White House meeting didn't fit in with the easing of tensions. Neither did the naval operation. The word "betrayal" flashed through Zorin's mind. Instinctively he placed Soviet forces on a higher level of alert. He ordered his emergency aircraft—the equivalent of America's National Emergency Airborne Command Post—taken out of its hangar. He knew the United States would detect both actions by satellite. He hoped they would deter any American tricks. Zorin was, of course, still unaware of the "sinking" of the *John Hay*. His frame of reference was obsolete.

It was 6:03 A.M. Washington time.

"We'd better get moving," the President said. He gave out a half yawn and fixed a rolled-up sleeve that was unraveling. "We only know that a Soviet attack has taken place. Admiral Anderson, the *Hay* would definitely know that the sub was Soviet, correct?"

"Correct, sir. She could identify the sub by sonar."

"No possibility of a mistake?"

"In this case, no, sir. The Soviet Union is the only hostile power that can fight under the sea."

"I am prepared," the President said, "to do whatever is necessary to defend the nation. I am ordering the reserves placed on alert. I am further ordering—"

A red phone behind Bixby rang. It was connected to the Situation Room and was faster than the CIS. Bixby reached back to grab it.

"Yes?"

There was a pause. Bixby looked concerned, then very concerned. He scrawled a note. The President leaned over to read it, and his face immediately showed that something new had entered the picture.

"Thanks," Bixby said, and hung up.

"Soviet forces have been placed on a higher level of alert," he reported. "Their radio traffic is increasing. Also, Zorin's emergency plane was taken out of the hangar and parked on the runway."

Eyes clicked from Bixby to the President. The Soviet emergency plane had never been used.

"Things are getting clear, aren't they?" asked Somerville. His voice was heavy. Although a hawk, he, too, was affected by the drama of the moment. Going to war was like going into surgery. There was a surrender to fate just before the act itself.

"They might be responding to this meeting," Anderson broke in.

"What?" the President asked. He didn't take kindly to the comment. Anderson knew that if the Chief needed a scapegoat, he had a perfect one in the man who had sipped drinks with a Soviet admiral the night before.

"Their people," Anderson went on, "probably picked up all this activity. Maybe they think we're planning something drastic in response to the *Hay*, and they're taking precautions."

"Of course they're taking precautions," Somerville said in a patronizing manner. "They know what their attack did. Now I suggest we also take some precautions."

"Name them," the President commanded.

"Number one, increase our alert. Number two, get to our own emergency plane."

Anderson could say nothing to counter Somerville's logic. In the light of Soviet action, Somerville's precautions were correct. The Soviets might be preparing a nuclear attack on the United States, and if Zorin actually took off in his emergency plane, it could mean that he was protecting the Kremlin leadership against a counterattack.

"Fred," the President ordered Bixby, "raise the alert. Order Haven readied. We're going to Andrews." Haven was the code name for the National Emergency Airborne Command Post.

There was a sudden movement. The tingling buzz of

118

zippers sealing overstuffed briefcases filled the room. Pencils dropped to the table. Every motion of every man spoke determination, resolve. Even those who may have had doubts about any strong action gave the appearance of going along with the mood.

"Hold it," the President said. "To put it mildly, the press is gonna notice there's no government in town. We've still gotta watch any panic."

He turned to McNamara.

"Mac, have one of your people put out something saying the CRITIC group is participating in an alert. My orders. Practice."

McNamara winced. It was that kind of offhand distortion that destroyed confidence in a President.

"Sir," he said, "that's a mistake. If war comes, and people see we've been lying, you lose credibility when you need it most."

"I'll take the chance," the President said. "We aren't even sure the *Hay*'s lost. Until we get the picture straight, I don't want a war atmosphere."

McNamara nodded his acceptance of the edict, but the pain ran deeper each time he had to face reporters and lie. Anderson wondered where his breaking point was.

The room started to empty. Three helicopters waited on the lawn to whisk the CRITIC group to Andrews Air Force Base or any alternative that the President might choose. They were always there when CRITIC met. They symbolized crisis.

Anderson looked out the White House windows as he moved toward the door. The first ray of dawn turned the white pillars a soft orange. On Pennsylvania Avenue the early shifts were just beginning to go to work. Trucks bearing the names of local dairies made their rounds. Anderson could hear, but not see, airliners from National Airport starting their morning business flights to the rest of the country.

As he left the mansion, Anderson again passed the cleaning force. He noticed one lady who seemed bewildered by the sudden mass of power parading by. But her bewilderment soon faded, replaced by a slow burn when she saw the CRITIC group stride over the floor she had just waxed. As the peace of the world appeared to fade, she had one overwhelming concern—scuff marks.

11

Frank Mario looked out at the Atlantic dawn from the porthole of his cabin aboard the Italian liner *Michelangelo*. This was his eighth crossing, a remarkable record even for a welder who had saved all his money for trips to his father's homeland.

The ocean fares were soaring, but Mario was afraid to fly. He didn't know how many more trips he could afford. At sixty he had to provide for his and his wife's future. So he savored every moment of this trip, even awakening to watch the sun rise. It was, he thought, one of the great joys of ocean travel. But he could not convince his wife of that.

Alone and dressed only in a bathrobe and slippers, Mario tiptoed from the cabin and walked to the guardrail. There he could lose himself in his thoughts, his recollections of past crossings. He looked out at the limitless sea. It was calm, and only a few clouds spotted the blue sky. He was practically alone at the rail, passed occasionally only by a deckhand or an officer. Everything was so serene, so perfect. He could not think of a better place to be.

But then, even with his failing eyes, he saw an object in the ocean. No, it was more than one object. There seemed to be two. The light was poor and Mario had trouble making out the shapes, but the *Michelangelo* was moving closer to whatever it was he saw. He started edging along the guardrail, staring, fascinated that things were actually floating this far out in the Atlantic. Within moments the objects became clearer. And then Frank Mario's stomach turned.

Bodies. Two of them. And near the bodies, just coming into view, pieces of wreckage.

Mario looked around frantically for someone to tell. There was no one. He ran up a stairway. About forty feet from the top, relaxing with a cigarette, was a young officer. Mario ran to him, jutting a finger toward the ocean as he approached. No words were exchanged. The officer looked out, saw the bodies, and immediately called the captain.

The captain ordered the *Michelangelo* stopped and notified the U.S. Coast Guard that bodies had been sighted. He had a boat sent out to retrieve them. Then he ordered a curtain strung across part of the main deck to shield the boatmen from view when they returned with their cargo. He didn't want to upset the early-rising passengers.

The boat carried six sailors, who hauled the bodies aboard and picked up some of the debris. Part of the wreckage bore the name USS *John Hay,* and the dead men carried U.S. Navy identification. This information was radioed to the Coast Guard.

Like all liners, the *Michelangelo* carried a small complement of coffins to accommodate sudden needs during the voyage. Two of the coffins became temporary resting places for the young victims of Richard Gillespie's grand design.

CRITIC climbed aboard its helicopters, the division of members among the three machines reflecting the realities of influence. Flying with the President were Bixby, McNamara, Somerville, Combs, Anderson, and the other Joint Chiefs.

The engines started, their whining sound piercing the ears of staff members remaining on the White House lawn. The rotor blades engaged and cut the air with the chopping noise that gave helicopters their nicknames. Inside the craft, though, there was only a soft purr. A new acoustic insulation made it possible for the passengers to speak at normal voice levels.

As the machines lifted off the lawn, Anderson looked

down to see the early traffic slow to a crawl, heads cran-
ing from the windows of cars and trucks. The sight of action at the White House was irresistible, especially in the
brooding atmosphere of semidarkness. Even seasoned
Washingtonians waved at the helicopters, hoping to get a
response from the President of the United States. Anderson knew that if the fates were wrong, all those smiling,
waving people would be turned into radioactive dust
within twenty-four hours.

He looked away.

The President's helicopter passed the Washington Monument and gained altitude. It approached the Potomac
River and flew just to the right of the Pentagon. The
phone beside Anderson buzzed, and he picked it up.

"Admiral Anderson."

As he listened to the message, he started rubbing his
lips together. His head seemed to drop slightly.

"Thank you," he said, returning the receiver. Then he
turned toward the President and took a deep breath.

"There's an Italian liner out there, the *Michelangelo*.
They picked up two bodies and wreckage from the *Hay*.
We can assume the ship is lost and that there's no hope
for recovery."

They had assumed it all along, of course, these rational
and experienced men. But, like close relatives of the ter-
minally ill, they had to have final confirmation. Somerville
slammed his hand sharply into the skin of the helicopter.

"We're at war."

"Now, just a second," Anderson said.

"Oh, come on, Admiral. Face reality!"

"I am," Anderson shot back. "The reality is that our
ship has been sunk. The reality is also that we were
falsely accused of sinking theirs."

Somerville looked at him with a skeptical expression
that made Anderson feel his sanity was being questioned.

"Mr. Secretary," Anderson said, "the men of the *Hay*
are dead. We can't bring them back. What we can do is
try to prevent more from dying."

"That's very noble," Somerville answered, "but the way
you guarantee more people dying is to show weakness.

123

I'm no warmonger. I hate war as much as anyone. But we've got to respond firmly to this direct enemy attack. The harder we hit back, the greater the chance of avoiding something big."

Anderson knew it was the classic Pentagon argument. You go to war to preserve the peace.

"I'd hate to see any action until their strategy is clear," he said. "It could be suicidal. Obviously they don't want all-out war. If they did, they'd have used nuclear weapons."

"So what's in their heads?" the President asked.

"It's conceivable," Anderson said, "that they could be trying for a slow-motion war."

"A what?"

"That's where they build up incidents one by one until they reach precisely the point they wish. They try to control things that way, for some objective we don't know about."

"The admiral has a point," Combs volunteered. "By starting with limited actions, the Soviets might hope to limit us. We'd respond, but cautiously. After all, escalation could be nuclear. You could have an endless series of small exchanges and battles. It could be very draining."

"Like a worldwide guerrilla war," the President said.

"Precisely," Combs replied, "if it worked their way."

"Well, now wait," Bixby broke in. "What if we don't go for their bait? What if we ignore the *Hay* and do absolutely nothing?"

"They'll simply manufacture another incident," Combs replied. "They'll keep doing it until we have to respond."

The President brought his left hand up to his chin in the "I'll be darned" gesture that Eisenhower made famous.

"So what in hell do we do?" he asked.

There was silence in the helicopter's cabin. A signal corps photographer, traveling on board, suddenly snapped a picture of the group with the Pentagon out the window in the background. It would be, Anderson thought, one of those classic historical photographs: NATIONAL LEADERS

124

But attention quickly returned to Combs' reply. "Mr. President," he said, sounding thoughtful and confident, "the worst thing we can do is fight on the enemy's terms. We must fight on our own terms. As Mr. Somerville said, hit back hard."

"Who said those are our terms?" Anderson asked.

Combs was contemptuous. "You want to crawl around, as we did in Vietnam, dragging ourselves up ten troops at a time?"

The President turned to Anderson. From his doubting expression it was clear that he had reservations about the admiral's caution.

"Mr. President," Anderson said, "if we must fight, every man in this helicopter is ready. But I recommend you begin your response by sending a stiff note of protest to the Soviet Premier. Let's see if we can determine what his strategy is. Get his response."

"Who cares about his response?" Somerville roared. "His deeds speak for themselves."

"I don't think remarks like that are helpful," Anderson shot back. "This is serious business, Mr. Secretary. Some of us have seen war."

Somerville's jaw dropped. Anderson recoiled slightly. He knew his comment was inappropriate, below the belt, out of line with the rule of civilian authority. But Somerville didn't answer. He couldn't find the words to express his rage, his sense of insult. All he could do was stare back at the admiral, incredulous and dazed.

There was another long silence. The President leaned back and looked out the window. The helicopter was passing over the Central Intelligence Agency in McLean, Virginia. The President closed his eyes, as if wanting a moment to escape from the strain and tension. If Richard Gillespie had been aboard, he would have congratulated himself. The very suspicions, uncertainties, and personal friction he hoped for were all there. These men were being conditioned for war. Even Anderson, the most cautious and farsighted among them, was prepared for com-

125

bat if necessary. The North Star Crusade was rolling toward success.

"Funny," the President said, "you look down at the CIA. It's so damned secret, but there it is. Right out in the open. I can't imagine anyone else doing that."

"That's democracy," Somerville said.

"Nope. That's Allen Dulles," Bixby replied. "He wanted a big building, just like his brother, Foster."

The President chuckled. It was just what he needed.

"Anderson's right," he finally said.

Somerville jutted forward, but restrained himself.

"Yup," the President went on, "I'll send a note to the Red SOB. There's no need to fly off the handle. Our forces are ready."

"Wise," Bixby said.

Bixby's remark surprised Anderson, who didn't know whether Bixby actually had a position. Bixby could be a valuable ally, Anderson knew. His office adjoined the President's, and in a town where geography spelled influence, that meant a great deal.

Rufus Combs rarely let his feelings show in his face, but now they showed. He removed his pipe from his mouth and looked at the President, incredulous. He knew he could not change the man's mind, but he wanted to make him feel as uncomfortable as possible. His face had a look which read, "You're the boss, but you're making a terrible mistake."

"Mr. President," he said, "considering your . . . decision, what do we say about the *John Hay*?"

The President turned to Anderson.

"It's traditional," the admiral said, "that when a sub is lost, we first announce that she's overdue. When we have positive confirmation that she's sunk, we announce that. Of course, that's procedure for accidents. Now—"

"Men have died from hostile action," Combs said, giving emphasis to Anderson's predicament.

"We can't say that," Anderson argued, "without destroying our negotiating chances with the Russians."

"Mr. President," Combs said, "that's unprecedented in American history."

126

Anderson pushed on. "There's another problem," he said. "This is the first time we've lost a Polaris sub. There are sixteen nuclear missiles on board. Even if the sinking was accidental, you'd have a public-relations problem. I recommend we simply announce the ship is overdue. We stress there's no danger of the missiles exploding."

"Can't do it," the President said. "You don't know Congress. All those clean-air-'n'-water types'll have coronaries on the White House lawn."

"Then what can we say?" Bixby asked.

"Nothing," the President replied. "That's what my bones tell me. It's tough to head off a bad reaction from up here. I don't need that headache right now."

"What about the families of the crew?" Anderson asked. "They're entitled to know. . . ."

"I regret it, but they'll have to wait."

"Sir," McNamara broke in, "those Italian sailors know all about this. They'll talk. The passengers'll talk. There are ship-to-shore phones."

The President thought for a moment. Of course, McNamara was right.

"Oh, Christ, look," he said, "that boat won't be in for hours. We'll take a chance that nobody yapped on the phone. I just can't worry about this now. If it leaks, I'll take the heat. I've got to get this note to the Russians."

Anderson saw that the President was becoming overwhelmed by the crisis.

Whitney Morath wrote for the New York *Times*. He was aboard the *Michelangelo* with his wife, having just ended a one-month vacation in Italy.

Morath was fifty-six. When he was sent to the European front in 1944, he was one of the *Times*' youngest correspondents. He stayed in Europe until 1948, when he was recalled to New York. Having gathered five years' experience in European politics, he was for a while—in typical *Times* fashion—assigned to cover the Parks Department.

He was sent to Korea for eight months, then served another stint in Europe, this time as correspondent in NATO headquarters. After that he returned again to New York, where he once more was assigned to trivial local coverage. He was now thinking of leaving the *Times* and buying a small newspaper in Vermont. He and his wife had gone to Italy partly to get the chance, far from New York, to talk about their future.

Morath saw some disturbed faces when he left his cabin to take a breath of ocean air. He saw hands pressed nervously to cheeks, and a woman with her head buried in her husband's shoulder. At first he assumed that a passenger had died on deck, but he asked an officer for details.

"American submarine sink," the officer said in halting English.

Smelling a story, Morath went from passenger to passenger, trying to find out more. An American college girl, more composed than most of the other passengers, told him that the *Michelangelo*'s crewmen had pulled two bodies and some debris from the water.

"The stuff said *John Hay*," she remarked.

His reporter's instincts working fully, Morath hurried to the ship's library, where he asked for a copy of *Jane's Fighting Ships*. He looked up the *John Hay* and saw that she was a Polaris sub. The key words raced through his mind—"nuclear," "missiles," "first time sunk." Morath hurried to the telephone room, suddenly feeling like the young *Times* man who froze with the troops at the Battle of the Bulge. After getting three bad connections, he reached the *Times* office in New York. New York then cabled the *Times*' Washington Bureau. The secret of the *John Hay* was unraveling faster than the President had expected.

Premier Zorin and Admiral Gorshkov nibbled at sandwiches. The report of CRITIC's flight to Andrews had just come in. Zorin was concerned, but not panicked.

"Do you think," he asked, "that the American flight

was caused by my moving our emergency plane to the runway?"

"How could that be?" Gorshkov answered. "Our plane is on the runway, but we are here. The plane will not run the government without us. The Americans know that."

"You're certain they know we're here, Gorshkov?"

Gorshkov looked at Zorin like an old man dressing down a grandson.

"Premier," he said, "half the drunkards in Red Square are CIA agents, and the other half are Israelis. They know when we brush our teeth."

Zorin threw up his hands. "So why do they fly?" he asked.

"They fly because they are involved in a plan," Gorshkov replied.

"And our response, Gorshkov?"

"We don't know precisely what they're up to. But at minimum we must equal their actions."

Zorin nodded in agreement. He pressed a white button mounted on his desk, and an aide soon appeared at the door.

"You will," Zorin ordered, "activate Purple Flower."

The aide raised his eyebrows in surprise and quickly disappeared. Purple Flower was the code signaling immediate use of the emergency aircraft. It would now be transmitted to alert all those assigned to the plane—crewmen, communications specialists, translators, military advisers.

Zorin thrust his chair back, then rose abruptly.

"The Americans will not get the best of us," he said. He slammed one hand into the other to try to show zeal, but the slam was hollow, for there was no zeal. Zorin was being dragged into a bizarre game of international chicken. He had no heart for it. He was deeply afraid. He packed some papers into a briefcase, then he and Gorshkov walked briskly toward the door. But they were interrupted by a sudden buzz from the intercom on the Premier's desk. Zorin walked back to take the call. He listened intently for a few seconds, then gradually slid back in his chair.

"The Hot Line is working," he told Gorshkov tersely. "We will wait." The look on his face showed slight relief. The use of the Hot Line symbolized peace, even though it could easily be used to send a message of war. Zorin waited, fidgeting with a paper clip. A long minute later a Red Army colonel entered the office carrying two copies of the Hot Line message. Zorin and Gorshkov took the copies, then read in tense, urgent silence.

MR. PREMIER:

AT 0446 THIS MORNING, OUR TIME, THE UNITED STATES NAVY RECEIVED AN EMERGENCY MESSAGE FROM THE SUBMARINE USS JOHN HAY, A MISSILE-CARRYING VESSEL ARMED WITH THE POLARIS WEAPON SYSTEM. THE MESSAGE INDICATED THAT THE HAY WAS UNDER ATTACK BY A UNIT OF THE SOVIET ARMED FORCES. . . .

Zorin looked up to see Gorshkov's expression turn from interest to anger. His own became cynical. The hope faded from within him. The message continued:

THE UNITED STATES MADE EVERY EFFORT TO LOCATE THE SHIP IN QUESTION, WITHOUT SUCCESS. HOWEVER, THE ITALIAN LINER MICHELANGELO INFORMS US THAT IT HAS RECOVERED TWO BODIES AND WRECKAGE DEFINITELY IDENTIFIED AS FROM THE HAY.

THE UNITED STATES PROTESTS IN THE STRONGEST TERMS THIS OUTRAGEOUS VIOLATION OF INTERNATIONAL PEACE, THE LAW OF THE SEA, AND THE SPIRIT THAT PREVAILED DURING THE VISIT OF OUR ADMIRAL ANDERSON TO YOUR SHIP LAST EVENING. THE UNITED STATES DEMANDS A COMPLETE EXPLANATION OF THIS INCIDENT.

IN ORDER TO SAFEGUARD OUR NATIONAL SECURITY, I HAVE ORDERED OUR FORCES PLACED ON A HIGHER LEVEL OF ALERT. I AM ALSO ORDERING THE USE OF THE EMERGENCY AIRCRAFT PLACED AT MY DISPOSAL. THE UNITED STATES GOVERNMENT IS FULLY COG-

NIZANT OF THE IMPACT THESE EVENTS COULD HAVE ON OUR TWO PEOPLES. IT WILL THEREFORE TAKE ALL REALISTIC STEPS TO AVOID PUBLIC STATEMENTS. WE HAVE ATTEMPTED TO ACT IN A SPIRIT OF UNDERSTANDING. WE REGRET THAT YOU HAVE CHOSEN TO FRUSTRATE OUR EFFORTS.

Zorin finished. Then he threw the American note down on his desk and spat at it.

"Disgusting!"

Gorshkov's expression again changed, this time from anger to smugness. His original assessment of the Americans had been proved correct. A secret ambition was about to be realized.

"They mock us," he declared. "They sink our destroyer, then they charge us with sinking a ship of theirs."

Zorin nodded his agreement. A new, strange militancy filled him. Proof of the American treachery seemed so clear. Zorin was approaching the point where the facts could overcome his reluctance to fight.

"We go to the airport," he said. His voice suddenly was commanding, and Gorshkov was pleased. As they left the room, Zorin had the stride of a man chosen to lead his nation through hell.

"I remember what you said," he remarked to Gorshkov. "This idea of their starting a naval war before our fleet grows too large. It fits together, doesn't it?"

Gorshkov did not reply. Events had answered the question for him.

Zorin and Gorshkov boarded an Mi-4P helicopter, which took off at once. They could see other military chiefs heading for an identical helicopter, which was waiting to take them to the emergency aircraft.

"I must respond to the Americans," Zorin said as his craft flew over the Kremlin walls.

"Why?" Gorshkov asked. "These shreds of paper mean nothing."

"For history," Zorin replied. "I want it known that we made every effort to avoid war."

131

"History has some value," Gorshkov mumbled, clearly uninterested in whether Zorin sent his message or not.

A few moments later the helicopter passed over the United States Embassy.

"They're reporting our flight to their people in Washington," Gorshkov theorized. "Their ambassador will probably be called home for consultations."

"We can intern him," Zorin said.

"We should do that. He would be a legitimate prisoner of war."

"Do you know Ambassador Gruening?" Zorin asked.

"I've met him," Gorshkov replied.

"Interesting sort. Not as grim or pompous as most ambassadors. A career man, like Washington always sends us. They think career men know more about Russia than the tractor manufacturers they make ambassadors to other countries."

"Do they know more?" Gorshkov asked teasingly.

Zorin paused for a moment. He reviewed in his mind the roster of distinguished Americans who'd been given the Moscow post.

"Yes," he answered, "they do. They're usually sensitive, subtle, intellectual maybe. In America they'd be failures."

Zorin looked out at Moscow. A sudden, awful vision formed in his mind: the city lying in ashes, its people turned to dust, great fires and windstorms raging on the outskirts. He looked away. And yet Zorin was better prepared psychologically for the sacrifice than any of the Americans. After all, he had history to contend with. If the Russians could lose thirty million to fight Hitler, was the current generation any less courageous? He knew that if war came, he would go to any extreme to win it.

He started writing his response to the American message. As he did, he saw Admiral Gorshkov take a piece of paper from a rack and begin making notes on his strategy in the conflict to come.

The Presidential helicopter bumped down in a desolate,

windy corner of Andrews Air Force Base, Maryland. The other helicopters landed moments later. Anderson looked out. Frustration crossed his face.

"Flap city," he said. Flaps—blunders—were an everyday occurrence in Washington, but this wasn't every day, and Anderson was annoyed by two mistakes. First, reporters were on the field. Emergency procedures specifically forbade that, but someone clearly didn't know the procedures. Second, Haven wasn't ready. Anderson thought that was incredible, appalling. With Soviet missiles potentially minutes away, technicians were still working on an engine. Anderson would later learn that the starter had not been properly connected.

The CRITIC group rushed to a hangar to wait for the repair. Reporters tried to get close, but McNamara and a small band of air police now kept them away. Anderson saw Doris Moffitt. They were separated by at least seventy-five feet, and a six-foot-three black trooper from South Philadelphia held Moffitt back when she tried to break through. But Moffitt held Anderson's attention by making a motion with her right hand, like a ship going down in the water. Then she placed both hands near the sides of her head and gripped air, like someone operating a periscope. She knew about the *Hay.*

Another leak. Anderson quickly walked over and took Moffitt aside.

Counterleak.

"Going flying, Admiral?" Moffitt asked.

"What do you know?" Anderson replied, ignoring the question.

"*John Hay,*" Moffitt said. "Sunk by the Russians. A Polaris sub, no?"

"Correct," Anderson replied. He assumed that Somerville had called Moffitt from his home after being notified of the sinking.

"War?" Moffitt asked.

"It's possible," Anderson replied. "But we're negotiating, or trying to."

"Are you sticking to your previous position . . . restraint?"

133

"For now, yes."

"No immediate retaliation?"

"No."

"Aren't the Russians going to question our toughness?"

Anderson smirked. The word—which seemed to have a magical effect on some people—always amused him.

"Toughness is not a policy," he answered with a slight touch of snippiness. "You have to decide what to get tough about. The Russians are impressed by strength, but only when it's wisely applied. Toughness and dumbness make a lousy combination."

"As in Vietnam?"

Anderson looked at Moffitt and smiled slightly.

They were alone, protected from the view of other reporters by the side of a toolshed. But a few Secret Service agents regarded them curiously, as if they were engaged in some dark plot. They were lit only by the haze of the rising sun and the rhythmic flashing of red landing lights. Their heads were close together as they continued their off-the-record discussion. They *looked* like plotters.

By now McNamara had rounded up the press for an impromptu news conference. Anderson could hear the shouted questions and answers. They seemed to come from another world, for only Moffitt had been tipped.

A reporter waved for recognition.

Question: "If this is an exercise, why wasn't it announced in advance?"

McNamara: "Because the President believed it would lose its value if everyone had time to prepare."

Question: "There's never been something like this before. Why now?"

McNamara: "Don't be so sure this is the first test of its kind just because no President has announced one before."

Question: "This is done regularly?"

McNamara: "I didn't say that."

Question: "Has this President used the emergency plane before?"

McNamara: "I have no comment."

"Mac oughtta write novels," Moffitt said to Anderson.

134

Anderson nodded indifferently. He felt more and more for the press secretary.

"Is there a plan to evacuate the cities?" Moffitt asked.

"Not right now," Anderson replied.

"How do you personally interpret the Russian motives?"

"I don't know, and we shouldn't assume there's a deep motive here."

"What do you mean by that?"

Anderson paused. He looked Moffitt up and down, focusing his attention on her press badge, pinned to a woolly sweater and blowing in the wind. For a moment he felt like turning and walking away from this persistent woman. But he had to counter Somerville's damage.

"Doris," he finally said, "I'm not sure I know what I mean. I've never faced a situation like this, and I haven't got any real answers for you. The American people like to think their leaders sit at long tables and say deep things. Frankly, we've been sitting around like kids making snap judgments about the other guy's Little League team. We have no idea where we're going, but we'll try to be careful along the way."

"Admiral," Moffitt said, "you're an honest man."

"Thank you," Anderson said. "That won't help me a bit."

Another reporter shouted to McNamara.

Question: "Mac, is this related to yesterday's alert?"

McNamara: "It happened to coincide. But no, it isn't related."

Question: "Isn't it awfully dangerous to pull something like this during an alert? With the President leaving town, the Russians might think we're attacking."

McNamara: "That's been taken into consideration."

Question: "Why aren't any reporters going?"

McNamara paused. Most of the reporters felt he was covering up. They were sensitive to the rumors of trouble with Russia, and their common sense told them the situation was far worse than McNamara was admitting. McNamara knew what the reporters felt. He seemed uneasy,

135

even a bit scared. He kept looking around, as if his past were peeking over his shoulder.

McNamara: "A tentative decision has been made that the presence of reporters on the emergency aircraft would be disruptive."

Question: "Even in a practice exercise?"

McNamara: "Yes, but I'll check further."

He hadn't thought of it before, but he could ask the President to allow a reporters' pool on the plane. He was trying to score points with his conscience.

A Secret Service man standing forty feet from Anderson received a terse message on his walkie-talkie. He started moving quickly toward the admiral.

"They're going to pull me away," Anderson said. "Doris, I just want to stress again what one loose word can do."

Moffitt nodded, and Anderson assumed she'd gotten the message. He could only hope she would show her usual journalistic good sense.

"One last question?" she asked.

"Sure."

"I'm not criticizing, but how does it feel to get out and leave the people of Washington exposed?"

The question wrenched Anderson's innards. Moffitt had not meant it harshly, but it was tantamount to asking a man how it felt to run away from combat.

"My wife is in Washington," he replied.

The answer disgusted him. It was evasive, and he knew he was playing for sympathy. It was also a half lie, for he knew Julia Anderson would not be in Washington for long. Under a secret Presidential order called Clearmind, all next of kin of CRITIC members were to be evacuated from target areas if there was imminent danger of nuclear attack. The purpose was to ensure that CRITIC's war recommendations were not influenced by the fear of losing close relatives.

The Secret Service man approached. "Sir," he said, "the President wishes to see you."

As he walked to the hangar, Anderson couldn't get Moffitt's final question out of his mind. It got to the very

136

heart of life in a democracy. He had once framed it in a speech at Annapolis:

> There's a first question in any war. Who goes? Whose kid serves behind the lines? Which eighteen-year-old fires a rifle? Which one stays in school to learn how to make money once the war is over?
>
> We all know the answer, and it's a rotten one. The people this country considers important stay at home. The ones we think we can do without get sent to die.

Anderson thought about that speech as the Maryland wind whipped at his skin. War had not yet begun, yet the question had already been asked . . . and answered. He himself was important. He would not be left to die in Washington.

Anderson couldn't know, as he left Doris Moffitt, how shaken she was. She had seen war. She had been shelled, bombed, shot at. But in that kind of war she could hide, wear a helmet, dive in a foxhole. Now all she could do was wait. She lived in northwest Washington, twenty blocks from the White House. Even if there were warning of an attack, the missiles would strike before anyone could escape.

Fearful thoughts flooded her mind. Run away. Quit the job. Vanish. Rush to friends in a small town.

But what of the other reporters? Tell them so they could get their families out? Then the secret of what was really happening would leak. There'd be panic.

And what of the people themselves? There was a thin line between reporting the government and becoming part of it. Keeping the *Dostoyny* incident out of the copy was right. It was in the national interest. But now the national interest presumably required another deletion: the possibility of nuclear war, the annihilation of millions. According to the rules of the game, what Anderson had said was strictly not for publication. But was secrecy now in the national interest just because Anderson had said so?

Breaking the rules would be a violation of journalistic trust, and the Moffitt career would be over. But the very panic the story set off might prevent a holocaust. Or it might save millions of lives by giving people a chance to take shelter. Or it might blow the negotiations and cause World War III.

Everything was "might" or "maybe" or "possibly." Morality was anything you wanted to make it.

Moffitt started writing her story. Maybe it was inertia, maybe it was faith in the United States government, maybe it was the ingrained belief that nuclear war, prevented for three decades, could never happen, but whatever the reason, Doris Moffitt played by the rules and revealed nothing. She used Somerville's leak and Anderson's counterleak purely for her personal guidance. Her story would seem slightly more informed than the ones others would write, but would still be, in effect, the party line.

Anderson entered the hangar, the smell of kerosene solvents hitting him and burning the tops of his nostrils. He saw the President standing amid oilcans and piles of rags. The chief's face was flushed with anger. He held a typewritten note in his hand as Somerville, Combs, and Bixby stood around him. Their faces, too, showed agitation. The President nodded nervously to Anderson and thrust the note into his hand.

"The funny papers."

Anderson read:

MR. PRESIDENT:

THE SOVIET UNION REJECTS TOTALLY AND COMPLETELY YOUR ABSURD AND INSULTING NOTE OF THIS MORNING, WASHINGTON TIME. THE INSOLENT TONE OF THIS MESSAGE AND THE IRRESPONSIBLE CHARGE IT CONTAINS LEAD US TO BELIEVE THAT YOUR POLICY HAS BECOME AGGRESSIVE. YOU HAVE SERIOUSLY UNDERMINED WORLD PEACE.

NO SOVIET UNIT ATTACKED YOUR SUBMARINE.

SURELY YOU KNOW THIS. THE SOVIET UNION ITSELF
WAS ATTACKED WHEN OUR SHIP THE DOSTOYNY WAS
SUNK BY YOUR FORCES. WE ATTEMPTED TO PREVENT
HOSTILITIES BY ALLOWING YOUR ADMIRAL ANDERSON
TO VISIT THE SOVIET SHIP SVIREPY. WE REGRET THAT
THIS VISIT WAS PART OF A DECEPTIVE SCHEME BY
YOUR MILITARY CLIQUE.

IN ACCORDANCE WITH MY RESPONSIBILITIES, I AM
TAKING THE NECESSARY PRECAUTIONS. MY EMER-
GENCY AIRCRAFT IS EQUIPPED TO COMMAND OUR
FORCES. IT IS ALSO EQUIPPED TO COMMUNICATE
WITH YOU.

BEAR IN MIND, MR. PRESIDENT, THAT WE ARE NOT
A FEARFUL PEOPLE. WE WILL DEFEND OUR HOME-
LAND.

Anderson handed the note back to the President.

"They're making fun of us," the President said. "We
rejected their charge yesterday, now they reject ours. But
we know they attacked the *Hay*. They're treating us like
children."

Anderson nodded sadly. He saw the emotion around
him and knew this was not the time for serious discussion.
But he kept firmly in mind one sentence from the Soviet
note: "It is also equipped to communicate with you."

He knew that sentence would play a critical role in the
hours ahead.

A ground crewman pressed a button on the hangar wall
and the huge door rolled upward, its steel wheels rumbling on their tracks like a freight train. A cool breeze
blew in to dilute the chemical smell. The Presidential
party stepped out and walked the forty yards to Haven.
The President, smiling, waved to reporters and photogra-
phers, giving the impression of a man going on vacation.
As he reached the top of the boarding ramp, he turned
around and waved again, setting a superb example of how
to maintain an official lie.

The CRITIC group entered the aircraft. Haven was an
E-4A, the military version of the Boeing 747, modified
for emergency use. It cost fifty-nine million dollars. Its in-

139

side looked like an executive suite—offices, a conference room, corridors. All carpeted. Each room was painted a different pastel color to make a long trip as pleasant as possible. There was something peculiarly uncrisislike about a beige command room or a mint-green communications center, but the psychiatrists who helped design the plane supposedly knew what they were doing.

Some called Haven a flying Pentagon, others a flying White House.

The President had been briefed on Haven's capabilities when he took office. He knew the plane was fully equipped to direct American forces all over the world and that it could maintain contact with foreign governments. He understood that Haven could also send or receive the most sophisticated codes. So he boarded the plane without any feeling of being cut off. He knew that at 30,000 feet he would still be in full control. As he walked down a corridor, an aide handed him an urgent message:

US EMBASSY MOSCOW—ISRAELI OPERATIVES REPORT ZORIN'S HELICOPTER HAS JUST LANDED AT MILITARY AIRFIELD FOUR. HE IS ABOUT TO BOARD HIS EMERGENCY AIRCRAFT.

GRUENING

The President knew that Zorin would soon be airborne and the Soviet government invulnerable to attack.

"Let's get out of here!" he ordered, and walked quickly to his oak-paneled office, sat down, and buckled up.

A ground crewman closed the main door with a loud clunk. The boarding ramp was rolled away. The four jet engines started their whine, and Haven came alive. The whine turned to a roar, the roar to thunder. Men with huge sound-resistant earmuffs ran under the wings and nose to remove the wheel blocks, and the plane lurched forward.

As Haven turned for its takeoff, Isaac Anderson popped two Chiclets into his mouth. The engines strained, and he was squeezed back into his seat as the huge plane hurtled down the runway, the morning sun glaring

140

through its windows and reflecting off the chrome appointments. Anderson looked out at the gathering of reporters. He picked out Doris Moffitt and fixed on her, even as she became a dot. It struck him that he had never really thought of reporters as human beings, with feelings and fears. They were simply part of the Washington landscape, ornaments around the seats of power. But now he saw Doris Moffitt as a potential casualty, and he realized how little he knew about her. He had trusted her with high secrets of the United States government, but he didn't know where she lived, whom she lived with, or what her religion was. He didn't even remember the color of her eyes. She had been, up to now, a thing.

Premier Zorin and his party entered their emergency aircraft. It had no name. Despite his Americanization, Zorin scoffed at the readiness of American Presidents to name everything in sight, from airplanes to homes. When Richard Nixon announced that his San Clemente compound would be known as Casa Pacifica, Zorin insisted on calling his apartment Flat Number Seven.

So only the Americans had a name for the Soviet aircraft. They code-named it Clamshell because of the shape of the thrust reversers on its four engines.

The plane was an Ilyushin Il-76 heavy freight transport, converted for the Premier's needs. It was smaller than Haven and dramatically different in outside appearance. Its wings came out of the top of the fuselage, rather than the middle. Its tail looked like a *T* with the elevators coming out of the top of the rudder. It was not the mightiest Soviet transport, but it had the valuable ability to take off from small, rough airstrips—the kind that might be left after a nuclear attack. It was fitted with extra fuel tanks for extended range.

Clamshell was not chic, its interior showing correct proletarian austerity. Everything, including the seat cushions, was gray, and all the furniture was made of lightweight sheet metal. The plane was divided into a communications room, a small meeting room, a military planning center, and offices for Soviet officials. The only visible amenity was a small refrigerator in the Premier's office.

As Zorin settled into his seat, he was handed two messages. One told him that the President had just taken off from Andrews. The other reported the progress of the Soviet alert: All submarines were either at sea or preparing to leave their bases. The strategic missile and bomber forces were ready. The army units along the NATO frontier were prepared to move. The reserves had been quietly notified. The air-defense system was in operation. The Soviet Union, according to the report, was ready to go to war.

And yet Zorin knew it wasn't so. Units always reported they were ready, but only a small percentage were ever up to standard. Military incompetence, combined with military boastfulness, was a worldwide problem. Zorin knew that neither he nor the President had an accurate idea of how effective their forces would be in actual war. Presumably, that was some kind of deterrent. But deterrence, Zorin realized, no longer seemed to be working.

Clamshell took off only four minutes after Zorin boarded. He flew away from Moscow, watching the city melt beneath the clouds.

"Good-bye," he said softly. "I'm sorry."

12

Nothing pleased Richard Gillespie more than hearing the uncoded transmissions from the *Michelangelo*. Reports of bodies, identity cards, spellings of names. Reports of debris, meticulously described. Here was his handiwork broadcast to the world.

He left the control room and walked to the missile compartment, where sixteen vertical cylinders stood positioned in two rows of eight. Each cylinder contained a Polaris "bird." A Crusade scientist told Gillespie that the fifth and sixth safety interlocks had just been bypassed. Only two remained. Delighted, Gillespie watched as one of his comrades clipped wires and soldered resistors inside a rocket engine, working with the precision and care of a surgeon. Gillespie felt a sense of well-being. He felt like a man about to enter history at the top.

What Gillespie could not know, however, was that a counterplot was being launched aboard the *Hay*. Its author was Captain Alan Lansing.

Lansing was kept in his cabin, under guard. He had no contact with anyone except for a Crusade member who brought him his meals. He realized that the crew had bought the Crusade's cover story—that the *Hay* was on a classified exercise with Gillespie in command. These men, Lansing knew, had the navy chain of command drummed into their heads. They might wonder, but they did not question. So Gillespie was wise not to announce the takeover on the bullhorn and make threats. The absolute requirement of navy men to accept the word of the control room was his best weapon in keeping order.

Some crewmen, Lansing sensed, might wonder why he

stayed only in his cabin, why his food had to be brought by one of the *Hay*'s "guests." But he knew they could dream up a logical reason, that perhaps it was the navy's way of testing crew discipline if a captain suddenly died on board. If the captain was seen by no regular crew member—including the steward who usually brought his meals—it would make the test that much more realistic. Such, Lansing mused, was the imagination of submariners.

So Lansing's first objective was getting the truth to his men. His plan revolved around his Parker mechanical pencil. Lansing managed to extract a small piece of the pencil's lead and jam it under the nail of his right index finger. A Crusade member entered forty minutes later bearing a tray with a pot of coffee and a cheese sandwich. The tray was placed in front of Lansing, who sat at his desk. His guard relaxed in the visitor's chair opposite him.

Lansing casually moved a napkin to a spot in front of the coffeepot, so that the pot would prevent the guard from seeing it. As he munched his sandwich, he slowly lifted his right hand to the tray and started writing on the napkin: "Takeover. Illegal. I under guard. Respond napkin."

The printing was minute. Lansing's hand hardly moved. He folded the napkin, hoping someone in the galley would see the note when the napkin was being discarded.

It was a distant hope, for this was Lansing's fifth attempt. He had started trying the evening before, and each time there had been no response. When the Crusade member returned for the tray and then left, Lansing again started hoping, praying.

When his next meal was delivered, Lansing instantly noticed that the napkin was not folded in its usual way, but he hid his feeling of elation. Watching his guard carefully, he began eating the meal without even touching the napkin. He intentionally spilled some soup on his uniform to give himself a natural excuse to open the napkin below desk level.

"We read you," the note said.

He used the same napkin to respond: "You will resist."

When the tray was returned to the galley, a regular

John Hay crewman removed the napkin and discreetly slipped it into the pocket of Lieutenant Commander Mark Price, the *Hay*'s engineering officer. Price was thirty-four, small, and pudgy. Like Gillespie, he was unmarried, and his career was his life. He was not particularly combative or physical, and one reason he enjoyed the navy so much was its emphasis on machines and strategy, rather than personal heroics.

But he knew his responsibilities now, and he realized they would probably involve violence. The prospect frankly frightened him, but he started passing the word to crew members to be ready to retake the ship. He went to his cabin to plan the attack, not knowing that he had sixteen hours and thirty-four minutes to succeed.

Anderson noted the time, 8:07 A.M. The first CRITIC meeting ever held aboard Haven was about to begin.

The room filled with tired, unshaven men. Each one sat down hard in his seat. None had gotten a full night's sleep, so minds were not at their sharpest. War or peace might be decided between yawns.

The conference room at the center of the plane was equipped with a wall-sized CIS. The table was oblong, with a metal top. Everything used on it—pencils, pads, cups, ashtrays—had a small magnet so it would not be thrown around if Haven hit an air pocket. The soft-cushion chairs were anchored on tracks for the same reason. There were no pictures of Presidents on the baby-blue walls, but there was a map of the world and a painted reproduction of the air force seal.

Although the air force operated the plane, the seal annoyed Anderson. Its very presence had a psychological impact. Combined with Haven's uniformed crew, Anderson thought, it contributed to a military atmosphere. At a time when restraint was needed, symbols of American power were all around.

The President sat at the head of the table. Next to him, on the floor, was a briefcase full of contingency plans.

"You all know the story," he began. His voice was

145

louder than usual, a response to the *whoosh* of the jet engines. "I can't, for the life of me, understand why they'd sink the *Hay,* then deny it."

"We're being strung along, that's why," Somerville said, "and we're putting ourselves at their mercy. We're responding to them. That's a defensive strategy, and I don't like it."

"Wait a second," Bixby said. "There's something spooky here. They sink the boat. They haul out the plane. But they haven't followed through. Why would they give us all this warning time?"

"Good question," the President said.

"But easily answered," Combs broke in. "Since we don't know their strategy, we don't know what we're being warned about, do we?"

Affirmative nods. Combs made sense.

Anderson lit a cigar and watched the smoke float toward a plastic vent in the ceiling. "Mr. President," he asked, "may I make a suggestion?"

"Of course."

"I proposed before that we wire the Soviet Premier to determine his strategy. His response is disappointing, and we haven't learned much at all. But there's one sentence that impresses me."

Anderson shuffled through some papers to find the note.

"He's discussing his plane and he says, 'My emergency aircraft is equipped to command our forces.'" Then Anderson gave added emphasis: " '*It is also equipped to communicate with you.*' "

"What's the big deal?" the President asked.

"We knew," Anderson replied, "that his plane had this capability. We'd discussed it with the Soviets. Why would Zorin mention it in his note except to signal that he *wanted* to communicate with you?"

"That's a theory," Somerville said.

"Of course," Anderson answered, "but I think it's a good one."

"Andy may have a point," Bixby said. "They're careful how they write these things."

"Mr. President," Anderson went on, "why don't you call Premier Zorin directly?"

"I'd oppose that," Combs announced. "They've attacked. Messages on the Hot Line are appropriate, but a phone call looks like we're begging."

The President turned toward Anderson. "He's got something there, Andy. Besides, you know how I feel about talking to Zorin directly. A slip of the tongue and the whole thing goes up. I like it in writing."

"But consider the impact of a call," Anderson argued.

"Mr. President," a well-modulated voice called out from a corner of the room. Eyes turned. Michael Sonderling, the UN ambassador, rarely spoke. Immediately Anderson sensed the President's coldness.

"Sir," Sonderling continued, "I think Admiral Anderson is absolutely right. You have an obligation—"

"Don't tell me what my obligations are!" the President snapped.

A moment of embarrassed silence.

"I think," Sonderling said, "you exaggerate the dangers of a personal call."

"No, I don't," the President replied. And that was that.

Ordinarily Anderson would have welcomed an ally, but Sonderling's support depressed him. Sonderling was the most unpopular man in the room and was there only as a sop to the far-left wing of the President's party.

At sixty-one Michael Sonderling went wherever fashionable opinion told him to go. If it was the year of the blacks, he was for the blacks. If it was Indian time, he forgot the blacks and supported the Indians. He had refused to denounce the Russian invasion of Czechoslovakia in 1968 because he thought it would damage Soviet-American relations, and he dealt with Third World countries at the UN as if they possessed some special wisdom. Among those he slapped on the back were the most brutal dictators of Africa and Asia.

So, being ideologically pure and often silly, Sonderling was, to the President, a perfect choice to be UN ambassador. His selection reflected the President's personal contempt for the organization. He felt it had slipped into an America-baiting club, and he now ignored it.

As the critical meeting continued, Anderson realized he had the worst possible man on his side.

But Sonderling's brief clash with the President provided a magnificent opportunity for Combs.

"Mr. President," the general said, "the time for theorizing has obviously come to an end. We all respect your hesitation, your caution. For more than a quarter of a century we've hoped this day would never come." He looked around at each face, pausing for effect. Haven climbed abruptly, pushing CRITIC members back in their seats, adding to the drama.

"But it *has* come!" Combs insisted with uncharacteristic sharpness. "True, no nuclear bombs yet. No missiles. But a subtle strategy that has already cost more American lives than any incident in the so-called Cold War. We have protested their actions, and their response showed open contempt. We cannot be pawns, Mr. President. Continued delay in meeting the Soviet challenge will simply encourage them. The result could be catastrophic for our country."

"What are you proposing?" the President asked.

"I am proposing, sir, a preemptive nuclear strike. . . ."

"Bomb their cities?" Bixby asked.

"Certainly not!" Combs answered, turning self-righteous. "I would never advocate a preemptive attack on population centers. I suggest a limited strike at their naval bases."

"Those are near civilian targets," Anderson said.

"Civilian losses could be minimized by careful placement of ordnance," Combs said, the lingo flowing like a river.

"They'd shoot back," Bixby insisted.

"Correct. We'd have to expect casualties. But we'd have shown our resolve and forced their hand."

"What if we forced their hand so much they hit our cities?" Anderson asked.

"They won't do that. Their objectives are obviously more limited. They may turn out to be diplomatic."

148

"I'll second General Combs," Somerville said. "A limited nuclear response has always been a reasonable option."

Sonderling waved his finger at Somerville.

"That's madness!" he said.

"Hold on!" Combs snapped back. "This is a national crisis, sir, and if you can't understand it—"

"I understand it fully," Sonderling said. "My brain isn't mesmerized by all the jewelry you boys wear."

The remark stunned the group, and it infuriated Anderson. "Mr. Sonderling," he said, a touch of anger in his voice, "you're the kind who would've stood up at Pearl Harbor, waved to the Japanese pilots, and said, 'Why don't we talk this over?'"

Laughter. Tense and nervous, but laughter nonetheless.

"I'm sorry you said that, Admiral," Sonderling remarked. "I generally admire your positions. I hope at this critical time you aren't going to join the military majority."

"I'm not a joiner," Anderson replied. "My opinions are my own. I'd just like to see peace preserved."

"So would I," Sonderling said.

"No doubt," Anderson answered, "but I'm not sure our approaches are the same."

In a way, it hurt Anderson to cut Sonderling down. But he had to separate himself from the man whose support was the kiss of death. It was cynical politics, and Anderson avoided Sonderling's glance for the rest of the meeting. He felt a tinge of shame.

Two members of the Joint Chiefs had not yet been heard from. General Wilbur Benson of the air force, a veteran of World War II, Korea, and Vietnam, sat silently. Anderson saw Benson as an intelligent, but not an intellectual man. He wasn't given to brash overtures or military arrogance. But he was a team player, generally taking the hard line expected of soldiers. Since he was regarded largely as a technician, the President generally did not call on him in international matters. But now it was important to get the views of each expert present.

"General Benson, what do you think?" the President asked.

"It seems to me," Benson replied, "that General Combs had summed up the proper military response."

Anderson and the President exchanged quick glances. Anderson was apprehensive that the President might feel forced to follow the majority position now taking shape. The President sensed that Anderson was holding back. He was correct. The admiral felt the time wasn't yet right for his rebuttal.

The President turned to the last member of the Joint Chiefs, army General Thomas Hartline. He had been appointed only three months before.

"What's your view?" the President asked him in the offhand manner reserved for freshmen.

"Sir," Hartline replied, "I have no particular recommendation. This is a naval matter."

The President was startled, angered.

"It's a *national* matter," he shot back. "I want your advice *before* you write your memoirs!"

Hartline glanced uneasily at Combs, then at Anderson. He seemed troubled. "I think," he replied in a halting, hesitant voice, "that General Combs spoke with much wisdom. Maybe, though, we ought to stall things until we can call ground reservists."

"Why?" the President asked.

"Our readiness should be maximized," Hartline replied.

Hartline was speaking nonsense, and he seemed to know it. The situation called for quick action, not the slow calling of reserves. Anderson was baffled. Hartline was a bright, articulate soldier, a tactician who knew better.

A buzzer sounded near the CIS screen. Aboard Haven that meant the device was about to operate. The letters clicked out:

STAND BY. SATELLITE SWEEP.

Anderson knew the CIS would show a selection of views from intelligence satellites.

The screen went blank. Then, a moment later, a four-engine Soviet jet came into view. At the bottom left of the picture the CIS operator superimposed CLAMSHELL. Then a data report flashed across the bottom of the screen:

CLAMSHELL FLYING NORTHEAST TOWARD SIBERIA—
GROUND SPEED 503 MILES AN HOUR—ALTITUDE
26,000 FEET—FLIGHT APPEARS NORMAL—SATEL-
LITE SURVEILLANCE SHOWS NO APPARENT MECHANI-
CAL PROBLEMS.

CRITIC seemed even more intrigued by this picture than by the earlier view of the action at sea. It was as if they were keeping an eye on the Kremlin. Their elation was tempered by the knowledge that Soviet satellites were watching Haven.

The picture changed to another satellite view—Soviet submarines leaving their bases in the Black Sea and diving. Anderson knew they would head for the Mediterranean, that their target was the U.S. Sixth Fleet.

A navy lieutenant walked into the room and whispered a message in Anderson's ear. The admiral winced.

"Mr. President," he said, "I've just been informed that the New York *Times* is asking about the *Hay*. They know the story."

"I needed this," the President moaned.

"You can't cover these things," McNamara said.

"Oh, shut up!" the President snapped back. "I don't want any more of that righteous crap, McNamara. You're no holier than the rest of us!" The President was strained, and it was affecting his demeanor.

"Meeting adjourned!" he announced. "Admiral Anderson, come to my office."

The room was stunned. Didn't the President understand the seriousness of the crisis? Didn't he realize the need for quick decisions? Was he up to this?

"Sir," General Combs called after him, "would you please wait? Please, sir!"

The President stopped.

"Sir, with all due respect, we've got to take action."

"I am taking action," the President replied. He turned again and disappeared out the door. The meeting broke up.

Anderson pushed back his chair and started to follow, puzzled about the President's summons to a private meeting. But Bixby sensed the meaning of the moment. He knew the President's habits and his responses to pressure. The President needed someone to solve a problem, and the first name to enter his mind was Isaac Anderson. Names entered the Presidential mind, Bixby knew, in order of Presidential favor. Favor was influence. Influence was power. Isaac Anderson was moving up.

Knots of worried men stood talking in the room. As Anderson maneuvered between them toward the door, he suddenly felt two light pats of encouragement on the small of his back. Glancing around, he was surprised to see Hartline smile and, ever so slightly, nod encouragement. Anderson discreetly nodded back and continued on.

There was no mistaking the meaning. Hartline sided with Anderson, but for some reason had refused to put his feelings on the line. Anderson wondered why. Perhaps Hartline was more than an assembly-line general, although his reluctance to speak up was not one of the great moments in the history of the army.

As Anderson walked down the corridor, Lieutenant Commander Mark Price completed his attack plan for retaking the *John Hay*. He put nothing on paper, for notes could be discovered. Under the guise of ship's business, he met in his cabin with three officers and secretly gave them their instructions, stressing the importance of precise timing and the probability that there would be only one chance for success. He also emphasized the constant lurking of guards. One suspicious action or glance, he warned his fellow conspirators, and the security of the plan could be destroyed.

As Price's counterplot went forward, Richard Gillespie was receiving more good news. Work on the seventh interlock was nearly complete. Work on the eighth, and last, was beginning.

When Anderson entered the President's airborne office, he found the Chief Executive seated and looking out the window.

"West Virginia," the President said. "You can always tell when it's West Virginia. The dullness just seeps up." He paused. "They're lucky, though. No big targets in West Virginia." He turned to Anderson. "Sit down, Andy."

There was a long silence.

"Andy," the President finally said, "I want you to know something."

"Yes, sir?"

"I'm in over my head."

Anderson was shocked, and it showed.

"I don't really understand all these theories you boys talk about," the President continued. "I never did. It was easy making tough speeches over there in the Senate, but frankly I didn't know what in hell I was saying. I had to become President to find that out." He looked at Anderson, a sadness in his eyes.

"I need you, Andy," he said. "You're the only one on this plane who's got any common sense."

"Sir, I don't think that's true."

"You let me judge that, will you, Andy?"

The President stopped for a few seconds.

"Well, I'll change that. Bixby's got common sense. But he's not up to this. Y'know, a guy's been second man for so long, it affects him. Like Anthony Eden. Remember? He was Churchill's man and did good. They put him in the top job and he screwed up. Strictly a second stringer.

"Or take Somerville. Now, I like Hank. All right, he's a goddamned hawk. So am I. They're usually right, y'know. All you have to do is look at history for the proof. It's not nice to say, but the hawks have their finger on the pulse of the world. They think everyone's lousy, and by God, it's true. Now, take Churchill again. . . ."

153

The President was rambling. The crisis was consuming him, and Anderson was worried. But in his emotional state, the President was giving an incredibly candid view of his closest advisers. Anderson was sure no one had heard this before.

"They laughed at Churchill in the thirties," the President went on, "but he was right. Somerville might be right, for all I know, but Hank never thinks. He's a one-line man and he scares me.

"Or Combs. Bright, but too ambitious. I'd go to the wall with that man in wartime, but I don't want a war-time. I mean it, Andy."

"I know that, sir."

"Andy, you know more about war than all those guys put together. Christ, did you hear that Hartline? He's strictly a tank driver."

The President suddenly stopped. He looked suspiciously around the office. "Christ," he said, "imagine if Nixon's tape thing was still in here."

He chuckled. The remark broke a little of his tension.

"I won't press the button first, Andy," he went on. "It's a risk, but you don't shoot in the dark. You showed me that."

"I'm gratified, Mr. President."

"The question is how we avoid war. I still won't talk to Zorin by phone."

"What about in person, sir? There's precedent for a summit conference. You'd meet as equals, and any slip of the tongue could be corrected right at the table."

"Maybe," the President said. "It could be dramatic."

Anderson reached to a shelf above the President's desk, pulled down a world atlas, and began shuffling pages. "Both this plane and Clamshell can be refueled in the air," he said. "We could arrange a summit for some point between here and Moscow and fly directly there. You could meet in a matter of hours."

"You think they would buy?" the President asked.

"There was that sentence in their note," Anderson replied.

"Andy," the President asked quietly, "will they see it as weakness?"

"No," Anderson said. "That's an American myth. Peace is weakness, war is strength. It's usually argued by people who did their wartime service in San Diego."

The President nodded knowingly.

"The Russians backed down in Cuba," Anderson continued, "and nobody thought they were weaker for it. It's hard to appear weak when you can wipe out the world."

The President pondered for a few moments.

"All right," he said, "let's move."

An elated Anderson went for the door. "I'll inform the CRITIC—"

"No!" barked the President. "I don't want them in on it. It's too much flak. Andy, you set this up."

Anderson winced. "Sir, wouldn't someone with diplomatic credientials be better?"

"Who?" the President asked. "Sonderling? He'd get on the phone and surrender."

"What about Fred Bixby? He's your closest aide."

"I want *you!*" the President snapped, slightly annoyed by Anderson's reticence.

The President stared directly at Anderson's five rows of ribbons. They comforted him. They made Anderson's views respectable. Anderson had earned the right to argue for peace by proving himself in war. The President might not have taken the same advice from a man in a business suit.

"I want you to get on the phone to Gorshkov," the President ordered.

"Gorshkov?"

"Yes. You talk to your opposite number. It keeps things neat. I know it'll come as a surprise to those Siberians to have you handling this, but there's a precedent. Truman made Marshall a diplomat."

The comparison flattered Anderson, who reached for a gray wall phone. "Connect me with Admiral Gorshkov of the Soviet Union."

His heartbeat quickened. Questions and nightmares raced through his mind. What would Gorshkov sound like? Would he suspect American intentions? What if the whole thing broke down in an argument? What if Gorshkov refused to speak with him?

Aboard Clamshell the target maps were out. They pinpointed each American target, including foreign bases.

"You will notice," Gorshkov told Zorin, "that there are excellent opportunities in this situation. Since we agree that the Americans are about to start an action, I advise a strike at naval bases along their eastern coast. Also, we should destroy some of their carriers in the Mediterranean. I am convinced that these blows will discourage them."

"They will retaliate," Zorin said.

"Of course," Gorshkov replied. "But I'm certain their response would simply match our action, which places us in a favorable position. Let them hit our bases. Our fleet is built around submarines, which can operate without these big installations. And our surface units are expendable, not like their carriers."

Zorin sighed at Gorshkov's glibness. "What if they attack our cities?" he asked.

Gorshkov thought for a moment, then delivered his answer like a professor lecturing a student.

"They will not do that. They would be desperately afraid that we would strike their cities in return. They're a soft people whose country hasn't been invaded since the 1812 war. They like to fight their wars somewhere else.

"Look," Gorshkov continued impatiently, "we must attack. We must not allow ourselves to be struck first . . . as with the Germans."

Gorshkov was a good psychologist. He knew that "Germans" triggered the same response in the Russian mind as "Pearl Harbor" did in the American. The word played on Zorin's conscience. No Soviet Premier could allow a repeat of the 1941 nightmare.

Zorin saw no realistic alternative to Gorshkov's plan. If he didn't authorize it, the Soviet military leaders aboard

Clamshell might simply seize power. Then there would be no restraint at all. He turned somberly to Gorshkov.

"You may proceed with your operation. As the assaults are carried out, you will immediately evacuate Soviet targets that the Americans are likely to strike in return."

Gorshkov felt a smile inside, but maintained his military demeanor. He stiffened in his chair.

"It will be done!"

Then he rose with pretentious solemnity and looked down at the braid on his sleeves. Gorshkov felt proud, like a man who had been anointed to save the motherland. He left the Premier's office and went to his own, where he would make final preparations for the attack.

For a man who had just ordered the use of nuclear weapons, Zorin felt little emotion. History had trapped him, and he saw himself as pawn rather than master. His thoughts were scattered, but they centered largely on the enemy. What will the Americans think when they see the nuclear flashes? Will their God be inside them?

Neither Zorin nor Gorshkov was aware of the sudden activity in Clamshell's communications room. A red light flashed atop a gray console, and a Soviet army officer looked up sharply. The light had only one meaning: A message was coming through from Haven.

The officer picked up a phone. At the other end an American announced in perfect Russian that Admiral Anderson wished to speak with Admiral Gorshkov. The Red officer rushed to Zorin with the message.

Zorin was baffled. Why would Anderson want to talk to Gorshkov? Did the Americans think Gorshkov was in power?

"Ask them why," he ordered.

The question was passed on, and the Soviet officer reported the reply: "Admiral Anderson wishes to speak with Admiral Gorshkov to make a proposal for peace."

Now the strange style of the American approach melted into the background. Zorin knew that Gorshkov's forces were only minutes away from an attack, and he was determined to seize any opening to stop it. He reached for the intercom and called Gorshkov.

"Come in here, please."

Gorshkov was in the midst of a battle plan. "Why?" he asked crisply.

"I asked you to come in here," Zorin insisted.

"Premier, I cannot leave the attack plan."

"Gorshkov," Zorin replied, his voice showing anger, "we have received a message from the Americans. I need you." He hung up.

A frustrated Gorshkov threw down his pencil and walked the thirty-three feet to Zorin's office.

"Their Admiral Anderson is on the phone with a peace proposal," Zorin said. "He wants to talk to you."

"Premier, you can't be serious."

"I am serious," Zorin replied.

"This is a joke, a charade. Anderson talk to me? Don't you realize what they're doing? They're trying to delay us."

"You will talk to him," Zorin ordered. "We will miss no opportunity for peace."

"This is an opportunity for disaster," Gorshkov snapped.

"Gorshkov, if you don't talk to Anderson, I will!"

Gorshkov believed himself better qualified to safeguard Russia's interests. He picked up a phone.

"This is Admiral Gorshkov," he said in Russian. "Translator, please." Although he spoke perfect English, Gorshkov considered it beneath him to use the language of his opponent.

In both Clamshell and Haven translators cut into the line. Zorin picked up an extension phone to listen in.

"Admiral Gorshkov, this is Admiral Anderson. . . ."

Gorshkov waited for the full translation. "Yes," he said coldly.

"The President has asked me to serve as his representative. I am making this call in the spirit of peace."

"Is this the same spirit of peace displayed in the sinking of our destroyer?" Gorshkov asked. Zorin gestured to Gorshkov to temper his remarks, but Gorshkov went on.

"Is this the same spirit you displayed when you made your absurd charge that we sank your submarine?" Zorin's face filled with fury. He gestured violently to Gorshkov.

"Admiral Gorshkov," Anderson replied, "I think it's best to leave specific grievances to the principals."

As Anderson said "principals," Zorin sensed what was coming. His face took on the look of urgent anticipation.

"What is your business?" Gorshkov asked.

"We believe," Anderson answered, "that it would be useful for the two heads of state to meet as soon as possible. We are prepared to discuss locations approximately equidistant between our two aircraft."

Zorin's eyes widened. Gorshkov's didn't.

"Your proposal strikes me as unnecessary," Gorshkov told Anderson. "Peace does not require such displays."

Infuriated, Zorin stood as though to take the phone from Gorshkov's hand.

"I will discuss it with the Premier," Gorshkov said hurriedly. "We will call back." Without another word, he hung up.

"You must not be led into that!" he insisted.

"Why?" Zorin asked, still furious.

"It's an obvious trick. The Americans will use this time well."

The Premier turned his back on Gorshkov and walked to the other end of his office.

"You know, Gorshkov," he said, "you have an excellent knack for seeing the dark side of everything."

"That is the job of a military man," Gorshkov shot back.

Zorin spun around. "And the job of a chief of state is to see every side!" He approached Gorshkov, stopping within six inches of the admiral. Zorin stood erect, as if underlining his determination. "You will proceed with your operational plan," he said, "but you will make no attacks without my direct order. First, however, you will contact Anderson and negotiate for a meeting."

Gorshkov gazed up at the ceiling, his expression now

showing that he regarded himself as more perceptive, perhaps more patriotic than the Premier.

"The nation will remember this as unwise," he said.

"You let me worry about wisdom," Zorin demanded. "You worry about the navy."

Gorshkov picked up the phone. "Get me the American admiral," he ordered in a tone of disgusted resignation.

The connection was instantly reestablished.

"Admiral Anderson," Gorshkov said through his translator, "I am instructed by higher authority to negotiate the circumstances of the Premier's meeting with your President. Obviously Soviet forces are prepared for any challenge in the interim."

Anderson was relieved, but carefully avoided the impression of an American "victory."

"Admiral Gorshkov," he said, "I have examined several sites. I suggest the Azores. As you know, it is approximately equidistant between our aircraft."

"You have a history of military bases there," Gorshkov said.

"But the Azores are not American property."

"We would have to pass over NATO countries. Rejected."

Anderson shrugged. The President, like Zorin, listened on an extension. The President smirked at Gorshkov's glibness.

"All right," Anderson said, "we propose the island of Iwo Jima in the Pacific. It is, of course, owned by the Japanese."

Gorshkov thought for a moment. "No. It would be wrong to meet on the site of an American military triumph, even over a common enemy. In the eyes of our Third World comrades the victory was won over the bodies of Asians."

Anderson was beginning to boil. With the future of civilization in the balance, the Russians were behaving like Russians. But he consulted some notes on his atlas and pushed on. "May I suggest the African city of Tananarive in the Malagasy Republic—"

"Admiral Anderson!" Gorshkov growled, "why don't you inquire about *our* choices?"

Anderson realized he had committed a diplomatic blunder. He had suggested the meeting, and he should have allowed Gorshkov to suggest the site. "I apologize," he said. "Please give us your views."

"I recommend Enderby," Gorshkov said.

"Enderby?"

"Yes." Gorshkov smiled, knowing he had caught the American off guard. Enderby was Enderby Land, the site of a joint Soviet-American research station in the Antarctic.

"Why the end of the earth?" Anderson asked.

"It's very private down there," Gorshkov replied. "Something like this should not be done in the sunlight."

Anderson pressed his HOLD button and turned to the President. "What do you think?"

"Jesus, I don't know," the President grumbled. "How long would it take?"

Anderson glanced at his atlas. "Offhand, approximately twenty-four hours."

"We're in the middle of a crisis, Andy."

"Mr. President," Anderson said, "I'm not sure the time factor is that critical. After all, you'd be in complete command of our forces throughout the flight, and you could instantly contact Zorin if necessary."

"True," the President said.

"And besides," Anderson continued, "the long flight may actually be a good sign."

"How do you figure that?"

"The fact that the Russians are willing to fly so far from their homeland could be significant. Both Zorin and Gorshkov are nationalists. If they were planning war, they'd probably want to be close to their people."

The President, still clearly skeptical, thought for a moment.

"Well"—he shrugged—"I could suggest better places, but I don't want to lose this. Okay, we'll go."

Anderson got back on the phone.

"Admiral Gorshkov, we accept."

Gorshkov was expressionless. "Very well," he said, "we

161

will now fly toward our destination." Then he simply hung up.

"We'd better change course," Anderson told the President.

Within a few seconds both Haven and Clamshell turned. Two heads of state, each believing the other responsible for the crisis, flew toward a confrontation they hoped would end it.

The President got on Haven's loudspeaker system.

"This is the President speaking." The familiar voice jolted drowsy men awake. "You'll be interested to know that we're heading for Antarctica. I will meet there with Premier Zorin. I expect the full cooperation of every man on board. Thank you."

Sonderling was delighted, but others were appalled. Somerville rushed to Combs' office.

"This is Anderson's doing," the Secretary said. "The Russians'll tear us up. We've got to reach the President."

"He's unreachable," Combs replied, his voice tinged with a bitter sadness. "He hears only those who tell him there's an easy way out. The President, if I may say so, lacks the will to fight."

Somerville nodded reflectively. "You're right. I'm afraid he's a weak man."

Anderson and the President now confronted the problem of the New York *Times*.

"You have to face it head-on," Anderson advised. "The secret is out."

"Well," the President replied, "why don't you draw something up?" Then, making his priorities clear, he turned away and started jotting notes for his meeting with Zorin.

Anderson left the President's office and walked to his own. He was aware of the glances along the way. Some suspicious, some hostile, some friendly, some deferential. As his influence had risen, so had the attention paid him.

He entered his office, took out a pen and pad, and began to write:

It is with deep regret that I announce that

'the USS *John Hay*, a missile-carrying submarine of our Atlantic Fleet, is overdue at her patrol station and presumed lost. The *Hay* carried 101 enlisted men and sixteen officers. The bodies of two crewmen have been recovered.

The cause of the loss remains undetermined. An active search for survivors is under way. The public will be kept informed.

I want to stress that there is no danger to mankind from the *Hay*'s missiles or her nuclear reactor. There is *no* possibility of explosion or radiation leak.

Naturally at a time like this we think first of the *Hay*'s crewmen and their families. As chief of naval operations I understand the anxieties faced by those who wait for further news. I am ordering navy personnel to do everything possible to assist them. All of us in the service share their grief.

Part of Anderson's statement was a pacifier intended to soften the blow for the *Hay*'s next of kin. He knew that rarely did anyone survive the sinking of a submarine.

After calling the Pentagon and arranging for his statement to be issued, Anderson studied route maps for the flight to Enderby. Haven's journey, he saw, would take it over Puerto Rico, then southeast toward Ascension Island, then farther southeast, passing a few hundred miles west of Cape Town, South Africa, southeast again to Prince Edward Island, then due south to Antarctica. The plane would make a final sharp swing to the east and into Enderby Land. Anderson ordered the nuclear attack submarines *Houston* and *Bangor* to cruise from their stations in the southern Indian Ocean to the seas just north of Enderby. They could be used, he reasoned, to evacuate the Presidential party should some problem prevent a takeoff.

Clamshell, Anderson anticipated, was flying a course that would take it over Rumania, Bulgaria, Yugoslavia, the Mediterranean, Syria, Iraq, Saudi Arabia, Yemen, and then down over the Indian Ocean to the meeting site.

The hours passed into late afternoon, Washington time. In both Haven and Clamshell there was a growing feeling that the international system was coming back under control. The feeling was wrong. Control still rested with Richard Gillespie.

13

Gillespie popped open a bottle of champagne, letting it bubble and fizz over his hands and drip to the deck of the control room. His comrades were around him. Scientists of the North Star Crusade had just broken through the eighth interlock.

"A toast!" somebody yelled.

Gillespie raised his cup. "To the United States," he said, "and to success in the postwar world." He placed the cup on a plastic console. "I'm going to Captain Lansing," he announced.

Gillespie left the control room and walked to Lansing's cabin. Lansing looked up as he entered, but offered no greeting.

"Good afternoon, Captain," Gillespie said. "I came to brief you on our plans."

Lansing raised his eyebrows. It seemed ludicrous to receive a briefing while a prisoner, but to Gillespie it was entirely natural. To him Lansing was still an officer of the United States Navy.

Lansing leaned back in his chair. Despite his contempt for Gillespie, he could not hide his curiosity.

"Captain Lansing," Gillespie began, "my group is called the North Star Society. Our goal is to start the Third World War—a war in which the Soviet Union will be destroyed and America's future secured. The men who boarded this ship are weapons experts. They have unlocked the safety devices governing our Polaris missiles."

Lansing was stunned. His insides began filling with revulsion—toward Gillespie's ideas, even toward himself, for he was the captain who had lost the *Hay;* he was responsible for Gillespie's success.

"Up to now," Gillespie continued, "I have taken several actions to increase tension between Washington and Moscow. Military traffic indicates the plan is going well."

"Gillespie," Lansing asked angrily, "do you realize how many millions of people—?"

"Captain Lansing," Gillespie interrupted, "the death of millions is tragic, but the sacrifice is necessary to safeguard our country." Ignoring Lansing's dismay, he went on. "Tension has now been raised to the point where a single incident could trigger nuclear war. That incident is about to take place. At midnight I will launch a missile attack from the *John Hay.*"

"You will . . . destroy Moscow?" Lansing asked, his voice shaking.

"No," Gillespie answered. "I have no intention of striking the Soviet Union."

Lansing looked confused. Gillespie gazed directly into his eyes.

"Captain Lansing," he said, "I will launch a nuclear attack on the United States."

Lansing was speechless.

"Permit me to explain," Gillespie went on. He stepped to a map and pointed to dots in the Soviet Union. "The Russians have thousands of targets," he said, "and we have sixteen missiles. If I were to attack them, damage would be minimal.

"Nevertheless, as soon as they detected our missiles, they'd assume they were under all-out American assault and they'd launch a counterstrike with everything they had. Their side, not ours, would have the first chance to attack *massively.* They could wipe out the American nuclear striking force.

"But if we launch missiles at the United States, the situation is reversed. The missiles will do little damage, but they will provoke a massive American counterstrike. The Soviet retaliatory force will be wiped out or heavily damaged. The Soviets could fight on with no hope of victory, or they could choose to surrender."

It was natural for the numbed Lansing to think instantly of his family in Groton.

"Your . . . targets?" he asked haltingly.

"There are eight," Gillespie answered. "I'm using only half our missiles. I'll use the other half as part of the American retaliation. Only two major cities will be struck—New York and Boston—both centers of the pacifist thought that has corrupted our nation. The other targets are military and industrial. None is vital to the war effort, but they make our attack look realistic, as if it were launched from a Soviet vessel.

"Captain," Gillespie continued, "I'd like to invite you to the control room just before midnight to witness the launch."

"Decline," Lansing said. "I have no desire to lend myself to this."

"I'll honor your wishes," Gillespie replied.

Lansing suddenly realized he had blundered. His being in the control room could help whatever plans the crew might be formulating for retaking the ship.

"Wait," he said, "I want to be there."

"Fine." Gillespie turned to leave, but when he reached the door, he turned back. "When this is over," he said, "you'll realize that I'm right." Then he left.

Lansing knew there was but one meal remaining in the day and that it was his only chance to alert the crew to the launch. When the meal came, he wrote on a napkin: "Launching. 2400. U.S. targets. Me in control room."

The time was 6:18 P.M. It would all be over in five hours and forty-two minutes.

Lieutenant Commander Price cleaned his .45 in his cabin, knowing that other men in the counterplot were doing the same. But their best weapons, Price realized, were surprise and the isolation of the control room. His objective was to retake the room in the moments before launch when Gillespie would be immersed in the countdown. He had learned, through an earlier message from Lansing, about the explosive charges carried by some Crusade members. He gambled that the speed of his assault would prevent their use.

After cleaning the pistol, Price set his alarm clock for 2300 hours—11 P.M. Then, knowing he had to be in top condition for the midnight ordeal, he went to sleep.

As midnight approached, Richard Gillespie dressed in a new work suit, then made his way to the control room. His movements were immediately reported to Price by a junior officer.

Members of the North Star Crusade replaced regular *Hay* crewmen at the missile-firing consoles. Their actions were rehearsed, polished. They had gone through this procedure hundreds of times onshore. The room gradually became solemn, as if the scene were being played out for the eyes of history.

Captain Lansing entered, escorted by his guard, and was permitted to sit in a chair from which he could watch the launch. His expression was blank, but occasionally he glanced toward the bulkhead separating the control room from the rest of the ship. He sensed that a battle was about to take place.

The *Hay* was 1,400 miles off the East Coast, cruising fifty feet below the surface. Sonar reported the ocean around her clear of ships.

"Gentlemen," Gillespie announced, "we are about to embark on the final stage of our Crusade. It's too early to claim victory, but not too early to thank each of you for what you have done and what you are about to do. Good luck." Then he threw the switches that began the firing sequence.

Lansing was gripped by a terrible tension. He had expected a great ceremony, but as the North Star Crusade got right down to business, the reality hit him in the gut. The tension yielded to terror, the terror to pain.

It was three minutes to midnight.

Cecil Kester and Edward Lent worked at consoles on

either side of Gillespie—the original triumvirate who had taken control of the *Hay* was now reunited for the ultimate moment. Green dots of light reflected in Gillespie's eyes from indicator signals. Everything was working. No problems. The green lights contrasted with the overall red glow from the night lamps, the same glow that had bathed two doomed sailors in the torpedo room the evening before.

Two minutes to midnight.

Lansing's eyes cut from the bulkhead to Gillespie. He listened for footsteps, anything that would tell him help was coming. He felt a brief needle of fear shoot up his spine. Maybe the messages had been detected.

Ninety seconds.

Silence in the control room. Gillespie watched his instruments. He saw the firing clock come up to one minute. He began counting.

"Fifty-nine, fifty-eight, fifty-seven. . . ."

Suddenly there was a solid *clunk*. Gillespie stopped counting and spun around, his eyes on the bulkhead. It flew open. A .45 glistened.

"Hold it!" Price shouted.

"Take him!" Gillespie barked.

North Star pistols flashed.

Price fired. The bullet whizzed past Gillespie's shoulder and struck Ed Lent squarely in the head. Gillespie hit the deck as Lent collapsed.

More shots. Shouting. Kester dived for the lights, and the control room went black.

Fists cracked jaws. Gun butts pulverized skulls. Moaning. More shots.

And then it was over.

Silence.

The lights came on. Gillespie looked around, shaken and frightened. The *Hay* was plunging at a twenty-degree angle. He quickly righted her.

Lent was dead, the side of his head blown off. Kester's collarbone was shattered. Price lay dead, four bullets in his chest. Two other allies of Lansing also were dead.

Lansing suddenly bolted from the control room, dashing down the passageways and ladders toward the galley. He was quickly captured by Crusade guards.

Gillespie recovered his balance. Strangely, he now felt almost gladdened by the episode. His Crusade had been challenged, and he had beaten back the challenge. He ordered four members of the *Hay*'s crew to remove the bodies from the control room and mop the blood from the deck.

Lansing was brought back in, this time in handcuffs.

"I respect your effort," Gillespie told him. "I hope you now respect our competence."

Deflated, Lansing responded with a slight affirmative nod.

But Gillespie had two problems. First, security had been broken. Obviously the *Hay*'s crew no longer believed his story about a "classified exercise." Second, the shots had severely damaged the missile-firing consoles.

As to the first, Gillespie ordered each member of the Crusade to keep his pistol out and an explosive pouch strapped to his shoulder. Then he got on the bullhorn:

"Hear this! Some people aboard apparently want to be heroes. Some of those heroes are now dead in the control room. Any further challenge to my authority will result in instant death for the offender, and any attempt on the lives of my men may result in the sinking of the *Hay*. Each one is carrying an explosive charge, easily set off. Think about that. That is all."

There was a stillness aboard the ship. Gillespie's tone was too convincing to be ignored. The revolt seemed at an end.

Gillespie's second problem was purely technical. He ordered repair work on the missile consoles to begin at once, with one of his scientists estimating that eight hours would be needed. Gillespie reset the firing for 9 A.M. and ordered every member of the Crusade to remain on duty until the launch was completed.

At 5:06 A.M. Washington time, Haven and Clamshell sighted each other 33,000 feet above the clear, unspoiled waters of the Indian Ocean. By agreement, the two planes then headed south in formation, each one checking the navigation of the other.

Tensions mounted as officials on both planes wondered what the other side would propose and demand. Both the President and Zorin were aware that a conference was itself no guarantee of peace. The Munich Conference led directly to World War II. The peace talks in Korea dragged on for two years, those in Vietnam for more than four. And the summit conference of 1960 between Eisenhower and Khrushchev blew up after Francis Gary Powers' U-2 went down over Russia.

The President called a final CRITIC meeting as Haven and Clamshell approached Antarctica. The members filed into the conference room, clean-shaven, their suits freshly pressed. The sight of Clamshell out the port window seemed to sharpen them, much as the sight of an enemy army on a battlefield might do. They "felt" the Soviet presence as they sat around the conference table, knowing the next table they surrounded would be in a converted mess hall at Enderby.

Haven and Clamshell flew to a point just east of the Riiser Larsen Peninsula, only 600 miles northwest of the Enderby airstrip. The temperature on the ice was thirty-six degrees below zero.

The President and CRITIC began reviewing the fine details of the coming talks. As their meeting continued, Anderson noticed that he had to swallow every few seconds. Haven was beginning its descent into Enderby Land.

North Star technicians completed their repairs at 8:46 A.M., fourteen minutes before Gillespie's 9 A.M. launch time.

The ritual that had begun a few minutes before midnight the evening before was now repeated. Gillespie took his place at the consoles, his eyes passing over the green indicator lights. The *Hay* once more cruised fifty feet below the surface. As 9 A.M. approached, Gillespie began the chant of the countdown.

"Fifty-nine. . . ."

He glanced toward the bulkhead, a reaction to Price's assault earlier. But there was no Price or anyone else. Nothing stood in his way.

"Thirty. . . . Twenty. . . . Fifteen. . . ."

Gillespie watched the clock. His heart pounded; his hands tightened on controls. He threw the final switches.

"Ten. . . ."

His whole consciousness focused on one last switch. He gripped it. After all the planning and details and worries the steel bar felt like velvet.

"Five. . . . Four. . . . Three. . . ."

Switch thrown.

"Two. . . . One. . "

A look at the clock. Nine A.M. and eight seconds.

A deadly *thump* resounded in Sherwood Forest, the missile compartment in submarine lingo. Then a shattering *whoosh*.

An eighteen-ton mass of steel, plastic, wire, fuel, and nuclear warhead roared from a thirty-one-foot tube and sliced into the Atlantic. It broke the surface, leaving a trail of turbulent foam. Its engine ignited, and the salt air was rent with crackling flame.

The Polaris A-3 shot upward, then gracefully arched over on its trajectory, disappearing into low-lying clouds.

Its performance was perfect.

Its target was New York City

Part II

14

The CRITIC meeting ended, and the members returned to their offices for the final approach into Enderby Land.

Anderson gazed out on the dismal Antarctic. The bleakness was broken only by the orange flares set by men at the Enderby base to guide Haven and Clamshell to the runway. Anderson now felt the bumps and shakes of air pockets as Haven descended. He tensed slightly, for in all his years as a pilot he had never gotten completely accustomed to turbulence. It was as though he were still a novice traveler—afraid that the wings would fall off.

Gorshkov contacted Anderson again.

"It is our wish," he told Anderson, "that you land first, with our landing immediately afterward."

"Fine," Anderson replied.

"There should be greetings on the field."

"Brief greetings," Anderson said. "We carry only light-weight snow clothing."

"Brief greetings," Gorshkov agreed. "Do you have a photographer aboard?"

"Yes, from the signal corps."

"Please restrain him," Gorshkov insisted. "The Premier does not wish photographs."

"No problem," Anderson answered.

"Perhaps you should leave him on your plane."

Anderson was annoyed with Gorshkov's pettiness.

"We have a right to have him with us. He'll photograph the President."

There was a long pause.

"Very well, but should he violate our understanding—"

"He won't," Anderson said sharply.

"Admiral Anderson," Gorshkov continued, "whatever our differences, I look forward to meeting you as a comrade-in-arms."

"I appreciate that," Anderson replied, surprised, "and I share your sentiments. Hopefully, we can make progress."

"That is our objective," Gorshkov said. "We have no wish to destroy—"

Suddenly, before Gorshkov could finish, Haven shook with the sound of a piercing, head-pounding klaxon horn. Anderson dropped the phone and slapped his hands to his ears.

One blast. Then, three seconds later, another.

Anderson was dumbfounded. The horn had only one meaning, confirmed by the immediate flashing of a red warning on the wall:

ENEMY ATTACK.

Anderson slammed down the phone and grabbed the intercom to the pilot.

"Let's move!"

He bolted from his office, heading for the conference room, bumping others along the way. As he dashed through the corridor, he felt the sudden thrust of Haven's engines. The floor tilted upward. Gravity threw him back. He grabbed a safety handle and began to pull himself forward. He reached the conference room just as the CIS was pounding out the news:

THE SUBMARINE-LAUNCHED BALLISTIC MISSILE EARLY WARNING SYSTEM REPORTS A SINGLE MISSILE FIRED FROM A SUBMERGED VESSEL. APPROX. 1,400 MILES OFF THE EAST COAST OF THE UNITED STATES AND FOLLOWING A TRAJECTORY TOWARD NEW YORK. . . .

STAND BY.

The system stopped, but eyes stayed firmly riveted to the screen. The President arrived, his face ashen, his hands trembling.

THE SUBMARINE-LAUNCHED BALLISTIC MISSILE EARLY WARNING SYSTEM REPORTS A SECOND REPEAT SECOND MISSILE FIRED FROM THE SAME VESSEL AND FOLLOWING A TRAJECTORY TOWARD BOSTON. . . .
STAND BY.

"My God!" the President moaned.

"Mr. President," Anderson said, "I'm sorry."

The President did not respond. Members of CRITIC filed in and took their places as an aide distributed red-covered manuals giving procedures for the first hours of nuclear war. Outside the conference room stood an air force warrant officer. He carried a small black bag with codes that could unleash the nation's nuclear forces. Bixby told him to sit beside the President.

The sound of a missile engine roared in Anderson's head. Images of New York and Boston as vast wastelands glared before him. The American deterrent had failed. The billions spent, the assurances to the world, the feeling of security in the nuclear age—all were mocked by the missiles heading for the United States.

His own advice to the President had been hopelessly wrong. Gorshkov, he knew, had shown him up as a gullible fool. He sensed the attitude of others toward him. The loathing, the contempt. They would say *he* was responsible for the Soviet attack. Had America struck first, as Combs and Somerville had urged, it might have been prevented.

THE SUBMARINE-LAUNCHED BALLISTIC MISSILE EARLY WARNING SYSTEM REPORTS A THIRD REPEAT THIRD MISSILE FIRED FROM THE SAME VESSEL AND FOLLOWING A TRAJECTORY TOWARD MARIETTA, GEORGIA. . . .
STAND BY.

"Lockheed," Somerville said. "They'll get Lockheed!"

"Mr. President," Combs added, restraining his anger, "this is a betrayal greater than Pearl Harbor."

The President turned to the warrant officer. "Open the bag, please."

The warrant officer opened the black bag.

"Remove the codes."

The codes were removed. The President looked toward Somerville.

"Do you have the target lists?"

"I do, sir."

Then the President winced, as if a new thought had struck him.

"Where is Clamshell?" he asked.

"Next door," Bixby replied.

The President glanced at Benson, the air force chief.

"Shoot it down!"

The order shocked the room. "This plane is not equipped for that," Benson responded.

"There must be a carrier somewhere," the President said.

"Sir," Anderson answered, "we have carriers in the Indian Ocean. We can shoot down Clamshell if she travels back to Russia, but I wouldn't recommend it."

"Why?"

"Because, sir, after the initial missile exchange you might want to negotiate. You *know* Zorin. You don't know who might replace him."

"I think we've had enough of your peace theories!" Somerville shouted. "Our country is under assault!"

"And we have to fight back!" Anderson replied. "But Zorin might be useful."

"Crap!"

"Mr. President," Combs said, "I must support Secretary Somerville. I don't like to attack another officer, but Admiral Anderson has consistently misled you. I ask him, as a gentleman and a patriot, to withdraw now from these discussions."

Dead silence.

No one expected a personal issue to bolt through the

178

crisis. A few men looked embarrassed. Only the President looked at Anderson.

"Admiral," he asked, "do you have something to say?"

"Mr. President," Anderson responded, "I am entirely at your disposal."

The President sighed. "Admiral Anderson," he said, a touch of emotion in his voice, "gave the best advice he could with the information he had. I accepted it. Nobody knows what would have happened if *other* advice had been followed. I regard the admiral as an intelligent, valuable man. He stays." The President stared for a moment at Combs, who looked coldly into space.

"Thank you, Mr. President," Anderson said.

"Clamshell will not be shot down," the President announced briskly.

Eyes shot toward the CIS.

THE SUBMARINE-LAUNCHED BALLISTIC MISSILE EARLY WARNING SYSTEM REPORTS A FOURTH REPEAT FOURTH MISSILE FIRED FROM THE SAME VESSEL AND FOLLOWING A TRAJECTORY TOWARD FORT JACKSON, SOUTH CAROLINA. . . .

STAND BY.

"Army base," Hartline said.

"When will the first missile hit?" the President asked.

"Within twelve minutes," Anderson replied. He knew there was nothing to stop it. Because of Congressional fund restrictions, only one antimissile defense installation had been built in the United States. It was protecting other missiles at Grand Forks, North Dakota.

Bixby's phone rang. He took a quick message, then hung up.

"Communications reports air-raid sirens are on in New York and Boston, but people are ignoring them. The emergency broadcast system is set to go into operation at your command."

"What's the use?" the President asked. "People will panic."

"I disagree," Combs said. "We still have time to get people into shelters, and some could evacuate."

"The President's right," Anderson insisted. "There's nothing you can do for New York or Boston. This attack might be limited. If you start scaring the whole country, thousands more could be killed. Our people aren't trained in civil defense."

"But evacuation," Somerville emphasized, "is possible."

"Put all those people on the road," Anderson said, "and you've got perfect targets with no fallout protection. I suggest holding any widespread warnings until we gauge the attack."

"Agreed," the President said. Again he was leaning on Anderson.

"I want all our missile bases, bomber forces, and submarines alerted for immediate retaliation," the President ordered. "Gentlemen, we must now decide on the scope of our action."

"I suggest," Combs said, "that our retaliation be designed to destroy completely the Soviet strike capability. That is the only way we can guarantee an ultimate solution acceptable to us. Even if their attack has limited objectives, we must demonstrate that it is as repugnant to us as an all-out assault."

"That's classic strategy, Mr. President," Somerville said. "Don't get drawn into fighting on their terms. You must demonstrate immediate superiority."

Again Bixby's phone rang. He picked it up and listened. His expression began changing—from blank, to curious, to angry, to curious again. He returned the receiver.

"Jesus," he said, looking at Anderson. "It's Admiral Gorshkov."

There was total silence for six seconds.

"Mr. President," Combs finally said, "this was not entirely unexpected. The Soviets, having attacked first, may now try to strike a deal from a position of strength."

"General Combs might be right," Anderson declared.

"What do we do?" asked the President.

"I wouldn't take the call," Somerville advised. "It would be like talking to the Japanese after Pearl Harbor."

"I disagree," Anderson said. "We should get a reading on them. That does *not* prevent our retaliation. We've talked and fought simultaneously in many wars."

"I'm inclined to go with Harley on this one," the President stated. "I don't think we oughtta talk to them until our missiles are in the air."

"Sounds reasonable," Bixby agreed. But as he spoke, his phone rang still once more.

"Bixby."

He listened.

"Wait a second," he said, then turned to the President. "Admiral Gorshkov has asked Admiral Anderson to hurry." He listened for more of the message, repeating it for CRITIC. "He says it's urgent. He says. . . ."

Bixby paused and seemed to grimace. "Say that again, please." He listened, then took a deep breath and put down his phone.

"He says they didn't launch those missiles."

Shock.

"Admiral Anderson," ordered the President, "get on that phone!"

Eyes shifted to Anderson as he reached for his telephone. The speakers in the room were turned on so all could hear.

"Anderson."

"This is Gorshkov," came the reply. The Russian sounded hurried, disturbed. "Admiral Anderson, our satellites have picked up the missiles. They are *not* ours!"

"Ridiculous!" Anderson shot back.

"I repeat, sir, we are *not* attacking you!"

Silence in Haven as members of CRITIC exchanged confused, worried glances.

"Then who is?" Anderson asked angrily.

"I don't know."

"Do you expect me to believe that?"

"Admiral Anderson, I beg of you. . . ."

The words were startling coming from Gorshkov. They reflected the pandemonium that had broken out aboard

Clamshell when word of the launchings was flashed from Moscow. Zorin stood beside Gorshkov, his breath coming hard, his face dripping with sweat, panic filling his eyes.

"Admiral Gorshkov," Anderson asked, "is it possible that one of your missile subs is loose?"

Gorshkov paused.

"It is possible," he conceded.

"Can you find out?"

"We are trying. Please believe me."

"When you have an answer, call me back." With that, Anderson hung up.

The President looked around the room, totally bewildered.

"Well?"

"Mr. President," Combs said, "there's a good chance that this is a master ploy. They sank our sub, then denied it. Their objective was to stall off our military response. Now they attack our country and deny that, too. In all the years of strategic thinking, the one contingency no one ever considered was a nuclear assault with its author denying responsibility. Yet look at the effect. Gorshkov's call alone has wasted valuable minutes, and we still have not retaliated."

The CIS started clicking:

THE SUBMARINE-LAUNCHED BALLISTIC MISSILE EARLY WARNING SYSTEM REPORTS A FIFTH REPEAT FIFTH MISSILE FIRED FROM THE SAME VESSEL AND FOLLOWING A TRAJECTORY TOWARD MAYPORT, FLORIDA. . . .
    STAND BY.

"The naval base," Anderson said.

The President turned sharply to Somerville. "Order our forces to run up their missiles to the point of launch."

"Yes, sir." Somerville quickly gave the order by phone.

"Question," Bixby said. "Why are all these missiles coming from only one sub?"

"It could be," Combs responded, "that they planned to sell us this idea of a Red sub on the loose. . . ."

"*I* was the one who brought it up," Anderson reminded the group.

"And if you didn't, they would have," Combs snapped back. "They're trying to keep us off-balance. It's a remarkable approach, a possible prelude to an even larger attack. They hit us, panic our country while we sit here debating, then hit us again."

"Just a second," Bixby said. "Why didn't they just go all out the first time? This seems like an awfully complicated business."

"Strategy is complicated," Combs replied condescendingly.

"You didn't answer his question," Anderson said bitingly, "and I'm not so sure you have the answer."

Eyes shot toward the admiral.

"I would still concede," he went on, "that the Russian denial probably is some kind of cover for their attack. But one point troubles me. They must know that this attack brings great risk of our total retaliation even before they launch the rest of their missiles. Would they take such a risk?"

"They have," Somerville said.

"And would they risk stranding Zorin in Clamshell, with the chance of his being shot down?"

"What are you saying?" the President asked.

"I'm not saying anything," Anderson replied. "But Gorshkov sounded like a scared man."

"An act," Benson volunteered.

"Maybe," Anderson responded, "and maybe one of his subs *is* loose."

"Do you believe that?" Somerville asked, contempt in his voice.

"It's a strange attack," Anderson answered. He looked at the President, who seemed fascinated but skeptical. Anderson understood the skepticism. He shared it himself.

"If it *was* a runaway sub, what could we do?" Bixby asked.

Anderson leaned back in his chair, took a cigar from his pocket, and lit it while framing an answer. He felt

183

more and more isolated among enemies who despised him and friends who doubted him.

"I don't know," he finally said. "We'd have a real problem. The Russians could easily think that we wouldn't believe the story and would therefore launch a counterstrike against them. They might try to preempt us by striking now, massively."

"In other words," Bixby said, "even if it was a runaway sub it could provoke a holocaust."

"Yes."

Eyes turned toward the screen.

THE SUBMARINE-LAUNCHED BALLISTIC MISSILE EARLY WARNING SYSTEM REPORTS A SIXTH REPEAT SIXTH MISSILE FIRED FROM THE SAME VESSEL HAS CRASHED IN THE ATLANTIC.

"Normal," Anderson said. "There'll be a failure rate."
Again the CIS:

RADAR TRACKING STATION ANVIL ESTIMATES IMPACT TIME OF NUMBER ONE MISSILE AT FOUR MINUTES IN NEW YORK CITY VICINITY.

"It can't be," the President said.

Gorshkov "knew" that a Soviet submarine had attacked the United States. After all, the Americans would not attack themselves, and other nations did not have strong enough motives. The fact that all the missiles came from one submarine proved the existence of a limited conspiracy. Only Russians, Gorshkov reasoned, had both the motive and the necessary equipment. True, Soviet ships had safeguards, but no safeguards were totally effective. Apparently the worst had happened.

Gorshkov sat with Zorin in the Premier's office aboard Clamshell, the tension and trauma still showing on both their faces. On the desk before them were unfinished notes for the summit conference that would never be.

Zorin occasionally stared outside, as if hoping that Haven would suddenly appear through the clouds, that the conference would take place, that all would be settled. But he quickly returned his eyes to Gorshkov.

The admiral was finishing a phone call from Moscow. He received the message and hung up.

"They say they have no information on any of our submarines performing improperly. But of course we cannot check without having the ships break radio silence and give away their locations. That would be disastrous if war broke out."

Zorin gestured his agreement, not really understanding what he was agreeing to. He was in a partial daze.

"This is the darkest day of my life," Gorshkov said. "My own navy did this. *My* men."

"That is not the point, Gorshkov. The point is what action we take."

"The Americans are considering whether to believe our denial," Gorshkov said.

"And if they do?" Zorin inquired.

"A number of possibilities. They may not strike back, but they might ask huge reparations for their targets."

"We would pay," Zorin said.

"Of course. But they may choose otherwise. They may insist on retaliating with exactly the number of missiles used against them to satisfy their public opinion and test our sincerity. We would agree to their action and the conflict would end."

"Gorshkov," Zorin asked after some hesitation, "do *you* think they'll believe us?"

Gorshkov looked directly into Zorin's eyes and shrugged.

"Would *you?*"

Zorin shook his head despondently. "Considering what has happened in these two days, my suspicions would be at their highest."

"You've answered your own question, Premier."

"So?" Zorin asked.

"The Americans will conclude they've been willfully attacked and betrayed. They will see the attack from one submarine as a prelude to others and will retaliate."

"When?"

"As soon as the first missile hits."

"How big a retaliation?"

"They can choose to match us missile for missile, but that is unlike them. They will go for the jugular—the very existence of our defense forces."

The phone that was linked to Moscow buzzed. Gorshkov answered.

"Gorshkov here." He listened intently, then turned to Zorin. "Premier, a seventh missile has been launched and is headed for an industrial complex in their Ohio. The New York missile is within three minutes of landing."

"We have three minutes?" Zorin asked almost angrily. "Three minutes to decide the fate of the world?"

Gorshkov continued listening to the Moscow message. "The Americans are opening their missile silos. They are communicating with their Polaris submarines."

The Premier's office fell silent as Gorshkov hung up. Both men lowered their heads and lost themselves in thought. Finally, after more than thirty seconds, Zorin looked up to speak, his eyes those of a desperate man.

"Gorshkov . . . what do we do?"

Gorshkov sighed deeply. The sigh was genuine, for he knew the consequences to the world that his advice would bring.

"Premier," he said, "we can sit here and agonize and bury ourselves in self-blame. We can pity our poor nation once it's destroyed. Or. . . ."

For the first time since the launching Gorshkov looked firm.

"Or . . . we can do what is necessary."

"Which is?"

"Forget who started it. Launch an immediate preemptive strike against the United States. Hope to destroy their missiles before they destroy ours."

Zorin's chest seemed to sag as he heard Gorshkov's strategy. "That is obscene," he said.

"But necessary, Premier."

"But necessary," Zorin mumbled. Again he gazed out the window as Clamshell headed back toward Russia. "You're certain there is no other way?"

"Premier," Gorshkov said, "if I may speak freely, your first obligation is the defense of our country. There is no other way."

Zorin nodded his reluctant approval. "Have them prepare the missiles for a total strike."

Gorshkov solemnly picked up the phone and gave the order. Zorin stared at him as he spoke, studying the admiral's eyes carefully, like a man looking for a clue. When Gorshkov hung up, Zorin continued staring. Gorshkov noticed and moved uneasily in his seat. He wondered at first whether Zorin was breaking. Then he sensed that the Premier's stare had a definite motive.

"Gorshkov," Zorin finally said, "I would like to ask you a question." Gorshkov stiffened. Zorin's tone had bite.

"Of course, Premier."

"Gorshkov, I am not certain that this launching comes from a runaway Soviet vessel."

"No one can give you guarantees," Gorshkov admitted, "but I myself have no doubt—"

"There is another possibility," Zorin said. He continued the long, penetrating stare into Gorshkov's eyes. "As you know, Gorshkov, military adventurism need not start on submarines."

Gorshkov's expression turned cold. He knew what Zorin was about to say.

"Even progressive elements in the United States," Zorin went on, "have raised questions about the mentality of soldiers. Their Eisenhower made his famous talk about the industrial-military complex. I just wonder, Gorshkov—"

"Premier, I must interrupt you!" Gorshkov snapped. "I will answer your question before you ask it. I did *not* order the launching!"

Zorin turned red. "No, no, no, I wasn't thinking of you, Gorshkov. But there are men in Moscow—"

"You were thinking of me," Gorshkov said sharply.

Zorin nodded sadly but affirmatively.

"I can understand," Gorshkov said. "You think I have dreams of grandeur, and I will concede that fighting the Americans at sea would interest me. But this . . . this genocide that is about to take place. . . ." He shook his head somberly. "I am not so stupid."

"Of course not," Zorin mumbled. But the suspicion refused to leave him, and Gorshkov knew it.

The admiral glanced at his watch. "In two minutes the first missile will strike."

The CIS aboard Haven clicked on:

> THE SUBMARINE-LAUNCHED BALLISTIC MISSILE EARLY WARNING SYSTEM REPORTS AN EIGHTH REPEAT EIGHTH MISSILE FIRED FROM THE SAME VESSEL AND FOLLOWING A TRAJECTORY TOWARD HUNTSVILLE, ALABAMA. . . .
> STAND BY.

"Redstone Arsenal," Combs said.
The CIS continued:

> RADAR TRACKING STATION ANVIL ESTIMATES IMPACT TIME OF NUMBER ONE MISSILE AT ONE MINUTE THIRTY SECONDS IN NEW YORK CITY VICINITY.

No one spoke as all eyes remained on the screen. Retaliation was ready. It was as if the nuclear blast over New York would provide the final moral authority for launching it.

> ADVISORY: SATELLITE SURVEILLANCE REPORTS ACTIVE COUNTDOWN OF SOVIET MISSILE FORCES.

"There it is," Somerville said. "As General Combs predicted, the submarine attack is a prelude."

"Stand by to launch," the President ordered.

Somerville transmitted the order by phone.

RADAR TRACKING STATION ANVIL ESTIMATES IMPACT
TIME OF NUMBER ONE MISSILE AT ONE MINUTE FIF-
TEEN SECONDS IN NEW YORK CITY VICINITY. TRAJEC-
TORY APPEARS SLIGHTLY SHORT.

CRITIC members jutted forward.

"How short? How short?" the President asked excitedly.

"Could be any amount," Anderson replied. "I wouldn't
get too excited at five miles. Queens isn't exactly a waste-
land."

The President slumped back. There was a dead silence.

RADAR TRACKING STATION ANVIL COUNTDOWN ON
NUMBER ONE MISSILE. . . . ONE MINUTE. . . .
FIFTY-FIVE SECONDS. . . .

The President closed his eyes as if trying to escape, but
he quickly opened them again and stared blankly at the
screen.

THIRTY SECONDS. . . .

15

Sol Ross stood on the Long Island Rail Road platform in Jamaica, the anger building within him.

He had just pulled in on the local from Far Rockaway. The conductor had chanted the ancient "Change here for trains to New York City," and as he had every morning for twenty-eight years, Sol Ross had changed. But there was no New York train. The Long Island had performed as usual.

Ross was fifty-two and heavyset. Today he was worried. He was scheduled to be at the most important meeting of his life in less than fifteen minutes. His lawyer would be there, and so would his creditors. The question was whether Sol Ross, practically bankrupt, would be allowed to keep his furniture-importing business. Being late was no way to make a strong impression.

The platform was crowded with at least 150 people waiting for the New York train. Shoes were tapping; watch arms were extended. Angry eyes and equally angry questions confronted a passing conductor, whose response was a grumble and a shrug. The dispatcher hadn't told him that the New York train was stalled four miles up the track with wheel trouble.

"The nerve," Sol Ross said to a man standing a few feet away. "All they do is increase the fare."

"Right," the other man said, looking up briefly from the *Wall Street Journal*.

"It's the unions," Ross said. "They were good at the beginning. But now . . . you know."

The man looked up and winked agreement.

Suddenly Sol Ross heard a strange noise from above.

He was used to aircraft noises from Kennedy Airport, but this was different. It was a rushing sound. Insistent. Hurried. Like a large object falling to earth.

Ross looked up, but the platform was covered.

"What the hell is that?" he asked. "Their roof caving in?"

The man with the *Wall Street Journal* also looked up as the sound grew closer.

Now others looked.

Closer. Fright crossed a few faces. For a moment Sol Ross forgot about his train and fixed his eyes on the station roof. He shuffled around nervously, as if wanting somewhere to run. His hand tightened on his briefcase. He stopped shuffling and froze.

Closer.

An approaching train suddenly drowned out the dread sound, like a hood over a doomed man.

Then a thunderous crash.

The roof split into blazing metal. Sol Ross vanished, along with twenty-three people standing near him. The man with the *Journal* lost his arms. Others screamed or gasped or fainted.

Then there was silence.

The CIS:

> NUMBER ONE MISSILE IMPACT NEW YORK REPEAT IMPACT NEW YORK.
> STAND BY.

"God rest them," Somerville said.

No one else spoke. Even breathing seemed suspended. But the CIS was relentless:

> ADVISORY: IMPACT NEW YORK—NO DETONATION.

"It didn't go off!" Anderson exclaimed.

"Christ!" the President yelled. There was sudden joy in Haven's conference room. The enemy had failed!

"*Will* it go off?" Bixby asked.

Eyes turned to Anderson.

"There's no rationale for a delayed trigger," the admiral answered. "It's a dud."

The joy was short-lived as reality came quickly back to mind: Six other missiles were streaking toward the East Coast.

"Mr. President," Anderson said, "there may be radiation danger at the impact site. We should advise them."

The President gestured his approval, and Somerville ordered the Pentagon to alert New York authorities.

The Pentagon's alert would reach the New York Police Department in four minutes and would take another two to be relayed to personnel at the crash site. For some, like Tom Shelton and Angel Lopez, it would come too late.

Shelton and Lopez were city patrolmen. Both were in their late twenties; both had fewer than five years on the force. Their car, number 851, had been cruising six blocks from Jamaica Station when the first Polaris came in. They had heard the crash and had seen the flying fragments. Now, after having raced to the station, they came on a scene that turned their stomachs. Mangled, charred bodies lay on the blackened cement platform. There was screaming and moaning. A few survivors stumbled along the track, dazed, while some others lay contorted over third rails, electrocuted when they ran in panic. The train that Sol Ross had heard in his last seconds remained just outside the station, its passengers squeezing against windows to get a better view of the disaster.

Sirens screamed through the neighborhood as Shelton and Lopez were joined by fire and police units. Civilians ran from nearby buildings, some with first-aid kits, others with cameras. Jamaica Hospital sent ambulances and staff doctors. Father Anthony Mancusi, who was buying a fountain pen in a nearby office-supply store when he heard the blast, hailed a cab and rushed to the station. The platform was soon crammed with emergency personnel and equipment—fire hoses, oxygen tanks, stretchers, blood bottles.

The crackle of walkie-talkies and the barked orders of gravel-voiced commanders competed with the cries of the dying. Shelton and Lopez tried to comfort a few victims, then let the arriving doctors take over. The two cops rummaged through wreckage, examining bits of the fallen "object."

"Musta been part of some plane," Shelton said as he picked up a jagged piece of metal.

"Yeah," Lopez agreed, examining the same piece.

"Amazin' it didn't crash," Shelton added. "You think it crashed?"

"Maybe it crashed in Jersey," Lopez said, "or in the water."

"Could be," Shelton agreed. "We'll hear."

Tom Shelton had a wife of twenty-four and one son, Tom, Jr., age two. Angel Lopez was also married and had two children, a boy and a girl. Neither Shelton nor Lopez knew it as they trekked through the debris, but they were slowly making their wives into widows. Fragments of the missile's warhead lay in the rubble, leaking radiation which was attacking the bodies of the two policemen—silently, painlessly.

Within an hour Shelton and Lopez would become nauseated. They would throw up and develop diarrhea. The symptoms would last for three days, then go away. But the number of white cells in their blood would begin to drop. Within three weeks they would feel an increasing malaise, and their hair would start falling out. Then they would notice small hemorrhages in their skin and mouth. They would bruise easily and bleed from the gums. Soon afterward ulcers would form in their mouth and throat. The diarrhea would return. They would lose their appetites, lose weight, and begin to run high fevers. They would not be able to eat by mouth. Their bruises wouldn't heal, but would instead become infected.

The number of red cells in their blood would then decline, and the white count would drop still further. With their bodies unable to fight infection, Shelton and Lopez would die.

Four others at the impact site would suffer the same

fate. Some forty-three more would experience other effects. Some would become sterile, permanently or temporarily. Others would develop lung cancer, still others cancer of the bone or eye cataracts. Some of these conditions would not appear for years.

The CIS:

> RADAR TRACKING STATION GUIDEPOST REPORTS COUNTDOWN NUMBER TWO MISSILE. THIRTY SECONDS. . . .

The CRITIC group sat hypnotized by the CIS' cold reports of the assault.

"You must give the order to retaliate," Combs told the President.

"I will retaliate when the first target is destroyed," the President replied.

Anderson sensed an uneasiness in the Chief. The strangeness of the attack, Gorshkov's plea, the failure to follow up immediately with a massive assault from Russia itself, the dud in New York—these things forced a reluctance, a sense of caution. Anderson's suggestion that a Soviet sub might in fact be loose was also apparently having its impact.

> TWENTY SECONDS. . . . TEN SECONDS. . . .

As with the first missile, the President closed his eyes, then opened them again and stared at the screen.

Herlihy sat outside his bar in South Boston, his massive legs spread apart, his paper open to the latest exploits of Dick Tracy.

It was a Herlihy habit. Five hours before he opened the saloon, the folding chair would appear outside and 300 pounds of Herlihy would squeeze down on it. The newspaper reading began with sports, then went to comics, then ended.

Herlihy was sixty. His wife had died of Parkinson's disease the year before. They had no children, but Herlihy was training a nephew to take over the bar, maybe turn it into a nice, respectable restaurant. Herlihy planned to retire, draw a small income from the business, and if the finances held, live out his years in Ireland.

He was just finishing *Tracy* when he heard the strange noise, like nothing he had heard before. It was distant, coming from above. He looked up, thinking it might be a new kind of airplane. He saw passersby stop and look up, too, then continue on. There was no plane, so Herlihy wondered whether some television set in one of the nearby apartment houses was on the blink and was turned up too high.

The sound continued. An object cutting through the air. It was the same sound Sol Ross had heard just minutes before.

Maureen Kennedy walked by, and Herlihy was momentarily distracted. "Chilly but nice and have a good one," he said to Maureen, giving the Herlihy weather report.

Maureen Kennedy stopped.

"Y'hear what just happened in New York?" she asked.

"No, what?"

"There was this plane accident. . . ."

Maureen broke off. She looked up. The strange sound came closer.

"Herlihy, somethin's wrong."

Herlihy tried to lift his 300 pounds, pushing against the back of the chair with his chunky arm. He breathed heavily, his face turning a beet red. Maureen helped him up. They both wanted to run, but there was nowhere. Instinctively Herlihy reached into his pocket for the key to his saloon. He turned toward the front door, opened it, and tried to push Maureen inside.

The last thing both of them saw was the mirror behind the counter start to shatter.

* * *

The CIS:

> NUMBER TWO MISSILE IMPACT BOSTON REPEAT IMPACT BOSTON.
> STAND BY.

> ADVISORY: IMPACT BOSTON—NO DETONATION.

"What the hell?" the President gasped.

"They're morons," Somerville declared.

"Mr. President," Combs said, "I would not let two duds deceive us. The Soviet missile forces are ready, and each minute that passes gives them more time to recheck their equipment. I recommend that you proceed with retaliation."

"I disagree," Anderson said. "The most difficult part of missile operations is getting the missile to target. Detonation is relatively easy, so the failure of these two warheads is suspicious. This does *not* look like a normal Soviet maneuver."

The discussion was broken off by the CIS:

> RADAR TRACKING STATION KING REPORTS COUNTDOWN NUMBER THREE MISSILE. . . . THIRTY SECONDS. . . . TWENTY SECONDS. . . . TEN. . . . FIVE. . . . ZERO. . . .

> NUMBER THREE MISSILE IMPACT MARIETTA REPEAT IMPACT MARIETTA.
> STAND BY.

> ADVISORY: IMPACT MARIETTA—NO DETONATION.

"Mr. President," Anderson insisted, "I am now saying there's a Soviet submarine on the loose."

"Manned by incompetents?" General Benson asked.

"We all know," Anderson replied, "that every missile submarine has safeguards. It's obvious that whoever took control of the Soviet ship broke through the missile safety net but failed with the warheads."

"I've heard of three duds in a row," Combs remarked.

"In a well-planned attack," Anderson countered, "every warhead would be examined and its trigger tested. You're up against the odds, General."

Combs smirked, as if Anderson were presumptuous in lecturing him. "Mr. President," the general said, "we must remember that the Soviets sank our submarine. They also issued a phony charge about our attacking their destroyer—"

"Wait a second," Anderson protested. "This runaway sub could've sunk the *Dostoyny and* our sub."

"Why sink their own boat?" the President asked. "You explained after the *Dostoyny* thing why the Red government might do it, but I can't see a runaway pulling that."

"I can think of several motives," Anderson responded. "Raising the level of international tension, confusing Washington and Moscow—"

"Speculation," Somerville said with a contemptuous wave of his hand.

"But it's *possible*," Anderson insisted.

Still another call came through on Bixby's phone.

"Bixby."

He paused.

"Mr. President," he said, "Admiral Gorshkov wants to speak with Admiral Anderson again."

RADAR TRACKING STATION KING REPORTS COUNTDOWN NUMBER FOUR MISSILE. . . . THIRTY SECONDS. . . .

"Hold Gorshkov," the President ordered. "Let's wait for this."

"Have Admiral Gorshkov hold on," Bixby told the communications room.

TWENTY SECONDS. . . . TEN. . . . FIVE. . . . ZERO. . . .

NUMBER FOUR MISSILE IMPACT FORT JACKSON REPEAT IMPACT FORT JACKSON.

ADVISORY: IMPACT FORT JACKSON—NO DETONATION.

"Mr. President," Anderson said, "I think the evidence is overwhelming."

"I don't know who's right," the President moaned, throwing up his hands in a gesture of futility. "Admiral, you'd better sound out Gorshkov."

Bixby quickly arranged for Gorshkov to be put through. Anderson picked up his phone.

"Anderson here."

"And this is Gorshkov. We are prepared to concede a runaway submarine. Obviously the idiots did not know how the warheads worked. You have, I hope, explained the safeguard system to your President."

"I have," Anderson said. "But some here think this is a trick." He looked directly at Combs.

"There is no trick. I swear it."

"Then take the first step by winding down your missile forces."

There was a long pause.

"We cannot do that."

Combs looked pleased by Gorshkov's admission.

"Admiral Gorshkov," Anderson went on, "we must have some gesture from you."

Another long pause. Zorin and Gorshkov hurriedly conferred.

Anderson kept watching the CIS as reports of the remaining missiles came across:

Number five . . . Mayport, Florida. No detonation.

Number six . . . already accounted for, confirmed down in the Atlantic.

Number seven . . . vicinity of Columbus, Ohio. No detonation.

Number eight, the last one . . . Huntsville, Alabama. No detonation.

Gorshkov got back on the line. "Admiral Anderson," he said, "we make this offer: Let us simultaneously suspend readiness procedures on *half* our respective missiles. We will watch each other by satellite."

"Admiral Gorshkov, you know that satellites cannot reveal all aspects of missile preparations. We cannot monitor your proposal closely enough to accept it."

Zorin and Gorshkov again conferred.

"Admiral Anderson," Gorshkov said, "we cannot offer anything more on missiles. So let us both be ready. But we pledge not to attack unless you do first."

"That's not very reassuring," Anderson said.

"Reassurance is difficult, isn't it, Admiral Anderson?"

Anderson didn't care much for Gorshkov's tone and knew he had to cut down the Russian to keep the negotiations balanced.

"Admiral Gorshkov," he said, "*your* side is responsible here."

"Who is denying that?" Gorshkov countered. "I am not one of your passers of the buck. I am determined to sink these criminals. In fact, I will let some of our officers board your antisubmarine ships to lead the search."

Somerville shook his head negatively, violently.

"Mr. President," he said, "they'd love to know all about our antisubmarine operations."

"Tell him no," the President ordered.

"We have to reject that," Anderson told Gorshkov. "We're prepared to sink the sub ourselves and ask you to supply technical data. You must bear the burden. If they get those warheads corrected, God help us all!"

"Your extreme suggestions are not helpful," Gorshkov said.

Anderson hesitated, trying to come up with an alternative that Gorshkov might accept.

"Admiral Gorshkov," he asked, "can you determine *which* submarine is at fault?"

"Not immediately," Gorshkov answered. "They don't admit these things."

"Let me suggest an approach," Anderson went on. "Eight missiles have been fired. Only two classes of your submarines—the Yankee and Delta types—can fire that many. Have all your Yankees and Deltas in the launch area come to the surface. Air reconnaissance could determine which one had empty missile tubes."

"You are naïve," Gorshkov responded. "A renegade would not follow surfacing orders."

"I'm not so sure," Anderson said. "It's in her interest to behave like a loyal ship. After all, she doesn't want to be hunted down. If you ordered the subs up, say, under some guise—"

"Give specifics!" Gorshkov demanded.

Anderson sensed Gorshkov's nervousness. He knew that the Russian was torn by guilt and conflict. Gorshkov, after all, was negotiating for the murder of his own men.

"You could say," Anderson answered, "that one of your air crews is down in the ocean and needs assistance."

Gorshkov pondered for a moment.

"That *might* work," he agreed.

"Of course," Anderson said, "there's another problem."

He paused for a moment, realizing that he was about to touch a raw nerve of any naval commander. "The renegade might not have been assigned to the area of the launch. She could have cruised there from her patrol station without your knowledge."

"Yes," Gorshkov said tensely, "so ordering up all *known* Yankees and Deltas in the launch area could be academic. The criminal could remain silent, and we would think she was somewhere else."

"Unless you contacted *all* Yankees and Deltas to confirm their locations."

"They would have to break radio silence!" Gorshkov snapped. "You'd know where they *all* were!"

"Regrettably."

"Regrettably or not, that is the reality!"

"Admiral Gorshkov, we're talking about the destruction of mankind."

Gorshkov didn't respond. Each man could hear the other breathing hard. The CRITIC group watched Anderson, fascinated by the unprecedented negotiations, but sensing that Gorshkov's silence was ominous. Anderson realized the next step would have to be American.

"Admiral Gorshkov," he said, "there is a possible compromise. You know when your Yankees and Deltas left their bases. Contact only those that have had sufficient time to reach the launch area."

There was brief talk between Zorin and Gorshkov.

"I will get back to you," Gorshkov said.

Both men hung up.

The President, his head dripping with cold sweat, turned to Anderson. "You handled him real good, Andy. But will they bite?"

"I don't know," Anderson replied. "If they don't we're at the mercy of that submarine."

"Can't we sink it ourselves?" Bixby asked.

"Yes, if we can find it. But I'm not optimistic. The renegades know from radio that they've failed. They'll probably drop down several thousand feet until they fix those warheads."

"Our sonars can't find them?" Sonderling asked incredulously.

"Sir," Anderson answered, "we're not much better at finding subs now than we were thirty years ago. Sure, detection has improved, but the subs have improved more."

The President turned to Combs. "General, you haven't said much. You change your mind or something?"

"Mr. President," Combs said, "I have given my advice. I sense that you prefer Admiral Anderson's theories."

"Well," the President said, "seven duds and Gorshkov's call make me think this runaway-sub story's got somethin' to it."

"If it doesn't?" Combs asked.

"You can answer that yourself," the President replied. "I'm playin' poker, General. The people elected me to make decisions, and I'm makin' 'em."

An intercom behind McNamara buzzed. The news secretary answered.

"Sir," he told the President, "it's the White House press office. They want a statement on the crashes."

"What're the reporters' questions like?" the President asked. McNamara relayed the inquiry.

"Sir," he said, "some airport radars got a glimpse of

201

those warheads in the last seconds, so the boys are wondering if a satellite broke up and came down. They're also asking if we had nuclear weapons in orbit, since all the crash sites are radioactive."

The President gestured to Anderson for advice.

"The satellite story is a good cover," Anderson said. "I'd confirm it. On the other hand, I'd deny that we had nuclear weapons in orbit. Say the radiation comes from scientific instruments that use radioactive materials, and issue a standard warning, as we did in New York. Of course, once they discover Red markings on those fragments, things'll get hot."

"Why not nail it on the Russians now?" Somerville asked.

"The public response could disrupt my negotiations with Gorshkov," Anderson replied.

With Presidential approval, McNamara transmitted Anderson's story.

Anderson knew that the administration was approaching the limits of credibility. Press leaks, military alerts, the use of Haven, and now the crashing of "objects" that would soon be identified as Russian all brought risk of panic. Should the renegade sub not be sunk soon, public or Congressional pressure could force war. The cover stories only bought time, and little of it.

The communications room reported that Gorshkov was back on the line. Anderson picked up.

"Anderson."

"Admiral Anderson, we accept your proposal. We hope you are conscious of the great risk we are taking for peace."

"I am."

"We are now contacting twelve submarines of the Yankee or Delta type. These are the only ships that could have reached the launch area from the time they left port. When we.... You will stand by, please."

Gorshkov got off the line, and Anderson guessed he was receiving a message from Moscow. The conference room was silent, edgy. There was relief at Gorshkov's acceptance, anxiety that the renegade might correct the warheads before being sunk.

"Gorshkov again."

"Yes, Admiral?"

"Seven of our submarines have responded. They are precisely where they should be."

The CIS started up:

ADVISORY: COMMUNICATIONS INTELLIGENCE REPORTS SEVEN SOV SUBMARINES EMPLOYING DETECTABLE RADIO CHANNELS. LOCATIONS MARKED.

"We appreciate your cooperation," Anderson said. He flipped a switch on an intercom and was connected with the communications room.

"Have Admiral Mann stand by at Norfolk."

Robert E. L. Mann, a four-star admiral, son of a late Georgia Senator, was commander of the United States Atlantic Fleet.

Anderson reached under his chair and took from a briefcase a file marked FLEET DISPOSITIONS. It told him the patrol locations of all navy ships.

"Admiral Anderson," Gorshkov said, "I have just been told that three more submarines have responded. Two are close enough to the launch point to have launched the missiles, but only one is equipped with missiles of sufficient range to be the renegade. That is number three-forty-three."

Anderson again contacted the communications room. "Gather all Defense Intelligence Agency data on Soviet submarine three-forty-three."

As he was speaking, the CIS kept up its regular reports:

ADVISORY: COMMUNICATIONS INTELLIGENCE REPORTS THREE MORE SOV SUBMARINES EMPLOYING DETECTABLE RADIO CHANNELS. LOCATIONS MARKED.

Gorshkov left the line again, but came back twenty seconds later. "We now have confirmations and locations on all twelve submarines," he said. "It is definite that only three-forty-three could have launched those missiles."

Men in Haven inched forward, their eyes riveted on Anderson. The climax was within reach. Time was all that counted.

"Admiral Gorshkov," Anderson inquired, "could this ship sink the *Dostoyny* and *John Hay* and still reach the launch point by the time the missiles were launched?"

"Let me check the times and distances," Gorshkov replied.

There was silence on the line for a full minute before Gorshkov came back. "My calculations," he said, "show the answer is positive. I am prepared to order three-forty-three to the surface. How will you sink her?"

Anderson checked his FLEET DISPOSITIONS.

"Our carrier *Forrestal*," he said, "is sufficiently close to sink three-forty-three by aircraft."

"That concerns me. As soon as three-forty-three detects your aircraft, she will dive again."

"All right," Anderson said, "we can have our planes already in the area when three-forty-three comes up."

"Good. Direct your air units to the target. Of course. . . ." He hesitated.

"Yes?"

"Number three-forty-three may still refuse to come up."

"If so, Admiral Gorshkov, we will have a deep-water fight on our hands."

"Let us hope," Gorshkov replied, "that these criminals are as gullible as they are incompetent."

"Let us hope," Anderson agreed.

"Admiral Anderson," Gorshkov said, a rigidity returning to his speech, "don't think that my cooperation in this matter signifies callousness toward Soviet personnel. I do not consider the instigators of this plot as members of the Soviet Navy. They are more typical of the kind of conspirators you have in America, like your Mr. Oswald."

Anderson understood that the insult was a face-saving gesture. After all, for the first time one side's command-

and-control system had broken down, and for Gorshkov it was a severe humiliation.

"I will take your comments under advisement," Anderson said.

Both men hung up.

Now the CIS came on with the data Anderson had requested from the Defense Intelligence Agency:

DIA ADVISORY SOV SUB 343: VESSEL IS A MISSILE-CARRYING SUBMARINE OF THE DELTA CLASS. SHE IS EQUIPPED WITH 12 LAUNCHING TUBES FOR THE SS-N-8 MISSILE SYSTEM, MAX RANGE 4,200 MILES.

NO. 343 WAS CONSTRUCTED AT SEVASTOPOL AND LAUNCHED ON 24 APRIL 1971. SEA TRIALS WERE MARRED BY SERIOUS VIBRATIONS IN HER PROPULSION SYSTEM, DELAYING COMMISSIONING BY THREE MONTHS, BUT THERE HAS BEEN NO APPARENT RECURRENCE OF TECHNICAL DIFFICULTY.

NO. 343'S HOME PORT IS MURMANSK. SHE WAS LAST SIGHTED DIVING IN THE NORTH SEA ON 10 OCTOBER. SHIP'S COMMANDING OFFICER IS V. K. SISLOV, WHO RESIDES IN MURMANSK WITH HIS WIFE AND TWO YOUNG SONS. SISLOV IS 37 AND IS GENERALLY REGARDED AS A CAPABLE OFFICER WITH SOME POTENTIAL FOR SENIOR LEADERSHIP. HIS FATHER, RUDOLF SISLOV, IS ONE OF THE SOVIET UNION'S FOREMOST ARCHITECTS.

NO. 343 IS CONSIDERED ONE OF THE MOST ADVANCED OF SOVIET SUBMARINES, AND HER SS-N-8 MISSILE SYSTEM IS THE MOST MODERN IN OPERATION IN THE RED FLEET. SHE CURRENTLY CARRIES APPROX 120 MEN.

"Get me Admiral Mann," Anderson ordered over the intercom. In an instant he was connected with Mann at Norfolk. He gave him a complete review of the situation and told him that a single Soviet submarine would be sunk by joint agreement with the Soviet Union. He ordered that no photographs be taken of the sinking to avoid embarrassing the Russians.

"Because of the extraordinary nature of this operation," he informed Mann, "I will be in direct command of all operational forces. Communications lines between these forces and this aircraft are to be kept constantly open."

The carrier *Forrestal*, cruising some 270 land miles away from No. 343, was alerted. With Anderson in command, the United States Navy was about to sink the first Soviet fighting ship in its history.

Nobody knew what Richard Gillespie was thinking as he stood silently in the control room of the *John Hay*. His face was blank as he continued listening to radio reports from American stations. The men of the North Star Crusade, showing considerably more anger and pain at their crushing defeat, stood around him.

Gillespie had tuned the radio soon after the eight missiles were launched. He had expected to hear the familiar "We interrupt this program . . ." followed by the terse announcement of a nuclear attack. He had expected to listen as a grim newscaster, his voice shivering with fright, announced that the station was leaving the air. He had expected to hear him tell listeners to turn to the emergency broadcast channels. And he had expected to hear the President of the United States come on and announce that the nation had retaliated and that the Soviet strategic forces lay in ruins.

He had heard none of that. Instead a New York radio station had broken into an old Percy Faith recording of "The Sound of Music" to report that an unidentified object had crashed through Jamaica Station. Gillespie had to wait for the next regular news broadcast to learn that other "objects" had fallen on Boston, Marietta, Fort Jackson, and three of his other targets. Later he had heard a White House reporter "confirm" that the objects were parts of a disabled satellite. The hottest speculation involved the rumor that the satellite carried nuclear weapons.

Now the radio reported Congressional reaction to the

forty-six dead and 173 injured in the morning's "satellite break-up." Gillespie finally showed slight emotion, smirking as liberal Senators expressed outrage at the danger from military satellites, smirking again as conservative Senators pointed out that there had never been any previous deaths from similar accidents. Gillespie had equal contempt for the orthodoxies of both sides. He regarded himself as an original thinker, and he thought of professional anti-Communists as dullards and ritual dancers—burdens rather than allies.

He disgustedly switched off the receiver. For a moment he stood sternly before his men and simply gazed at them, one by one, as if trying to guess who had screwed up. The mood was grim, even funereal. All the years of planning gone to waste, the dream of saving the nation seemingly dashed. Some of the scientists wondered whether a saboteur had infiltrated their ranks. A few entertained the thought that one among them had had last-minute qualms and had intentionally disarmed the missiles. But these ideas quickly evaporated. These men had known one another too long to have doubts.

Gillespie cleared his throat. His hands began to tremble, so he clasped them behind his back. His skin seemed pale. Yet, still trying to affect the poise of a strong leader, he purged all emotion from his voice.

"Gentlemen," he said, "we have failed. We have failed ourselves and we have failed our country."

There were sad, affirmative nods. Tears welled in the eyes of nine of the twelve men before him.

Only one man in the room was happy.

Captain Alan Lansing sat thunderstruck by what he had witnessed. The joy was all inside, for he knew that to release it might bring a quick bullet to the brain. He watched Gillespie intently, wondering how the self-proclaimed strategist would extricate himself. Thoughts of testifying against Gillespie flashed through his mind. Visions of Gillespie in prison, his comrades in cells around him, hurried by briefly. But Lansing sensed they were premature.

"Obviously," Gillespie told his men, "failure can be

temporary or permanent. It can be the end, or it can be the beginning of resurrection."

Lansing couldn't figure what Gillespie meant. Was he hinting that the North Star Crusade had some future? Maybe he was. Lansing knew it was common for men in deep depression to have sudden illusions.

"The navy's experts," Gillespie went on, "will analyze the fragments from the crash sites. That might take minutes, hours, or days, but eventually they will learn that those fragments came from Polaris missiles. They will salvage the warhead serial numbers from the wreckage and trace them to this ship.

"And then they will hunt for us. They will try to kill us or capture us. I have no doubt that, given the time, they will succeed." He started pacing, like a military commander whose men faced their most desperate mission. "And that," he said, "gives us a number of options. . . ."

The men of the Crusade followed him with their eyes. The glamour had been drained from the mission, and now many of them were frightened.

"We can surrender," Gillespie said. "All we have to do is contact Groton and announce where we are. But it would be an admission that our Crusade has lost its meaning, and it would be cowardly.

"Rejected.

"Or we can all commit suicide. How we do it doesn't really matter. But suicide is for those who don't have the guts to face the future.

"Rejected.

"We can go the escape route—beach the *Hay* on a remote part of a foreign coast and hide like the Jap soldiers did after the war. But that's running away, and we'd probably never make it before the antisub forces got us.

"Rejected.

"Then again, we can try to get back to the States. That would mean surfacing at night just offshore and making the final distance in rubber rafts. But the navy will anticipate our trying that, and the antisub patrols near the mainland will be brutal. Not much chance.

"Rejected."

Gillespie paused to give dramatic effect to his next words.

"There's another option—the only one that makes any sense at all. We can hold our ground and try to correct the problem in the warheads. We have eight missiles left. We can try again. If we've got to die in this ship, let's at least die like Americans!"

There were vigorous nods of agreement from the men of the Crusade, but on Lansing's face there was only astonishment.

"You seem surprised, Captain Lansing," Gillespie said.

"I can't believe you're serious," Lansing responded.

"Why?"

"Because your whole plan was based on the idea that Washington would strike the Soviet Union if nuclear missiles exploded in the United States. But that could work only if our people thought the missiles were Russian. They'll have those fragments analyzed and this ship identified long before you correct the warheads. Do you really believe Washington will go to war over an attack they know is coming from an American sub?"

Gillespie smiled. "Captain Lansing," he said, "the answer is yes."

"That's crazy!"

Gillespie chuckled at Lansing's self-assuredness. "I submit to you, Captain, that when eight warheads explode on American soil, our country will *have* to strike the Soviets. Public opinion will demand it. You think the nation will believe some slick story about a renegade American sub? The fury of her people will send America into war even if the President has to be dragged behind."

"That makes no sense at all," Lansing declared.

"Not to *you*," Gillespie replied. "You still think in conventional terms. You don't give proper weight to psychology, mass hysteria, the American's love of fighting back."

He turned to his group. "Does anyone disagree?"

There was no disagreement. For the men of North Star, disheartened by their earlier failure, the prospect of success was dazzling.

The group broke. The scientists hurried to Sherwood

Forest to find out what had gone wrong with their calculations and to correct the remaining eight warheads. Gillespie stayed with Lansing in the control room, the captain turning silent now, convinced that nothing he said could penetrate the glib logic of what he had just heard. The North Star Crusade, seemingly finished a few minutes before, had been reborn. It would go forward aboard a submarine that Isaac Anderson believed was at the bottom of the sea. It would drive toward victory while the United States Navy prepared to destroy a totally innocent Soviet ship.

16

Anderson walked briskly to Haven's command room, just forward of the wings.

The room looked like a small movie theater. At one end were four rows of purple seats, reserved for CRITIC staff aides. The seats faced a huge CIS wall with six screens. Between the rows of seats and the wall was an eight-sided table for CRITIC itself. The table was white matte so that a projector in the ceiling could throw maps and battle charts onto the surface.

Now the row seats were filling with men who would relay orders or give briefings on specific problems. Anderson and the rest of CRITIC took their places at the table. The lights were dim. The table glowed with a projected map of the Atlantic showing the positions of the carrier *Forrestal* and Soviet submarine 343. The map bled onto the faces of CRITIC, making the highest officials in the land look like performers in a circus.

One CIS screen showed a satellite view of the carrier, her flight deck teeming with half her eighty-four jets.

Anderson glanced up at the screen and picked up a phone.

"Get me the *Forrestal*."

Commander J. R. Haber paced expectantly on the *Forrestal*'s bridge. He led the ship's air group.

Haber was forty, with a crew cut, a Nebraskan whose two sons called him "sir." He had flown seventy-eight missions in Vietnam and saw combat as a "job." He had no interest in the political arguments surrounding it, pre-

ferring instead to talk about "surgical" air strikes, "kill ra-
tios," and "protective reaction."

As the call from Anderson came through, a second CIS
screen in Haven flashed on. Anderson could see the five-
foot-ten Haber, who was already in flight gear.

"Commander Haber? Admiral Anderson."

"Yes, sir."

"I assume Admiral Mann has briefed you."

"He has, sir."

"You understand the Soviets are cooperating."

"I do, sir."

Anderson watched the picture of Haber carefully,
searching for any sign that he might be inadequate for the
mission. He saw none. Haber, the professional, did not
move a muscle when Anderson mentioned Soviet cooperation in the sinking of their own ship.

"Commander, you and your men have no need to know
the circumstances surrounding this operation. You will
not speculate among yourselves. When you return, you
must never mention the incident again. Do you follow?"

"I follow, sir."

"Commander, have your crews man their planes."

Gorshkov faced a problem. His communications were
monitored in Moscow, so other admirals would know he
was helping Anderson sink the 343. He had to head off
the shock, the disgust, the suspicion of betrayal. He sent
an urgent message to Admiral V. M. Grishanov, chief of
the political directorate, Soviet Navy:

I REGRET TO INFORM YOU THAT ONE OF OUR SUB-
MARINES, THE 343, HAS APPARENTLY BEEN SEIZED
BY REACTIONARY ELEMENTS. NUMBER 343 HAS EN-
GAGED IN ACTIONS THAT THREATEN THE PEACE AND
SECURITY OF THE USSR AND, AS A RESULT, MUST BE
DESTROYED. BECAUSE OF HER LOCATION, THIS OPERA-
TION MUST BE CARRIED OUT BY THE UNITED STATES
NAVY. I HAVE MADE THE NECESSARY ARRANGEMENTS.
NUMBER 343 IS A DISGRACE TO THE SOVIET FLEET.

THOSE WHO NOW CONTROL HER MUST BE VIEWED, NOT AS FELLOW OFFICERS, BUT AS CRIMINALS.

Then Gorshkov added a thought to keep his people in line:

OBVIOUSLY THE POLITICAL DIRECTORATE SHOULD BE ON GUARD AGAINST THOSE WHO QUESTION OUR ACTIONS. THE CONSPIRACY ABOARD 343 MAY EXTEND ELSEWHERE. YOU WILL CONDUCT A FULL INVESTIGATION OF ANY WHO DO NOT EMBRACE OUR OPERATION WITH THE EXPECTED ENTHUSIASM.

The implication for those opposing Gorshkov was clear.

Captain Sislov of the 343 was baffled.

He had never been asked to break radio silence. Now he was asked for position reports every few minutes. If war broke out, he knew, he would be a sitting duck. But he could not defy the admirals.

Not that Sislov was so enamored of Soviet leadership. Privately he questioned its competence and even questioned the Soviet system itself. He despised the lack of freedom, the constant presence of the KGB. His loyalty was to the motherland, to the soul of Russia.

The message came through: 343 was to pick up a downed Soviet air crew on the surface. Sislov got on the bullhorn to inform his 120 men, and most of them were strangely enthusiastic. It was rare that anything exciting happened on a cruise.

A second message assured Sislov that no American units were in his sector. It told him that Soviet long-range bombers would fly overhead while he was making his assist.

There was no way for Sislov to find out that the official messages were deceptions. His sonar, designed to track ships, was not sensitive enough to tell him there were no airmen on the surface of the sea. And his radar could detect the presence only of overflying planes. It would take human eyes to tell their country of origin, and by that time they would be in attack position.

Haber climbed aboard his Lockheed S-3A Viking. It was a 43,000-pound antisubmarine bomber, ten times deadlier than any previous antisubmarine aircraft. Besides Haber, there were three crewmen.

Haber revved his two turbofan engines and pulled up to the starboard-bow catapult. Steam hissed from the catapult slit that extended to the forward edge of the flight deck. Haber observed that the day was perfect. Blue skies, a few clouds. Three other Vikings approached the remaining catapults.

Deckmen in tight-fitting work suits hooked Haber's sweptwing Viking to the catapult cord. A deckman's hand went up. Suddenly it thrust toward the bow.

A roar of jet power.

Haber's helmet slammed back against his seat as the Viking lurched ahead. The huge *59* on *Forrestal*'s deck blurred past him. Then only the sea was below.

Other Vikings followed. Twelve in all. They started their 270-mile run toward the 343.

The flight of the Vikings took slightly more than half an hour. Haber roared in over a peaceful patch of sea where, cruising—submerged, unsuspecting—was his target.

From Clamshell, Gorshkov passed the order to Sislov: "Prepare to surface!"

Activity quickened aboard 343. Crewmen assigned to rescue the "Soviet airmen" donned life jackets and broke out medical kits. The galley warmed soup. Sislov himself rechecked his instruments to be sure he would surface at the location ordered.

Anderson was on the line with Gorshkov. "Admiral Gorshkov, our planes are ready."

"Very well," Gorshkov replied crisply.

There was a pause. The critical moment had come. Anderson and Gorshkov each felt a sudden exultation, yet they also shared a feeling of pain. Men brought up in the tradition of fair, open combat sensed that what they were doing was a violation of honor.

"Surface!" Gorshkov ordered.

Air tanks blew the ballast from the 343. Quickly, gracefully, she rose. The first section to cut through the foam was her X-band surveillance radar, code-named Snoop Slab by the United States. As it slid upward, it started its sweep. Immediately twelve contacts appeared on Sislov's scope. They were, he assumed, the Soviet bombers Moscow had told him about.

His ship rose farther, starting to reveal her 425-foot length. Two Vikings peeled off and began their attack run.

Anderson watched, leaning toward the screen. His breathing quickened. He clasped his hands together on the table, the blood squeezing from his fingers.

Gorshkov appeared calmer. It was appearance only. His insides felt as if someone had punctured his neck with a meat hook, then ripped downward. For him this was tragedy compounded. *His* renegade.

"Commander Haber," Anderson ordered, "fire at will!"

The first two Vikings roared in.

As 343's bridge popped through the waves, Sislov rushed upward to the main hatch. He threw it open and looked out.

He saw.

Vikings, their snub noses coming at him. Americans, not Russians.

"Dive!" Sislov screamed. He jumped down, slamming into the deck below. He heard a loud snap and felt a burning pain in his right ankle. Limping, grimacing, he got back to his control room as 343 started slipping under.

But it was too late.

A single 250-pound bomb arched downward. Then another. The first missed, showering the sub with shrapnel that sounded like hail to the frightened sailors inside. The other hit squarely atop her missile tubes, puncturing the hull, igniting rocket fuel. The ocean erupted in flame.

"No!" Sislov shouted. He shook his fist in defiance of the Americans. Despite the damage, he maintained the dive. He ordered the missile compartment sealed off, trapping eighteen screaming sailors inside. Anything to save the ship.

Another Viking flashed in. The pilot released a 580-pound Mk 46 torpedo. It slapped the water, racing toward the 343, its acoustic detector picking up the sub's sounds. The eight-foot torpedo slammed into her stern, destroying the control system, throwing her into a nose-first dive.

Crewmen rushed toward escape hatches as the Atlantic flooded in. They clawed their way past one another—scratching, gouging, kicking. But 343 continued down. She was too deep for escape.

Sislov knew he was dying. Now, in his final moments, confused by images of his family, he wondered whether the orders from Gorshkov had been fakes. Maybe the Americans had broken the Soviet code. Or maybe there had been a blunder in Moscow. War, obviously, had broken out.

"They didn't warn me," he mumbled as he heard grown men starting to cry. "They didn't even warn me."

Crewmen were able to seal some emergency bulkheads. But for those not already drowned in flooded compartments, death would come another way.

The 343 reached 1,000 feet. Fifteen hundred. Eighteen hundred. Finally Sislov heard the steel hull start to crumple like a cigarette pack in the hands of an angry man. The ocean pressed inward, and the hull burst. Water and fish and slime thundered in.

Then all was quiet.

"God help us," the President said. He rose slowly from the table, looked around at each man, then stopped at Anderson.

"Thank you, Admiral. Well done."

He turned and slowly left the room.

Somerville, Combs, Bixby, McNamara, Benson, Hartline, Sonderling—none uttering a sound—followed. The men in the row seats, like the audience at the end of a

tragic film, also rose and silently filed out. Anderson, a reluctant hero, was left alone, the sign of his triumph reflected in the bobbing pieces of the 343. Gently, almost
reverently, he picked up the phone that was linked to
Clamshell.

"Admiral Gorshkov," he said, "on behalf of my government—"

"Stop!" Gorshkov ordered. "This is not the time for
soothing words. What is done is done. We are military
men."

Anderson understood Gorshkov's reluctance to be
drawn into an emotional exchange. He couldn't see that
Gorshkov's eyes were red, that his hands, for the first
time in his naval career, trembled. The Soviet admiral felt
an overwhelming guilt.

"I *do* want to say, though," Anderson insisted, "that I
personally appreciate your cooperation . . . and your
thoughtfulness . . . throughout this episode."

There were moments of awkward silence.

"You are a good man," Gorshkov replied, surprising
Anderson with his personal touch. "It has been a long day
for both of us. A very long day."

"It has," Anderson agreed quietly. "Good-bye, Admiral
Gorshkov."

"Good-bye, Admiral Anderson."

The call ended. Anderson rose from the table, feeling empty and weak. He glanced for one last time at the
CIS. The wreckage from 343 was spreading out, a single
body floating in its midst.

Anderson walked slowly out of the command room, the
muffled thumping of his steps on the carpets accompanied
only by the whine of Haven's engines. The room went
dark, the CIS screens blank. Crewmen silently moved in
to empty ashtrays, clear away scratch pads, sharpen pencils. In a few moments all signs of what had happened
were gone. The room was restored to its neutral, antisep-
tic look.

Anderson returned to his office and slumped in his seat.
Peace had been restored. The crisis was over. Haven and
Clamshell headed for home.

217

17

By agreement between McNamara and the Russians, Moscow issued the following statement:

> THE SOVIET GOVERNMENT HAS CONCLUDED THAT ONE OF ITS SCIENTIFIC SATELLITES PLUNGED TO EARTH TODAY AND STRUCK VARIOUS LOCALITIES IN THE UNITED STATES.
>
> THE SOVIET GOVERNMENT DEEPLY REGRETS THE LOSSES THAT RESULTED FROM THIS ACCIDENT. IN LINE WITH ITS PEACEFUL POLICIES, THE SOVIET GOVERNMENT HAS INSTRUCTED ITS AMBASSADOR IN WASHINGTON TO OFFER FULL REPARATIONS.
>
> THE RADIOACTIVE MATERIALS ABOARD THIS SATELLITE WERE DESIGNED FOR SCIENTIFIC PURPOSES ONLY. THEY HAD NO MILITARY APPLICATION WHATEVER.

Haven had been flying more than twenty-four hours, refueled in midair. On her return she landed in Cape Town, South Africa, where she was checked for the rest of the trip. The South African government had no idea the President was aboard. Haven bore ordinary air force markings.

Clamshell headed for Dar es Salaam, on the east coast of Africa, where she, too, was serviced.

Members of CRITIC felt an increasing sense of ease. They napped, then caught up on routine work. McNamara informed the White House that the President would return the next morning. The official line was that the exercise was over and had been successful. Haven would land just three hours before the Shah of Iran arrived for a state visit, a visit the President felt was good fortune because it would divert official attention from the "satellite" crashes.

Richard Gillespie's radio picked up the admission from Moscow, and Gillespie heard the announcement of the President's return. While he couldn't understand the reasoning behind the Soviet statement, it seemed obvious to him that the United States had not yet learned the spent missiles were American.

Gillespie had no idea that a Pentagon decision had given him a reprieve. Since the crisis was over, the Pentagon reasoned, there was no rush about examining the "Russian" missile fragments. That was now a routine intelligence job. So the fragments were ordered crated and sent to the Philadelphia Navy Yard. Examination could begin the following day.

Time was all that mattered to Richard Gillespie, and time had tilted in his favor.

Soon after leaving Cape Town, the President called Anderson to his office. The admiral walked wearily down the aisle, still conscious of the stares that greeted him. His prestige was now at its height. He had been correct; his counsel had prevented war.

As he entered the office, he saw that the President now looked refreshed, his hair combed, his eyes clear. His breathing was regular, and his hands were steady. He turned toward Anderson, smiling.

"I've had better flights," he said.

Anderson laughed at the understatement, then sat down.

"Y'know what I thought about during all that?" the President asked.

"What, sir?"

"I thought about my tombstone. Y'know, the Presidents have stuff like 'Soldier, patriot, thirty-third

President of the United States.' I thought they'd put on my stone, 'Hell of guy and last President of the United States.' "

"Sir, you didn't think that bombs would start—"

"I did."

The President stared out the window toward the west coast of Africa, now fading into the distance.

"Been there?" he asked.

"Once," Anderson replied.

"You should go again."

"Why, sir?"

"Important place," the President said. "Man like you, your brains, you should get to know those people. Let 'em see you."

"Mr. President," Anderson said, "I don't think they'd care about an admiral whose career is almost over."

"Naval career," the President said.

"Sir?"

"You heard me." He slapped his hand on his desk as if saying, "Let's talk business."

"Andy," he asked, "what do you think of military men taking government jobs?"

"I don't like it," Anderson replied.

"Why?"

"It blurs civilian control. People never think of those men as civilians. Look at Grant or Eisenhower. After Eisenhower left the White House, people called him 'General.' It was ridiculous."

"That all?"

"No. They usually don't do well. Admiral Raborn was a great officer, but flunked as CIA director. Then you have—"

"What about George Marshall?"

"An exception."

"I'd say Isaac Anderson is an exception."

Anderson nodded modestly. "Thank you, sir."

"Enough of an exception to be Secretary of State."

Anderson was flabbergasted, expressionless. He froze, fearful that even a movement might seem brash.

"Well?" the President asked.

"Sir, I. . . ."

"George Marshall made it, Andy. Won a Nobel Peace Prize. Y'know, Charlie Safrin was my closest friend. When he was at State, I could sleep better, and that's the way I feel about you."

"You honor me, sir."

"And let me tell you . . . it doesn't have to stop at State. You're fit, trim. You get some Cabinet experience, and who knows? I'll run again and . . ."

He slurred his next words, offering them as an enticement to the still-dazed admiral.

". . . and everyone knows what I think of the Vice President."

Anderson squirmed. State was an appointed post, an outgrowth of the Marshall tradition. The national ticket was politics, something he could never stomach. He wasn't even a member of the President's party.

"What do you say?" the President asked, a broad smile breaking out.

"Sir," Anderson replied, "obviously I'm grateful. But I'd ask your indulgence while I think it over. I want to talk with Mrs. Anderson. . . ."

"Well, that's fair enough. Wives usually encourage husbands to go higher. You just let me know."

"I will, sir. And . . . thank you."

Anderson rose, saluted formally for the first time during the flight, and left. As he walked down the aisle, he blocked out everything but the President's offer. What lay before him was an opportunity to expand his commitment to peace, yet he knew the opportunity was also a minefield. His naval career had been distinguished. Politics could tarnish his name and drag it into the mud. There was nothing so pathetic, he thought, as a decorated officer who tried a civilian job and failed. He tried to feel modest, to keep the offer in perspective. It reflected the opinion, after all, of only one man . . . and one not known for deep thought. But he could not fight the feeling that he was heir to the Marshall legacy.

The future glittered. Isaac Anderson had only to say yes.

Navy Captain Ian Alleyne threw his overnight case on the baggage scale at National Airport in Washington. His trip to Philadelphia had been planned quickly.

Alleyne was forty-two, prematurely gray, tall, and slightly stooped. He was a naval intelligence officer, a specialist in missiles. He headed the team that would analyze the "Russian" fragments at Philadelphia. Alleyne was a graduate of Cal Tech, with a PhD in physics from Columbia. His career had begun in the Navy Special Projects Office, the same unit that had launched Richard Gillespie and his North Star scientists. Alleyne knew Gillespie and respected him. He also knew most of the men who now made up the North Star Crusade. During his cab ride from the Pentagon he had thought of calling one of them for help in analyzing the fragments. But, realizing that new security clearance might take weeks, he dropped the idea.

Alleyne boarded the twin-jet Eastern plane and made the quick hop to Philadelphia. He went immediately to a small brick building—L-39—in the Navy Yard's dock area. Ordinarily it was used to store lathes, but now it was the deposit point for crates of missile fragments. As Alleyne arrived, he saw that one crate had preceded him. It was marked FORT JACKSON IMPACT. A second arrived a few minutes later bearing the label BOSTON IMPACT.

The captain looked around. Building L-39 was set amid the obsolete remains of America's reserve fleet. Ancient destroyers were bunched at a nearby mooring, and off in the distance were the battleships *Iowa* and *Wisconsin,* two names on Isaac Anderson's scrap list.

Alleyne set a meeting of his staff for 10 A.M. the next morning, when analysis would begin. Until that hour the fragments would stay sealed. No man would see the tiny imprint on miniaturized parts: UNITED STATES NAVY.

18

Haven landed at Andrews Air Force Base at 8:36 A.M.

Anderson slipped by waiting Congressmen, even by Doris Moffitt, who lost him in a crowd. He wanted to get home to Julia. He had some time to make up and a Presidential offer to discuss.

When he arrived home, however, he was disappointed to learn that Julia was still in the secret shelter for CRITIC relatives in Maryland. Although there had been no attack, Pentagon "realism" rules required medical examinations and debriefings before the relatives could go home. These things were still under way.

So Anderson went upstairs to rest and continued pondering his possible future as Secretary of State. He set his alarm and dozed off. In a few hours he would be due at welcoming ceremonies for the Shah.

As Anderson slept, Ian Alleyne briefed intelligence officers outside building L-39, giving them details of the radiation danger, telling them what to look for in the fragments. He was particularly interested, he said, in any evidence that the Soviets were using new metals in their warheads.

After the briefing Alleyne and his eight men entered L-39 dressed in radiation-resistant clothing. They had microscopes and cutting tools, but detailed examination was still hours away. First there was the indexing, cataloguing, and weighing of fragments. It was 10:41 A.M. Alleyne set the time for the first examination at 12:10.

* * *

Anderson awakened at 11, disappointed to find that Julia was still not home.

He dressed in his best blue uniform, with full decorations. He was itching to have Julia know about his new prospects, so he scribbled a note on a piece of her stationery:

> J.A.:
> Welcome home! You'll be interested to know that I might be getting a new business address. State Department. One of those Cabinet-type jobs you know, gray suits and European shoes. What do you think?
>
> I.A.

Anderson placed the note against a lamp on Julia's bed table, then left for the White House.

The time was 11:28.

Ceremony. As common in Washington as a coffee break in Dayton.

The Joint Chiefs, the staff of the Iranian Embassy, the press, invited guests, all waited patiently on the White House lawn. The temperature was in the fifties, and a soft, hazy sun shone down. The day was fitting.

At precisely noon a glistening helicopter appeared in the distance, beyond the Washington Monument. A protocol aide phoned inside the White House to signal its approach.

The President of the United States, without his wife, emerged from the West Wing and the United States Army Trumpets raised their instruments to their lips. "Ruffles and Flourishes" blared out, followed by "Hail to the Chief." The President stood at attention, but his mind wandered back to the terrible moments that had just faded into history.

The helicopter came closer, its whirring blades beginning to stir up the dust. Elegant ladies grabbed their hats or pressed their hair as the aircraft landed on the lawn and its engine stopped.

The Shah of Iran, gray-haired, smiling, stepped out and gingerly descended the small ramp. The army trumpets gave forth with a pompous welcome. The President walked along a spotless red carpet to greet the monarch with a firm handshake, then both men turned and walked down the same carpet, receiving the applause of the guests. They mounted a reviewing stand trimmed in red, white, and blue crepe and covered with still more red carpet.

A military band played the national anthem of Iran, followed by the "Star-Spangled Banner." Cannon in the distance boomed their twenty-one-gun salute, smoke from their barrels partially obscuring the Jefferson Memorial. Following the anthems both leaders stepped down and inspected platoons representing the American armed forces. Then they passed an honor guard of fifty servicemen, each carrying the flag of an American state.

As the President and Shah reviewed the troops, Captain Alleyne placed fragments on an examining table in building L-39. They were pulverized and, to the casual observer, useless. But to Alleyne they possessed a wealth of technical data. He placed one fragment under a Leitz microscope and began focusing.

The time was 12:08.

The Shah and the President remounted the reviewing stand. Isaac Anderson watched closely, knowing *he* might soon be the pivotal figure in these diplomatic visits. He wondered, as he observed the polished, sophisticated civilians, whether he had the poise for the job.

The President stepped forward to speak.

"Your Majesty, you are so welcome here."

Vigorous applause.

"Relations between our two nations are warm, cordial, and exist in an atmosphere of mutual respect. . . ."

More applause.

"Americans have come to know you as a wise and forceful leader. . . ."

Applause, especially from the Iranian diplomats.

The time was 12:10.

Ian Alleyne brought his microscope into sharp focus, made a note about the first fragment, and placed a second under the lens. A puzzled expression came across his face. He peered closely, and puzzlement turned to concern. He removed the fragment and inserted another. Again he focused.

"Stan!"

The sharp call was to a navy commander, an expert in nuclear warheads.

"Stan, come here, will you!"

Bespectacled, more scholarly-looking than a navy officer should be, Stanley Kearn walked over.

"Take a look," Alleyne said.

Kearn peered into the microscope. Suddenly the muscles in his face became tight, intense. He stood up and turned to Captain Alleyne, a touch of fright in his eyes.

"My God."

Alleyne slipped quickly out of L-39 and dashed to a nearby office. He commandeered a phone and ordered the place cleared so he would not be overheard. Then he dialed the Pentagon number for the chief of naval operations.

The President concluded:

"You, Your Majesty, are making a major contribution to the stability of your region. The great Persian culture is emerging once more. . . ."

Suddenly a navy ensign burst out of the White House and slipped by the crowd, carrying a note. He approached Anderson from behind and tapped him on the arm. Surprised, Anderson looked back as the ensign whispered in his ear.

Anderson braced, and his face reddened. He grabbed

the note from the ensign's hand, reading rapidly. As the President finished and the Shah moved forward to speak, Anderson rushed to the rear of the reviewing stand. The Secret Service was appalled, as were the diplomats. This was unheard of.

"Mr. President," the Shah began, "how pleased I am to be in this great country. . . ."

As the applause started, Anderson gestured toward the President, who saw that he was disturbed and stepped down a step. The Shah, his back to the President, was oblivious.

"I have always admired the American people, their greatness, their strength. . . ."

The President leaned over a rail.

"Andy, what's up?"

"Sir," Anderson whispered, "the missiles that hit the East Coast yesterday. . . ."

"Yes?"

"Sir, they were American."

The President was silent. He stood staring at Anderson, the admiral's words slashing across him like the knife of a crazed assassin. The Shah's speech became a blur.

"Yes, Mr. President, our two nations can move forward with a common purpose. . . ."

The President glanced around at the crowd. He knew that he could not show emotion, anger, frustration without tipping the world to a new crisis. "Andy," he said, with armor in his voice, "do what you have to."

Anderson slipped away, trying to look unconcerned, while the President took his place near the Shah.

"Both my country and yours, Mr. President, share the great dangers and opportunities. . . ."

Anderson rushed to the Situation Room in the White House basement, grabbed an office, and sealed it off. There was an immediate problem. The missiles were American, but was the sub? Anderson knew that one other nation—Great Britain—used Polaris missiles made in America. Conceivably some parts could have been shipped with U.S. Navy markings.

Anderson called London and in moments was speaking

with Admiral Sir Anthony Redman, Chief of the Naval Staff, First Sea Lord, and an old friend. Anderson did not give Redman the full facts, fearing a leak in London and resulting panic. He simply said there had been some confusion in submarine contacts. Could Redman confirm the locations of Britain's missile subs?

Anderson knew there were four—*Renown, Repulse, Resolution, Revenge*—each armed with sixteen Polaris missiles.

Redman thought the request curious. But, as befit the close relations between the American and royal navies, he was totally cooperative and came up with the answer in three minutes. *Resolution* and *Repulse* were in port. *Renown* was in the Mediterranean, in sonar contact with the carrier *Ark Royal*. *Revenge* was just leaving the Channel. She had surfaced the day before to practice reconnaissance maneuvers.

Now Anderson was sure. The submarine was American.

He summoned CRITIC. As each member was notified, he was read an Anderson memo giving the grim details. Anderson also sent an urgent message to Moscow:

MR. PREMIER:

THE UNITED STATES URGENTLY INFORMS YOU THAT ANALYSIS OF FRAGMENTS REVEALS THE MISSILES THAT STRUCK US YESTERDAY WERE POLARIS A-3 WEAPONS OF AMERICAN MANUFACTURE.

THE UNITED STATES SHARES YOUR DISMAY AND SHOCK AT THESE FINDINGS. WE ASSURE YOU THAT A RELENTLESS SEARCH FOR THE RENEGADE SUBMARINE IS UNDER WAY. IT WILL CONTINUE UNTIL THE VESSEL IS DESTROYED.

REGRETTABLY, ANALYSIS ALSO SHOWS THAT MISSILE WARHEAD NUMBERS, WHICH WOULD IDENTIFY THE SUBMARINE, HAVE BEEN OBLITERATED. IDENTIFICATION WILL HAVE TO BE MADE BY OTHER, UNFORTUNATELY SLOWER METHODS.

THE UNITED STATES WILL KEEP YOU INFORMED OF ALL DEVELOPMENTS.

Members of CRITIC rushed to the Cabinet Room still dressed formally for the Shah's arrival. Faces showed bewilderment, fright, anger. So severe was the shock that only half the members remembered to rise as the President entered. He didn't notice, but, rather, whipped off his jacket and tossed it to a chair. It fell to the floor, a Presidential pen popping out and rolling to a corner. No one picked it up.

The President slammed down in his seat. He said no hellos.

"I don't want cryin'," he began, the strain torturing his voice. "I don't want any finger pointin'. This is too serious." He turned to Anderson. "Andy, let's roll."

Eyes shot toward Anderson. Despite the President's words, he felt a sense of guilt, just as Gorshkov had before. *His* ship. *His* men. The nation betrayed by *his* navy.

"Mr. President," he said, "we're vulnerable again. The renegades have eight missiles left, and we must assume they'll correct those warheads. They may try for Washington."

There were uneasy movements as men contemplated their own deaths.

The phone behind Bixby rang.

"It's Gorshkov. For Admiral Anderson."

The room tensed for the Soviet reaction. Anderson felt awkward, ashamed to speak to the man whose ship he had wrongly sunk. Slowly he reached for his phone as the room speakers came on with a low hiss.

"Admiral Anderson."

For a few moments, nothing. Then, from a dimly lit study in his Moscow apartment, Gorshkov spoke.

"Anderson, you people are idiots!"

The President bridled, but Anderson raised his hand to calm him.

"We understand how you feel," he told Gorshkov.

"You understand," Gorshkov replied mockingly. "Your words are so soothing, Anderson, like your advertisements for Cadillacs. Do you understand about the *Dostoyny*? Do you understand about three-forty-three? Are these mere toys to be played with by your incompetent lackeys?"

"Admiral Gorshkov," Anderson replied calmly, "I share your grief."

"Tell me," Gorshkov asked, "have your geniuses learned why an American ship would attack the United States?"

"No."

"This gangster might strike the Soviet Union!"

Gorshkov had a devastating point. Anderson knew that a strike against Russia would subject Premier Zorin to enormous pressure to retaliate. The source of the strike would be irrelevant.

"We'll do all in our power to prevent that," Anderson said. "We may need your help."

Gorshkov gazed at a picture of a Soviet cruiser as he weighed Anderson's remark. His face showed anger, but it was tempered with fatigue. "Assistance will be rendered," he said coldly, "in line with the interests of the Soviet people. But let me warn you, Anderson, that I must consider whether this new claim of yours is a lie. You might see a chance to attack us by pretending your ship is loose."

"I assure you," Anderson replied, "that is not the case."

"I wouldn't expect you to admit it, but ponder the consequences."

Gorshkov slammed down the phone.

"SOB," the President muttered.

"He's in a tough spot," Anderson said. "He's had a lot of explaining to do on the three-forty-three, and this makes him look like a fool. And he's serious about suspecting an American stunt. He's *got* to suspect it."

"Mr. President," Somerville said, "we must protect the government. Shall I arrange for our alternate headquarters?"

"Yes."

"That's unwise!" Anderson declared.

The room was astounded.

"Consider the situation," Anderson continued. "We've just returned, and the Shah is visiting. If we clear out, we send a shock wave through the nation . . . through the *world*. There'd be instant panic."

The President leaned back slowly. Anderson's argument was worth considering.

"Something else," the admiral went on. "If you make the government invulnerable to attack, you increase Soviet suspicions. They may get jumpy and try something."

A touch of panic crossed Somerville's eyes.

"Admiral Anderson, are you suggesting that the highest officials of the land remain in a *target* zone?"

Every eye in the room riveted on Anderson. He ignored the stares and looked directly at the President.

"That is my recommendation."

Dead silence as minds turned automatically to the White House shelter. But these men knew modern weapons. They knew that many hydrogen-tipped missiles were accurate to within 500 yards, the newest to within ten *feet*. The shelter was useless.

"Admiral Anderson," Somerville asked, "if the sub attacks us, how much warning do we have?"

"What you're really asking," Anderson replied, "is whether we could get away."

"I'm concerned about the President."

"Depends on where the sub is. We've lost more than a day. Our subs can travel close to a thousand miles in that time. If this ship headed toward our coast, warning time would be almost zero."

"If it was farther away?" the President asked.

"We'd have a chance."

The President smirked. "It's goddamned Russian roulette."

"Yes, sir."

The President paused, weighing his strategy. He gazed up at the Woodrow Wilson portrait, then at a few members of CRITIC. He knew that his decision could be a death sentence for himself and his closest aides.

"The admiral makes sense," he said tersely. "But only those *essential* to the crisis should stay. Of course, that means me, Admiral Anderson. . . ." He looked searchingly around the Cabinet Room. "General Benson, General Hartline, this is naval. You will go to an underground headquarters and stay in contact. Mr. Sonderling, you will return to the UN. General Combs—"

"I volunteer to stay," Combs said.

"Fine. Harley. . . ." Attention turned to Somerville.

"I'm at your discretion," he said. But he had failed to volunteer, and there was a weak, pathetic look in his eyes, as if he were pleading to be sent to a safe place.

"I need you here."

Somerville said nothing.

"Fred. . . ."

Bixby shrugged. "I'll stick around," he said grumpily. "Always wanted to see an H-bomb up close."

The President smiled ironically. "Fred, order the helicopters to stand by. And make sure the CRITIC families are kept in their shelter. Mac, tell the world it's routine—somehow. By the way, I'm asking you to stay, too."

"Yes, sir."

"Those of you who are going," the President said, "go now. If anyone asks, you're inspecting facilities."

Those assigned to leave slipped quietly out of the room. As they left, the room began to feel empty, eerie, the remaining officials experiencing a sense of unbearable isolation.

But the issue was still a runaway sub.

"All right, Admiral," the President said, "what is our approach?"

"Regrettably," Anderson answered, "the pulverizing of the warhead numbers puts us at zero. We must identify the sub the same way the Russians did the three-forty-three—by having our Polaris ships break radio silence and give us their locations."

"The Russians'll pinpoint them!" Somerville said.

"As we did with theirs."

"Yes," Somerville protested, "but isn't there a chance they're behind this? Couldn't they have *captured* one of our subs . . . like with the *Pueblo*?"

Anderson saw the sudden tensing of the President's

face. The name *Pueblo* sent a nervous chill up the man's spine.

"The technology is much more difficult," Anderson replied, "and no sub has radioed for help. I consider a capture extremely remote."

"But *possible*," Somerville insisted.

"Mr. Secretary, the realm of possibility can include almost anything." Anderson turned to the President. "Sir, I regard Soviet action as so unlikely that it should not occupy us. I request permission to contact our subs."

"I don't see what else we can do," the President said.

Anderson reached for the phone.

Gorshkov and Zorin sped through the chilly Moscow streets, heading for a secret military base outside the city. From there they would fly to their war headquarters.

The streets, dampened by a brief shower, were deserted except for an occasional stroller or periodic drunk. Zorin looked away disgustedly whenever he saw one of the drunks. They reminded him of the severe alcohol problem that plagued the Soviet Union—a sign that the Leninist dream was far from complete.

Gorshkov's ear was sealed to a phone. He knew his conversation would be jumbled by a code box and made unintelligible to foreign intercepts. He listened, nodded a few times to himself, then hung up.

"The Americans are contacting their submarines," he said.

"Then they must be telling the truth," Zorin replied.

"Possibly," Gorshkov answered. "But there's something else. Their leaders are remaining at the White House."

"So?"

"Why would they stay if a submarine was really on the loose, a submarine that could destroy Washington?"

Zorin turned somberly to Gorshkov.

"You're suggesting, Gorshkov, that there is *no* submarine loose, that they remain because they know they're safe?"

Gorshkov shrugged. His technique was simply to inject the thought.

"But," Zorin said, "if that is so, then the Americans might be planning some action against us, and the President would have to consider our counteraction. He would still *prepare* to leave Washington."

A slight smile came to Gorshkov's lips.

"Premier," he said, "I was just informed that helicopters are standing by on the White House lawn."

Gorshkov's comments revealed a flaw in Anderson's thinking. Anderson had completely misjudged the Russian reaction to keeping the government in Washington.

Zorin was glum. He looked out at apartment buildings and darkened stores, as forlorn now as when he had left Moscow earlier in the crisis.

"I was sure it was over," he said quietly. "This is slow torture."

"We must be prepared," Gorshkov insisted, "so I am reestablishing our alert. I am also sending our northern antisubmarine forces into the Atlantic. If this is an American scheme, we will be ready. If there *is* a renegade, I would love to avenge the three-forty-three."

"Go play with your toys," Zorin mumbled coldly.

"There is honor in the Soviet Navy," Gorshkov said.

Richard Gillespie listened as the Pentagon contacted the Polaris fleet. Now he knew the Americans realized that the renegade was theirs. He was sure they would soon find out it was the "sunken" *John Hay*.

Gillespie ran the ship down to 1,000 feet and cut all engines. The *Hay* became a silent dot in the Atlantic, an overwhelming challenge for even the most modern detectors.

North Star scientists reported that work on the warheads was moving faster than expected. The first might be ready in forty-eight hours.

As Anderson waited for the Pentagon to contact the Polaris subs, his mind was wrenched by the illogic of the situation. An American submarine had apparently sunk a Soviet destroyer, then the *John Hay,* and then had launched a missile attack on its own country. It seemed totally bizarre. And yet the very effectiveness of these actions and the evasiveness of the renegade convinced him that an incisive mind and a careful strategy were at work.

Anderson understood his disadvantage. His opponent was an American submariner who undoubtedly knew every weapon, every search device, every tactic that his navy was ready to throw at him. He could not be defeated, Anderson realized, by the book. The crisis called for the same gifts of reasoning and imagination that Isaac Anderson had displayed as a young officer a generation before.

19

Commander James Hughes Leonard had never been asked to reveal his position in six years as a Polaris submarine captain, so the request from Washington came as a jolt. He assumed something was wrong. He wondered whether a review had turned up some defect in his ship, the USS *Will Rogers,* or whether some tragedy required the evacuation of one of his men.

Leonard was thirty-nine, a 1957 graduate of Brown University, and a product of navy ROTC. He had hopes of becoming an admiral in a service that traditionally reserved the top spots for Annapolis men. Leonard was medium-sized, a reciter of such popular poetry as "The Face on the Barroom Floor." He was married, the father of six.

The *Will Rogers* was the last submarine of the Polaris program. She had been built by General Dynamics in Groton and christened in 1965 by Mrs. Hubert Humphrey.

Leonard's first instinct when the call from Washington came was to check the radio signal. He feared a Soviet ruse, but his checks showed the call was genuine. So he responded, realizing the Soviet Navy would pick up his transmission and that he would be tracked by Soviet ships for the rest of his mission.

Leonard could not know it, but the *Will Rogers* was now the subject of intense scrutiny by the commander, Submarine Force, Atlantic Fleet.

Cruising sixty miles from the *Rogers* was the Polaris submarine USS *George Washington Carver,* en route to her station in the Mediterranean. Commander George

Bigelow, *Carver*'s captain, was also upset by the order from Washington to reveal his position and insisted on confirming it four times.

Bigelow had commanded the *Carver* for two years. He had just received new orders, to take effect at the end of this cruise, giving him command of the USS *Memphis,* a new attack submarine. The *Memphis,* Bigelow knew, symbolized the growing significance of the undersea navy, for at one time only cruisers were thought important enough to name for cities.

Bigelow was one of the navy's progressives, a protégé of Admiral Elmo Zumwalt, chief of naval operations in the early seventies. Zumwalt had pushed for integration in the navy and for better treatment of minorities. Bigelow's own knowledge of human relations proved especially useful aboard the *Carver*, since he had a unique problem: Some crew members resented serving in a ship named for a black.

The *Carver* had been built at Newport News, Virginia, and christened by Marian Anderson. A sister ship of the *Will Rogers*, she, too, carried sixteen Polaris missiles.

Bigelow responded to the navy's call to reveal his position. Like the *Rogers,* the *Carver* was now under careful scrutiny at Norfolk.

Anderson listened to a report from the Pentagon, then put down his phone.

"Mr. President," he announced, "we have now heard from all our Polaris subs, and their routes have been analyzed."

The President leaned forward somberly.

"Which one?"

Anderson grimaced, then shook his head in frustration.

"There are *two* possibilities, the *Will Rogers* and the *George Washington Carver.*"

The President knew the implications of Anderson's words. No one could be sure which sub was the renegade, which the innocent. The choice was desperate: Find out . . . or destroy them both.

The President sighed heavily. "Make sure the Russians know."

"The Pentagon has put it on the Hot Line," Anderson said.

Suddenly the CIS came on:

> SATELLITE SURVEILLANCE SHOWS HEAVY MOVEMENT OF SOVIET NAVAL UNITS TOWARD THE ATLANTIC. GENERAL ALERT UNDER WAY THROUGHOUT SOVIET FLEET.
> STAND BY.

The room was still, eyes welded to the screen as CRITIC waited for the second message.

> US EMBASSY MOSCOW—DISSIDENT SOURCE INSIDE SOV GOVERNMENT REPORTS ZORIN AND GORSHKOV PROCEEDING BY CAR TO UNKNOWN DESTINATION OUTSIDE CAPITAL.
> END TRANSMISSION.

"That's not good," Somerville said. The silver pen came out of his pocket, and his eyes narrowed. He started jabbing the pen at the President.

"Sir, I think we've been too casual about possible Soviet action here."

"They're taking normal precautions," Anderson cut in. "We would do the same."

An agitated Somerville was about to answer when Bixby received another phone message.

"Admiral Gorshkov," he reported.

Anderson grabbed his receiver. The room speakers came on.

"Anderson here."

"Anderson," Gorshkov said, the Moscow streetlights flickering on his face, "we have your report."

"Yes, Admiral. . . ."

"You will naturally sink both ships."

Anger swept the Cabinet Room. Satisfying the Russians

was critical, but Gorshkov's absolute demand was so abrupt and brutal.

"Admiral Gorshkov," Anderson replied quietly, "we intend to find out which ship is guilty."

"That is ridiculous sentiment! Peoples on two continents are in danger!"

"I have a plan," Anderson pressed on, "that will allow quick identification. The Pentagon has already sent attack planes from the *Forrestal* to the areas where the two subs are cruising. When the planes are overhead, I will order the ships to surface. Then I will order each captain to fire *nine* missiles, set to self-destruct at twelve hundred feet. The innocent sub, having all her sixteen missiles aboard, will be able to fire the nine. The guilty ship, having already fired eight, will have only eight left. That will establish guilt, and we will attack."

"You thought of no such humane plan for the three-forty-three," Gorshkov said.

"There was no dispute over guilt," Anderson replied.

"What if your renegade refuses the order to surface?"

"We know his location. He's a dead duck."

"What if he realizes he's trapped and fires his eight missiles at a live target instead of destroying them?"

"There'd be no effect. If he had already corrected his warheads, he would have attacked earlier. We can assume his warheads are still unarmed."

"Plan rejected," Gorshkov announced.

"Why?"

"I don't have to answer your questions. Look, Anderson, stop quibbling. What's a couple of hundred lives? You will sink both of them."

There was a click as Gorshkov hung up.

The President was furious. "Andy," he said, "we're not butchers. Your plan is a good one, and it doesn't kill a second of time. You go ahead. We'll handle the Russians."

For the first time since the message from Captain Alleyne arrived, Anderson smiled.

"Yes, sir."

The CIS came on. The screen was split between two

flights of American warplanes. J. R. Haber was again in command as the planes roared toward the *Rogers* and the *Carver.*

"Mr. President," Anderson said, "I have another thought. I couldn't discuss this with Gorshkov because of his attitude."

"Shoot."

"The amphibious assault ship *Tarawa* is with the *Forrestal* and has marines aboard. We can fly the troops to the area of the subs. We would establish guilt by the method I've described, then, *if* the option is open, the marines could effect a capture. This conspiracy could be widespread, and we would gain valuable information."

Combs looked skeptical. "Admiral, I doubt if a renegade would just sit there and be taken. She'll probably go way down."

"I agree," Anderson said. "But we should be ready."

"I'm never against readiness," the President said. "Have the marines go."

Anderson transmitted the order to the *Tarawa,* a new ship that symbolized a new concept. She looked like a World War II aircraft carrier—a large straight flight deck with an island jutting up from its starboard side. But she carried only helicopters. The deck could handle nine at a time. In addition, *Tarawa* had a large well deck below that could be flooded to allow landing craft to ,pass out through an opening in her stern. Helicopters from above, landing craft from below. She was the total assault ship.

Now eighty combat-ready marines, baffled by their sudden call, assembled on *Tarawa*'s flight deck and boarded four Boeing UH-46 Sea Knight helicopters. Some of the men were issued pistols rather than rifles, adding to their sense of wonder. Anderson had thought pistols more useful in seizing a ship. The helicopters—lumbering, awkward, ungraceful—lifted off and headed out over the ocean, immediately passing a French tanker. The tankermen waved, oblivious to the drama going on around them.

As Anderson watched the operation on the CIS screen,

e ordered a special phone connection and got on the
ine.

"This is the chief of naval operations."

His voice boomed in the Cabinet Room and was car-
ied to the earphones of jet crewmen and the cold, metal-
ic cabins of the marine helicopters.

"I am speaking to you from the White House. We are
confronted with a serious problem, which you have been
sent to solve."

In the planes, in the helicopters, quizzical faces turned
grim. Anderson's words had the tone of war.

"There are two operations under way, each directed
against an American submarine. One of these ships might
have to be sunk."

Incredulous men looked at one another aboard the flying craft. Anderson's announcement was beyond compre-
hension to American fighting men. Some of the air crews
had flown against the 343 and were mystified by this
latest turn.

"You have no need to know the whys of your mission.
If ordered, you will attack the American submarine."

Anderson outlined his plans precisely as he had done
for the President. Then he and CRITIC waited for the
planes and the much slower helicopters to reach their targets.

Gorshkov and Zorin arrived at the small base outside
Moscow, where they boarded helicopters and made the
eight-minute trip to their underground headquarters. They
went immediately to the command center, 300 feet below
hard rock.

The center was the size of a school auditorium and
consisted of fifteen horseshoe-shaped tables extending
back in rungs. The rungs faced a theater-sized intelligence
screen. A constantly moving "stock ticker" ran under the
screen, reporting every movement of American forces.
Zorin, Gorshkov, and the rest of the high command sat in
the first rung, the rungs behind being occupied by other
defense officials in descending order of importance.

241

The intelligence screen now split into four frames, each depicting a different scene. Gorshkov got on the phone to Anderson.

"What are these helicopters?" he asked.

"Marines," Anderson replied.

"You don't need marines."

"Admiral Gorshkov, let *us* handle this."

"Yesterday we let *you* destroy our three-forty-three."

"You had no forces in the area."

That was the statement Gorshkov was waiting for. He looked smug, suddenly self-satisfied.

"Anderson," he said, "I have been informed that our submarine two-eighteen is tracking your *George Washington Carver*. I am ordering two-eighteen to attack."

"You can't!"

"The cause of mankind, Anderson. . . ."

"You haven't established guilt."

"Anderson, your planes haven't arrived. The criminal might correct his warheads and fire in the next few seconds!"

Gorshkov was right. Millions could die because of Anderson's attempt to determine guilt. If the Russians were in a position to attack, logic insisted that they sink the *Carver* on the chance that she might be the renegade.

The American planes were still eight minutes away.

"I now give the attack order," Gorshkov said.

Men of CRITIC sat paralyzed. There was nothing they could do. There was nothing they *dared* do. Outside, through the windows facing the Rose Garden, Anderson saw workmen rolling up the red carpet from the Shah's reception, a pathetic counterpoint to the reality of the Cabinet Room.

Suddenly Anderson decided to chance a desperate way out.

"Admiral Gorshkov, I am ordering the *Carver* to fire nine missiles and destroy them twelve hundred feet above the sea."

"We rejected that!" Gorshkov shouted. Eyes in the command center shot toward him in surprise.

"Admiral Gorshkov," Anderson replied, his volume

watching Gorshkov's, "look at your map! *Carver* is out of missile range of your country. *You* are not in danger."

Zorin turned to Gorshkov, suddenly placing his hand on the admiral's arm.

"He makes a point."

"You're letting him twist you again!" Gorshkov snapped.

"Let *them* handle this!" Zorin ordered. "If we sink their ship over their objection, there might be repercusions."

"If we let them control us," Gorshkov shot back, "*then* there will be repercussions!"

"Gorshkov!" Zorin roared. Conversations in the center ceased. Soviet eyes, alert to subtle shifts in power, riveted on the two men at the front.

Anderson didn't wait. He got on the phone to the Pentagon and instructed the National Military Command Center to send surfacing and firing orders to the *Carver*. The sub was told that the firings were part of a surprise readiness test and that warheads were to be unarmed.

Captain Bigelow received the order and instantly prepared to obey. He started the same countdown procedures that Richard Gillespie had employed the day before.

Admiral Gorshkov—tense, bitter—watched the spot of ocean above *Carver* on his screen. He quickly convinced himself that the sub was taking too long and got on the phone to Anderson.

"What is the delay?"

"We've ordered *Carver* to the surface for the launch," Anderson replied.

"It is a stall."

"Admiral Gorshkov, be reasonable!"

"How long will it take?"

"Once their first missile is off, they'll go at a rate of one a minute."

Carver surfaced. Radar reported a freighter nearby, but Anderson ordered *Carver* to ignore it.

Bigelow's countdown neared its end. He checked his control panel. Signals showed everything normal.

The countdown ended.

Firing order.

The first missile left its tube.

Crewmen on the nearby freighter were horrified to see the flaming rocket vault upward. Some panicked, running for cover behind deck equipment. Others watched in rapt fascination. But fascination turned to fright as the missile blew up 1,200 feet over the ocean, fragments coming down only 300 yards from the peaceful ship.

The second missile. The third, the fourth. Planes from the *Forrestal* were now overhead.

Not a word was uttered in the Cabinet Room or in the Russian command center.

The air bursts looked like a daytime fireworks display, perhaps more spectacular as burning fuel fell to the sea and kept burning on the surface.

Fifth missile. Sixth. Seventh. Eighth. Then the ultimate test.

"Fire nine!" Anderson ordered.

They waited. Inside Washington. Outside Moscow. Thirty seconds, forty, fifty. One minute.

Launch.

The ninth Polaris tore into the sky—straight, perfect—an acquittal for *Carver*.

But a death sentence for the *Will Rogers*.

Gorshkov got on the phone.

"You have your evidence, Anderson. The Soviet Union demands appropriate action!"

"We're on our way," Anderson replied.

To demonstrate his resolve to the Soviets, Anderson ordered the aircraft headed for the *Carver* diverted to the *Rogers*. Now every available plane and helicopter sped toward a single target. They overflew merchant ships, providing a wartime thrill for passengers who thought they were seeing some great exercise.

"I still see helicopters," Gorshkov insisted. "Why?"

"Admiral Gorshkov," Anderson replied, "the helicopters are an added measure. If possible, we may attempt a capture."

"No!"

"Only if *possible,* Admiral. It's best for all of us."

"There is no sense!" Gorshkov shouted. "You must attack. Anderson, you have reneged. You cannot be trusted, and the Soviet government will draw conclusions!"

"Andy," the President said, "we're buggin' him. We *know* the *Rogers* is the black sheep here. I'd rather sink her than fool with the Russians."

Anderson pushed his hand toward the President, as if to say, "Give me a chance."

"Admiral Gorshkov," he said into his phone, "it would be useful to have prisoners."

"You didn't need them for the three-forty-three," Gorshkov replied. "You tell me now that Americans are more valuable than Russians?"

"Certainly not!"

"You don't convince me, Anderson."

"Then I'll go further. There are those here who believe your side has captured the *Will Rogers.* If we sink her, those beliefs will remain."

Gorshkov turned red, but his anger melted into thoughtfulness, as if Anderson had struck a responsive chord. Zorin also showed concern.

"Is there any danger in trying a capture?" the Premier asked.

"They could probably do it," Gorshkov replied. "It is their attitude that upsets me, their high-handedness. And we always give in."

Zorin pondered for a moment.

"They agreed to our conference site in Antarctica."

"An exception."

"But, Gorshkov, if they think we are responsible, it could affect their foreign policy for years."

Zorin looked around, realizing that others had overheard him. He worried about sounding too soft, too accommodating. Hard-liners were already questioning his loss of the 343.

"Let them try a capture," he quietly ordered Gorshkov. Then he added, in a much louder voice, "But if there is any hostile action by their submarine, they must sink it!"

Gorshkov resented the order, but he knew he couldn't

talk Zorin out of it. He passed on the Premier's comments to Anderson.

"We accept Premier Zorin's conditions," Anderson replied.

Gorshkov still wanted to show his annoyance at Anderson's tactics. He knew the locations of the American Polaris subs from their breaking of radio silence and saw by his charts that two of them were within sonar range of Soviet attack submarines. Gorshkov ordered his ships to close, to harass the Americans under the sea, to harass them relentlessly.

The CIS:

COMSUBLANT REPORTS PROBABLE SOV ATTACK SUB CROWDING USS JOHN MARSHALL APPROX 124 MILES WEST OF LISBON. MARSHALL FORCED INTO EVASIVE ACTION. COMSUBPAC REPORTS SIMILAR MOVE AGAINST USS THOMAS A. EDISON IN BERING SEA, APPROX 400 MILES WEST OF ATTU ISLAND. EDISON SCRAPPING PLANNED EXERCISE TO ALLOW FULL EVASION.

STAND BY.

US AIR GROUP APPROX THREE MINUTES FROM POSITION OF USS WILL ROGERS. MARINE CHOPPERS FOURTEEN MINUTES FROM SAME.

Colonel John Rawl Williams commanded the marine detachment aboard the *Tarawa*. Now he was in the lead helicopter, heading for the *Will Rogers*.

Williams was forty-six, a West Point graduate who had transferred to the corps. He was a marine's marine—devoted to "manliness," discipline, and the fabled marine belief that a small war is better than none at all. In Vietnam he had personally killed sixty-three "Cong" and unnumbered "gooks." Clean-cut, six feet five, 270 pounds, he would not have been Anderson's choice for a job so delicate as capturing a submarine, but Anderson didn't know him.

"Colonel Williams," Anderson called through his phone, "this is the chief of naval operations."

"Yo!" Williams replied. "Yes, sir."

"Colonel, there has been a change. Your objective is now limited to one submarine. You will, under a plan to be transmitted, capture it. Your opponent may try to scuttle his ship or otherwise resist. If capture is impossible, try to take prisoners, but do not shoot except in self-defense."

"Yes, sir." Williams' eyes lit up as he listened. This was far better than marching drills on the deck of the *Tarawa*.

Captain Leonard received the order to surface and, like Captain Bigelow, was told it was a surprise test. American planes, the Pentagon informed him, would be overhead.

Leonard immediately passed the order to his crew. The *Will Rogers* broke through the waves, her radar picking up the air armada of Vikings, Phantoms, Tomcats, and, behind them, marine helicopters. The marines were ready, but so were bombs, torpedoes, and rockets. One odd move by the *Rogers*, one misinterpretation of her orders, and Anderson would send her to the bottom.

Anderson got on the line to Leonard. A weird feeling passed through him. Was Leonard the head of the conspiracy? Or its victim?

"Captain Leonard?"

"Yes, sir."

"Captain, during this operation you will not open your missile hatches." Anderson was concerned that open hatches might disturb Gorshkov. "Is that clear, Captain?"

"It is clear, sir."

The voice was steady, Anderson noted.

The planes began lightning runs over the *Rogers* from bow to stern, seconds apart, 100 feet off the water. Hardly an instant passed without some plane directly over the ship. The sub was neutralized.

The plan worked. Watching his screen, even Gorshkov saw no cause for complaint.

The helicopters approached, inching their way toward the *Rogers*, churning up the sea below.

"Captain Leonard," Anderson announced, "you are about to be boarded by marines. They have a classified mission, and you will cooperate in every way."

"Aye, aye, sir."

Williams' chopper slid over the submarine's missile hatches, under the flickering shadows of streaking jets. It hovered a foot above the steel deck while Williams and twenty marines gingerly jumped down. Slowly Williams led his men toward the sail, the part of a submarine that juts up from the hull and contains periscopes and radars. They climbed the sail to the main hatch at its top.

"Captain Leonard," Anderson ordered, "have your people open the hatch."

The hatch swung open, and Williams, a transmitter strapped to his back, climbed down the main ladder.

"I am inside the ship," he said.

Anderson felt a sudden fear that the marines would be slaughtered as soon as they were all inside, but it faded when Williams was greeted cordially by Captain Leonard.

Now was the crunch. Anderson would formally establish that the *Rogers* was the hub of the conspiracy.

"Colonel Williams," he ordered, "you will take four men to the missile compartment and determine the status of each tube."

Anderson could hear the chatter as Williams chose his four men. He cut Gorshkov in on the line so he, too, could hear. The lack of resistance, the absolute cool of the *Rogers* crew, was amazing, suspicious.

Anderson waited and listened.

Footsteps. Marine boots, still wet from the walk along the hull, squeaking down the steel passageway. The clunking of bulkheads. Finally the footsteps slowing and coming to a halt. Anderson could hear the bulkhead to the missile compartment swing open.

"I am inside the compartment," Williams reported. He stepped to the first missile tube and examined it, then, one by one, inspected the remaining fifteen.

"I have completed the inspection," he announced.

248

"And what have you found?" Anderson asked.

"Sixteen Polaris A-three missiles in place and ready."

Chairs lurched back in the Cabinet Room. Pandemonium broke out at the Soviet command center.

"Anderson!" Gorshkov shouted.

Anderson didn't respond. The blood drained from his face, already lined with fatigue.

"Answer me!" Gorshkov demanded.

"Admiral Gorshkov," Anderson finally said, "I'm as shocked as you are."

"Ah!" Gorshkov snarled. "The shocked American! The man who rubs his chin and says your 'gee whiz!' "

"Admiral Gorshkov, stay calm."

"Calm? You planned this. You will claim you don't know which ship is loose. Then you will have a submarine attack us!"

"I will do nothing of the kind!"

Suddenly Bixby's phone rang. He picked it up and looked toward Anderson. "For you. Very urgent."

"Admiral Gorshkov, stand by," Anderson said. He grabbed a second phone.

"Anderson."

Every eye focused on him. He grimaced slightly as he listened, then picked up a pencil and flipped it down in frustration. Finally his face filled with resignation, acceptance.

"Thanks," he said quietly, and hung up. He picked up the Moscow line. "Admiral Gorshkov," he said, grim but firm, "I ask you to listen, to listen very carefully."

Gorshkov sensed the urgency. "I am here," he said.

Anderson turned to the President. He crossed his arms on the polished table, the thick gold stripes on his sleeves underlining his experience.

"Mr. President, that was Captain Ryan of the National Military Command Center. He had computed the routes of our Polaris submarines and identified the *Carver* and the *Rogers* as the two that could have launched those missiles."

"He screwed up," the President said.

249

Anderson raised his hand to prevent interruption. "He just gave me additional information."

The admiral paused. Men lurched forward in their chairs.

"There was a third submarine."

Looks of confusion.

"Understandably Captain Ryan didn't report it earlier because . . . because it didn't exist."

Now looks of anger, annoyance.

"But he followed our action against *Rogers* and *Carver* on his CIS. He reports that the only other submarine that could have launched the missiles . . . was the USS *John Hay.*"

Silence. CRITIC looked at Anderson as if he were crazy. "The *Hay*," said the President coldly, "is at the bottom."

Anderson let out a deep, heavy breath. "Sir," he replied quietly, "I'm afraid she isn't." He looked around the room, sensing the dismay, the unreality. "We *thought* she was gone. So did Ryan. That's why he ignored her when she appeared as a possibility. We had no reason to doubt the distress call and the bodies, but that evidence could have been provided by the *Hay* herself. With *Rogers* and *Carver* now eliminated, we must conclude that the *Hay* falsified her own sinking and fired her missiles. The mathematics of routes and speeds don't lie."

"Where does that leave us?" Somerville asked.

"At the mercy of the *John Hay,*" Anderson replied.

"And the Soviet Union!" Gorshkov announced, his voice booming through the Cabinet Room. "Your so-called explanation creates difficulties, Anderson. You give no proof!"

"I have none to give. But in the next few hours we will mount the largest antisubmarine effort in history. *That* will be our proof."

"I warn you, Admiral Anderson," Gorshkov went on, "the situation between our two nations . . . is very, very grave."

There was a click. Gorshkov was off the line.

A sense of doom hung over the Cabinet Room. The

President leaned forward with a look of determination and pressed a clenched fist onto the table before him.

"Admiral Anderson," he said, "find that goddamn submarine!"

20

"I am ordering a maximum antisubmarine effort," Anderson told CRITIC, "but we must face reality. We can't be sure of finding the *Hay* before she launches her missiles."

"Mr. President," Combs said, "we must evacuate our cities."

"We can't," Anderson replied. "It's the same as the President leaving Washington. The Russians could interpret it as proof that we're planning war."

"What about our people?" Somerville asked. "Don't you care?"

"Of *course* I care. The *Hay* can produce terrible casualties. But if we trigger a Soviet strike by evacuating, casualties might be twenty times as high."

"You're saying," the President responded, "that we must decide here and now to accept the casualties the *Hay* could produce."

"Mr. President," Anderson answered, "we have no choice. We must do *nothing* to disrupt the international order. Yes, sir, we may lose five million lives to save a hundred million."

The President slumped slowly in his chair. "I can't believe we're talking this way."

Anderson nodded sadly. His demeanor was strong, but his innards were sickened at the thought of nuclear genocide. "Mr. President," he said, "the worst thing is *not* to talk." He glanced toward Combs. "We should not accept traditional military answers."

"What if the *Russians* evacuate?" Combs asked pointedly.

"Then we could do the same," Anderson replied. "I'm just saying that we can't precede them. This is an *American* sub, and they have legitimate suspicions."

"Andy," the President asked, "what is your plan?"

"Sir," Anderson answered, "I assume the *Hay* knows she's being hunted. She's probably gone to maximum depth, where detection is extremely rough. I'll have to take some radical action, and I'll need your authorization."

"Shoot."

"The search area is infested with submarines. That will slow us because every contact has to be identified. I'd like to surface all American submarines in the area where our computations show the *Hay* could be hiding."

"That's absurd!" Somerville exclaimed. "If war breaks out, those subs are finished."

"The Russians already know where our Polaris subs are," Anderson countered. "We broke radio silence."

"But they don't know where our attack subs are," Somerville snapped back, "and they're the ships that keep the sea lanes open."

Anderson went for his phone. "Get me Admiral Gorshkov."

"What are you doing?" the President asked.

"Trying to make a deal. It's not enough to have *our* submarines come up. The Russians have to surface theirs. If they agree, both fleets are neutralized and the Secretary's objection becomes moot."

"This is Gorshkov," came the voice from the Soviet command center.

"Anderson here. Admiral Gorshkov, I'm sure you see that a massive American effort has just begun."

Gorshkov glanced up at a television view from a Soviet trawler. It showed six destroyers in a line, heading out from Hampton Roads, Virginia. Each one carried AS-ROC, a nuclear-tipped rocket that dived underwater to seek out enemy submarines.

"Very impressive," Gorshkov said, "but I have seen maneuvers before."

"Admiral Gorshkov," Anderson went on, "you know

the difficulty of finding this renegade. Our task, and the cause of peace, would be served if both of us surfaced our submarines in the search area."

"What are you saying?" Gorshkov roared. "You *know* the Soviet Navy is built around submarines. You are asking me to paralyze our operations. Anderson, every word you speak makes me more suspicious."

Anderson paused long enough to see the looks of grim satisfaction on the faces of Somerville and Combs.

"I understand your apprehensions," he said, "but with the permission of the President, we might be willing to surface, say, ten of our submarines as a first step. We would ask you to match that. There would be mutual neutralization, stage by stage."

Eyes turned toward the President.

"Is it *absolutely* necessary?" he asked.

"Yes," Anderson replied.

The President gave an affirmative but unenthusiastic nod.

"The President approves," Anderson told Gorshkov. There was a lengthy pause on the line.

"Rejected!" Gorshkov said. "Ten is not enough. *All* your submarines will have to surface before we can even *consider* your request. We have an excellent idea how many submarines you have in the region, so cheating would be futile. This is a test of your goodwill, Anderson."

The line went dead.

"That kills that," Somerville said.

"Just a sec," Bixby broke in. "Seems to me—and I'm just an old backroom pol—that our Russian friend kinda left the door a mite open."

"Fred is right," Anderson said. "Gorshkov is just bargaining. Mr. President, I ask you to take still another serious risk for peace. I would like to bring twenty-five submarines to the surface. It would be a powerful demonstration, and we might be able to move the Russians."

"That's a hell of a risk!" Somerville insisted. "Mr. President. . . ."

The President waved for Somerville to stop. He looked

into Anderson's eyes, then down at the chestful of ribbons, then down farther to the gold stripes. Ultimately he, like most Americans, respected expertise, and Anderson was the only naval expert in the room.

"Do you think the Russians'll budge?" he asked.

"Mr. President," Anderson replied, "I can't even guess at that. I can only urge that we give them the maximum inducement."

All eyes turned to the President.

"Raise the twenty-five subs," he ordered.

Zorin and Gorshkov watched their intelligence screen as the USS *Theodore Roosevelt* cut through the waves and surfaced 800 miles east of Washington, D.C. Immediately an aide slipped a data sheet to Gorshkov. It told him that the *Roosevelt* was 380 feet long, was the third Polaris submarine built, and had been constructed at the Mare Island Naval Shipyard in California. It had been launched by Alice Roosevelt Longworth.

A few moments later a satellite camera zoomed in on a sudden turbulence in the ocean 320 miles north of the *Theodore Roosevelt*. The superstructure of the USS *Lafayette* appeared, the soaking metal glistening in the sunlight. Another data sheet: *Lafayette* was 425 feet long, a product of Electric Boat in Groton, and had been launched by Jacqueline Kennedy. She carried sixteen Polaris missiles.

Zorin was encouraged. The Americans were proving their goodwill. But Gorshkov was cautious, skeptical. Where were the attack subs?

Four minutes passed. Then, at a spot 1,230 miles east of Atlanta, Gorshkov's question was partially answered. USS *Sea Devil*, a 292-foot attack submarine, came to the surface, the number 664 on her hull clearly visible. But even the appearance of *Sea Devil* did not remove the suspicion from Gorshkov's gut.

Zorin noted the number of surfacing subs. "Eight, nine . . ." he mumbled as two came up simultaneously. "Gorshkov," he said, "we must believe the American story about the *John Hay*."

"Why?" Gorshkov asked.

"Because they'd never take a risk like this if it wasn't true. I know them."

"You only know your own prejudices, Premier."

Zorin turned sharply to his naval chief.

"I warn you of such comments!"

Again eyes rose in the command center. Zorin's authority was being tested. Geographically he was in a poor position compared with Gorshkov—in a military center, surrounded by officers.

Eyes turned toward the intelligence screen as another attack sub came up.

"When it came time," Zorin said, "the Americans revealed the location of their Polaris fleet. Why, Gorshkov? Why, if they were planning war?"

Gorshkov was silent. Another attack sub appeared.

"Gorshkov," Zorin ordered, "bring five submarines to the surface."

Gorshkov turned to Zorin, an expression of seething contempt on his face. "You can't be serious."

"You will do what I say!"

"Premier, you may be ordering the destruction of our Atlantic forces."

"Don't give me your theatricals, Gorshkov. I'm an old man. I've heard too much."

Gorshkov came to a rigid sitting position. He flipped a yellow switch on a console in front of him. In clipped, military style he passed on Zorin's order. But he did not look at the Premier. Instead he turned to the officers behind him, his expression of disgust signaling his complete break with Zorin's policies.

The CIS:

COMSUBLANT REPORTS ONE SOV ATTACK SUBMARINE SURFACING 918 STATUTE MILES EAST OF CAPE MAY, NEW JERSEY. . . .
    STAND BY.

CRITIC turned to the screen. Grim looks gave way to

anticipation, eagerness. A tense, hesitant smile came to Anderson's lips as he saw his plan begin to work.

> COMSUBLANT REPORTS SECOND SOV ATTACK SUB SURFACING 473 STATUTE MILES SOUTHEAST OF WIL-MINGTON, DELAWARE. . . .
> STAND BY.

A map of the Atlantic appeared on the screen showing the locations of the two Soviet ships. In the next five minutes the CIS reported three more surfacings. Anderson got on the line to Gorshkov.

"Admiral Gorshkov, may I congratulate you on your cooperation. Your gesture toward peace—"

"Save your words," Gorshov answered. "You go and sink your ship. If we detect it first, we shall attack. We don't need your permission."

He clicked off the line. For a few moments there was new apprehension in the Cabinet Room. Was true Soviet policy reflected in the five surfacings? Or in Gorshkov's arrogance? The first hint came in a message on the Hot Line, relayed by phone to Bixby:

> MR. PRESIDENT:
> IN VIEW OF YOUR SURFACING OPERATIONS IN THE ATLANTIC, THE SOVIET GOVERNMENT WILL COOPER-ATE IN ANY MANNER NECESSARY TO MEET THE RENEGADE'S CHALLENGE.
>
> ZORIN

Then the CIS:

> COMSUBLANT REPORTS FOUR MORE SOV SURFACINGS IN USS JOHN HAY SEARCH AREA.

The apprehension faded.

"Mr. President," Anderson said, "we need a further refinement. The *Hay* is picking up our surfacing orders. It is conceivable she could already have disguised herself as a sister ship by repainting the number and name on her hull, if only to gain a few hours. I'm going to start a check. Our people will contact each sub on the surface and ask a single question that can be answered only if the sub is giving its real name. For example, 'What is the birth date of your commanding officer?' We'll check the answer against navy files. The *Hay* couldn't fake that."

"Fine," the President said. Anderson's canniness appealed to him.

"Sir," Anderson went on, "I'll need your approval on several more points. First, I want to use nuclear weapons to sink the *Hay*."

The idea disturbed Bixby. "Admiral, you sure you want to put an A-bomb in the middle of the ocean?"

"In a crisis like this . . . yes. It's the surest means of knocking out a sub."

"You've got my okay," the President said.

"Further point," Anderson continued. "Any news leak about the *Hay* could provoke worldwide panic. I suggest the White House prepare cover stories to fit all contingencies. For example, merchant ships will sight some of those subs on the surface, and so will airline crews."

The President looked toward McNamara. "You do that."

"Now, Mr. President," Anderson said, "we've got to practice a little psychological warfare. I'd like to try to contact the *Hay* to harass the conspirators into giving up. If they hear my voice naming their ship as our target, they may decide that holding out is hopeless."

"I have no objection," the President said.

Anderson got on the phone to Captain Ryan, now coordinating the Pentagon's search efforts.

"Captain, I want you to switch on your recorder. I am about to make a statement to the *John Hay*. You will send it immediately and repeat it every three minutes unless there's a response. Of course, you will use secure channels to prevent other nations from picking up my voice."

Anderson waited for Ryan to switch on his equipment. He cleared his throat. There seemed a special solemnity to the moment as the United States government attempted for the first time to contact the conspirators aboard the *Hay:*

"This is the chief of naval operations speaking. I am addressing those in control of the USS *John Hay*.

"You know by now that your attempt to launch nuclear missiles against the United States has failed. You must also know that a massive search is under way for your ship, a search that will ultimately succeed.

"We offer you the opportunity to surrender rather than die. You need only contact Atlantic Fleet Headquarters at Norfolk. If you have a radio problem, come to the surface and fire flares. Our satellite cameras will detect you.

"I strongly urge you to weigh this offer carefully. Your destruction could come at any time."

Richard Gillespie heard Anderson's voice. There could be no further doubt that the *Hay* had been identified.

Gillespie despised Anderson. Anderson was the decadent American, the man afraid to fight. Yet Gillespie did not greet Anderson's message with the traditional jeers reserved for surrender calls. Instead a sudden terror sliced through him, a sense of entrapment. It had been easy to feel heroic in the hours after the missiles failed, when the destruction of the *Hay* was an abstraction. Now it was all too close. The hunters had become the hunted, their ship helpless, its missiles still unarmed, its engines silenced to evade sonar. Men who had set out to give their nation a rebirth were targets of the very countrymen they sought to serve.

But progress on the warheads was greater than had been expected. The original estimate of forty-eight hours to arm the first missile was reduced to eight, with one missile ready every four hours after that. Gillespie knew there might not be time to arm all eight missiles before the antisubmarine forces found him. But with four or five, he reasoned, his plan might still succeed. The men of the Crusade threw themselves into their work with the zeal of kamikaze pilots.

Captain Lansing knew his fate. He had felt the dive to 1,000 feet, the engines coming to a halt. Although still kept in his cabin, he easily deduced that the *Hay* was being hunted. If Gillespie retained command, he knew, death was only a matter of time, and that fact alone changed his thinking. Whereas another attempt to retake the *Hay* had seemed futile, now it was the only rational course. Failure could accelerate the certainty of death, but success might prevent it.

How, though, could it be done? Lansing was cut off from everyone, and each of his food trays was now searched before and after his meals. For him to organize a conspiracy was impossible. His hope was that others aboard the ship, understanding the situation, would take action.

His hope was partly justified, for a number of crewmen were considering new counterplots. They realized, of course, that isolated acts of sabotage or resistance would be useless. They would do nothing to dislodge Gillespie's grip, which might even result in a Crusade member's setting off his explosive charge and sending the *Hay* to the bottom. Their ideas, rather, centered on a new go-for-broke assault on the control room. But there was no plan, no organization—just a blunt realization that this was the only way to save their own lives.

The CRITIC meeting broke. The President stayed at the White House, determined to keep his scheduled conference with the Shah and give the appearance of normalcy. But a portable CIS was installed in a room adjoining the Oval Office to bring him close to any development.

Anderson sped to the National Military Command Center, from which he would direct the assault on the *Hay*. He quickly gave the operation a code name: Haystack.

Haystack's command post was an overheated converted classroom in the NMCC's Action Center. It was painted an uneven light brown. Anderson sat in the middle of a long table, facing a CIS screen and an electronic map of the Atlantic. The map showed a dot for every American antisubmarine unit and also showed the spot from which the dud missiles had been fired. Around the spot was a constantly expanding circle indicating how far the *Hay* could have traveled since the time of the launch.

Anderson knew there was a similar map in the Soviet command center, that the Soviet Navy was searching for the *Hay* with its most sophisticated equipment. He was sharply aware of Gorshkov's boast to sink the ship if the Russians detected her first. Now he felt a deep, competitive urge to beat his opponent, to have the United States Navy solve its own problem. He desperately wanted to avoid the humiliation imposed on the Russians when American planes sank the 343.

But Haystack was producing no results. Grimly negative reports flashed by on the CIS. They rang with the lingo of antisubmarine warfare:

HAYSTACK REPORTS NO VDS CONTACT.
STAND BY.

VDS stood for Variable Depth Sonar—sound domes lowered from ships and helicopters. They were positioned beneath the layers of water near the surface that often confused sound waves. They listened for the noises of submarines.

HAYSTACK REPORTS NO MAD CONTACT.
STAND BY.

MAD—Magnetic Anomaly Detector. Carried by planes, it reported disturbances in the earth's magnetic field, such as those caused by a submarine's steel hull.

HAYSTACK REPORTS NO SONOBUOY CONTACT.
STAND BY.

The sonobuoys—428-dollar expendable listening devices dropped into the sea by aircraft and helicopters.

SOSUS—Sound Surveillance Under the Sea—a network of microphones on buoys and on the ocean floor. They detected passing subs and flashed the information to Norfolk.

The CIS kept up its stream of bad news. Huge sonars listened in on the entire Atlantic from their stations off the coasts of Norway, the Shetlands, Iceland, and Greenland.

No results.

Massive sound makers that rang in the ocean like a bell were activated, and receivers then "read" the sound waves that came back.

No results.

Planes were sent out equipped with infrared devices that detected the minute changes in ocean temperature caused by submarines.

No results.

Undersea picket lines, connected by cable to land stations, listened in on coastal regions.

No results.

Anderson was not surprised. The inner ocean, with its ability to confound sonar and every other detection device, was a far better hiding place than even the outer reaches of space. The only answer was the one he was giving—sheer brute strength, a massive concentration of antisubmarine forces.

Anderson watched the clock. It was 2:20 P.M. What realistic chance, he wondered, did the world have of avoiding catastrophe?

Then at 2:46:

URGENT—HAYSTACK REPORTS CONTACT APPROX 630 STATUTE MILES NORTH NORTHEAST OF MISSILE LAUNCH POINT.
STAND BY.

Anderson braced in his chair, and the eyes of uniformed men snapped toward the screen. Again the room fell silent, waiting for the CIS to continue.

URGENT—HAYSTACK REPORTS CONTACT IDENTIFIED AS SUNKEN VESSEL.
END TRANSMISSION.

Anderson leaned back, slowly drew a cigar from his inside jacket pocket, and accepted a light from an officer behind him. He glanced up at the map. The circle expanded still more. He prepared for a long ordeal.

At 10:12 P.M. Washington time, Richard Gillespie could celebrate once more. North Star scientist Jack Rains informed him that the first missile warhead was armed and ready and that Crusade scientists were sure it would detonate. They had made tests on the *Hay*'s computers, actually running the warhead up to the point of explosion. Everything had functioned.

Four hours later the second missile was ready. Now a sense of anticipation began to build. The two live "birds" gave Crusade members a feeling that anything was possible, that their martyrdom was near. But there would be no champagne to celebrate the victories, nor would there be any sleep.

This was launch day.

21

It was 10 A.M. in Moscow. The Soviet command center was quiet. Gorshkov and Zorin had remained until 4 A.M., Moscow time, 8 P.M. the previous night in Washington, then had retired to an adjoining quarters building.

Now Admiral Gorshkov reentered the center, and officers quickly realized that he did not seem rested at all. He was wearing the same uniform as the night before—he apparently had not taken it off—his eyes were red, his whole demeanor less polished than usual. It was as if he had never slept. He walked over to another admiral and whispered something. The admiral seemed upset. Other senior officers came over. There was hushed, hurried talk. Junior men inched forward, trying to hear. A few picked up key words:

"Zorin . . . stroke. . . ."

The discussion among the senior men ended, and Gorshkov slid into his seat. He checked his watch, then checked it again. He was agitated, expectant. He kept looking back toward the rear door of the command center. A crackling, forbidding tension filled the room.

Twelve minutes later the rear door opened. Heads turned to identify the visitor. A silence fell over the rear rows of officers and spread downward toward Gorshkov. Typewriters stopped. Conversations ended in mid-sentence. Hands froze on pencils.

Gorshkov turned around and stiffened. His emotions clashed—subtle contentment mixed with fear. He looked directly at the man who stood just inside the doorframe. He knew him.

Everyone knew him.

Yuri Vladimirovich Andropov returned Gorshkov's stare. Tall, bespectacled, a former telegraph operator, he had been Soviet ambassador to Budapest during the Hungarian Revolution of 1956. Now he was the director, Komitet Gosudarstvennoy Bezopasnosti, the Committee for State Security—the KGB. America hater, hard-line propagandist, brutal grabber of power.

Andropov stepped forward, a bodyguard at his side. He walked slowly down a carpeted aisle to the top military commanders, who followed him hypnotically with apprehensive eyes. Unsmiling, he shook hands and exchanged brief, impersonal greetings. He reserved Gorshkov's hand for last, gripping it more strongly, more positively. A signal.

Then he sat in Zorin's chair.

22

It was 2:38 A.M. Anderson was exhausted. A bed had been set up for him near the Haystack command post, and he was planning to retire in the next few minutes. There had been no news from the fleet.

He started gathering papers to take to his room. Then, as he rose to leave, the CIS clicked on:

ADVISORY: URGENT TRANSMISSION UPCOMING.
STAND BY.

He sat down again. All eyes in the room turned to the screen.

URGENT: US EMBASSY MOSCOW. ZORIN OUT.

Anderson shoved his papers aside and grabbed the White House phone. The connection was instant. A voice in the Situation Room told him the President was sleeping, but was being awakened because of the news from Moscow.

The CIS:

URGENT: US EMBASSY MOSCOW. TASS REPORTS ZORIN REMOVED FOR MEDICAL REASONS. CONDITION UNKNOWN.
STAND BY.

Anderson wondered whether the official reason was false, whether Zorin had been replaced for his overly cordial relations with the United States. His suspicions were wrong. At that moment Zorin was near death.

The President came on the line, still half asleep, yawning and slurring his words. "Mornin', Andy. Helluva thing. What do you make of it?"

"I don't know, sir. There's been no Soviet military move." Anderson paused. "One second. . . ."

The CIS:

> URGENT: US EMBASSY MOSCOW. TASS REPORTS ZORIN REPLACED BY Y. V. ANDROPOV.

"Andropov!" Anderson announced over the line.

"Oh, Christ!" the President groaned.

"I guess," Anderson said, "Premier Zorin was too much to hope for."

A navy aide rushed in with a message from the Hot Line. Almost simultaneously a White House assistant handed the President the same note:

> MR. PRESIDENT:
> YOU UNDOUBTEDLY KNOW BY NOW, BOTH FROM OUR OFFICIAL ANNOUNCEMENTS AND YOUR SPY NETWORK, WHICH RELIES ON SO-CALLED DISSIDENTS, THAT I HAVE SUCCEEDED PREMIER ZORIN, WHO IS IN FAILING HEALTH. YOU ALSO KNOW THAT I AM A MAN OF PEACE AND FRIENDSHIP. HOWEVER, I ASSUME RESPONSIBILITY AT A TIME OF GREAT DIFFICULTY IN SOVIET-AMERICAN AFFAIRS. YOU HAVE MADE OUTRAGEOUS REQUESTS OF OUR NAVAL FORCES. REGRETTABLY, PREMIER ZORIN, IN WEAKENED CONDITION, AGREED.
> THE SOVIET GOVERNMENT TAKES AN EXTREMELY GRAVE VIEW OF THE ACTIVITIES UNDER WAY IN THE ATLANTIC. IT MUST TAKE STEPS TO PROTECT ITS FORCES AND CARRY OUT ITS COMMITMENTS. IN THIS CONNECTION, I DEMAND THAT YOU RESOLVE THE PROBLEM OF YOUR MISSING SUBMARINE AT ONCE, IF SUCH A PROBLEM ACTUALLY EXISTS. DO NOT UNDERESTIMATE OUR SUSPICIONS IN THIS MATTER.

I LOOK FORWARD TO LONG AND CORDIAL RELA-
TIONS WITH YOU.

ANDROPOV

"Long and cordial," the President mumbled.

Anderson knew that Andropov's dark perception of the United States, not the tactical situation in the Atlantic, would determine Soviet policy. "Mr. President," he said, "everything has changed."

The CIS:

> SATELLITE SURVEILLANCE SHOWS INTENSE SOV NA-
> VAL ACTIVITY IN ALL ATLANTIC, MEDITERRANEAN,
> BLACK SEA, AND NORTHERN COMMANDS.

Anderson relayed the report to the President.

"Andy," the Chief said, "you'd better get to the White House."

Anderson sped to the Executive Mansion in the predawn darkness. On the way, he received a call giving him a new CIS report:

> SATELLITE SURVEILLANCE SHOWS 40 BE-12 TYPE
> AIRCRAFT PREPARING FOR TAKEOFF AT BENGHAZI.

Anderson knew that the Be-12 was an amphibious flying boat with advanced antisubmarine equipment. It had four turboprop engines. Its presence in Morskaya Aviatsiya—the Soviet naval air arm—made Russia the only country besides Japan that used military flying boats. Anderson assumed the forty planes based near Benghazi, Libya, would fly into the Atlantic to protect the surfaced Soviet submarines. They would land in the ocean for refueling by destroyers.

Anderson arrived at the White House and rushed to the Oval Office, where members of CRITIC were assembling. The faces were tired, apprehensive. These officials, like most Americans, had been conditioned to fear changes in Soviet regimes, and the accession of the icy Andropov had only underlined that fear. They collapsed into soft chairs, waiting for the President's first words.

The portable CIS, which looked like an oversized television set, was operating. The words STAND BY flashed on the screen.

The President pulled out his rolling desk chair to sit with the group, then glanced out the window. He was reassured by the two helicopters on the lawn, ready to evacuate CRITIC in case of attack.

"Okay," he began, "we've got a problem in Moscow. . . ."

The CIS started clicking:

> HAYSTACK REPORTS SOVIET SUBS DIVING THROUGHOUT ATLANTIC SEARCH GRID.
>   STAND BY.

"Well," the President said, "that ends Soviet cooperation with our search for the *Hay*. Andy, what do you think?"

"Mr. President," Anderson replied, "we're back in position one. There's a distinct chance now of tracking a Soviet sub and thinking it's the *Hay*. In a situation like this we could destroy a Soviet ship."

"I am," the President said, "putting our forces on DefCon Two."

Everyone knew the meaning of the term. The levels of Defense Condition (military alert) ranged from one to five, with one being the most critical. It had never been reached. Two was as close as the nation could come without going to war.

The CIS:

> URGENT: HAYSTACK REPORTS US NAVY ORION PATROL BOMBER FIRED ON BY SOV DESTROYER IN SEARCH AREA.

"Those SOB's!" Somerville said. "Mr. President, some action is called for."

"Wait a minute!" Anderson broke in. "I know things look grim, but let's not forget our main objective—to find the *Hay*. We've absorbed harassment before, and we may have to absorb more. Andropov's an extreme man. He sees the Russian submarines on the surface as a humiliation, and he's trying to balance it by belligerence. We can't let him rattle us."

"I'll buy that . . . for now," the President said. "But, Andy, I want to show 'em we're on top of things. I want you to fly to the fleet and direct from there."

"Mr. President," Anderson replied, "the facilities are just as good in Washington."

"Andy . . . it's style."

Anderson felt a sudden sense of guilt. *He* would be leaving the target zone while the President remained behind. But he could not contest a direct order.

"Aye, aye, sir."

The CIS:

URGENT: HAYSTACK REPORTS WARNING TORPEDO FIRED BY SOV SUB AT USS SPRUANCE.

Anderson turned to the President. "Mr. President," he said, "stay calm."

The President was reassured by Anderson's steadiness. "Andy," he said, "you'd better get out to the fleet."

Gillespie heard the announcement of the change in Moscow at 5:20 A.M. Washington time. It was a tremendous lift. As a moderate, Zorin might have gone to the wall to preserve peace, but there would be no such problem with Andropov. Gillespie despised him for his Communist beliefs, yet blessed him for being the right man at the right time.

All was going well. The third missile had been armed an hour ahead of time. If that pace could be continued, Gillespie calculated, all eight missiles would be "go" before 9 P.M.

He walked to Lansing's cabin to tell him of Andropov,

of the progress on the missiles. Keeping Lansing informed remained a point of pride with him, an expression of respect for navy tradition. To Gillespie, Lansing was still "sir" and "Captain."

Lansing saw that Gillespie was buoyant and riding a new high. With three missiles the Crusade was already in a position to launch a nuclear strike. Lansing inwardly conceded that his own men, held down by the constant surveillance, could not execute a counterplot in time.

As Gillespie left to return to the missile compartment, Alan Lansing gave up all hope that the North Star Crusade would fail. Within hours, he was sure, nuclear warheads would explode in the United States.

23

The CRITIC meeting broke. Anderson strode down the halls of the White House, encountering some groggy, grouching reporters roused from bed by their home offices because of the convulsion in Russia. Among them was Doris Moffitt, who slipped alongside the admiral as he was leaving the mansion.

"What was *that* about?" she asked.

"Come on, Doris," Anderson replied with a half grin, "there's been a shake-up over there."

"I hear there's an alert."

"Routine precaution."

"This other flap—the Red destroyer. . . ."

"Over," Anderson answered. He was relieved. It was obvious that Moffit didn't know about the *Hay*. Somerville had not leaked it, he reasoned, because it reflected badly on the American military.

Anderson finessed his way through Moffitt's questions, then left the mansion for Andrews Air Force Base. To avoid the appearance of alarm, he used a staff car rather than a helicopter, instructing the driver to begin the trip at normal speed. From Andrews he was flown to the aircraft carrier *Saratoga,* 400 miles off the East Coast. She was a sister ship of the *Forrestal,* almost identical in design. Anderson thought it ironic that she should be his command ship for a nuclear crisis, for *Saratoga* had been named for the only carrier ever to be sunk by an atomic bomb. The old *Saratoga* was intentionally destroyed in 1946 to test the bomb's power against naval vessels.

Anderson was ushered to the admiral's cabin, which was equipped with plush furniture, a deep-pile blue carpet, and a CIS screen built into one wall. He was immediately given a handful of reports:

No progress on the *Hay*.

Soviet harassment of American ships continuing, but nothing critical.

A few press inquiries on naval activity at Norfolk, fielded without problem.

Only the first report worried Anderson. He opened his cabin door to watch as planes from the *Saratoga*, back from the search for the *Hay*, landed in the dawn mist. Then he walked back inside, frustrated, feeling more like a symbol at sea than a commander. He could give routine instructions, but little more. Three carriers, forty destroyers, fifty-two submarines, more than 200 planes, all probed the Atlantic for the renegade. Their crews knew what to do without Isaac Anderson telling them.

He waited and paced.

Then, at 7:10 A.M., his CIS suddenly snapped on:

URGENT: ATTACK SUBMARINE INDIANAPOLIS REPORTS
CONTACT 330 MILES SOUTHEAST USS SARATOGA.

Anderson bolted to his desk and grabbed a direct line to the Haystack command post. Captain Ryan rattled off the data: *Indianapolis,* cruising on the surface, had picked up a dim signal on her magnetic detectors. Pentagon experts thought it *might* be from a stilled submarine trying to hide in the depths. *Indianapolis* was going down to search.

Captain Donald S. White gave the order to dive, and SSN-697 slipped beneath the waves in pursuit of the *John Hay*.

White loathed the mission. He knew that the captain who destroyed an American submarine, even under orders, would be seen as a curiosity for the rest of his life—a freak, a cursed man, a bringer of bad luck.

There was another reason for hating the assignment. White was an admirer of Isaac Anderson, one of the few

273

navy officers willing to say so. Like Anderson, he was re-pelled by war and by killing.

He was thirty-nine, a former Rhodes scholar. Married. Two children. Both adopted.

Indianapolis dropped to 100 feet, still diving.

She was the most modern of attack submarines, carry-ing both conventional and nuclear torpedoes. She also carried SUBROC—a rocket that is fired from a torpedo tube, rises to the surface, flies to the vicinity of a target submarine, reenters the ocean, and destroys the enemy ship.

As *Indianapolis* continued her dive, Captain White was reminded of the sub's bizarre legacy. She had been named for the cruiser *Indianapolis,* which transported the first atomic bomb to the B-29 base at Tinian. A few days after delivering the bomb, cruiser *Indianapolis* was sunk by tor-pedo in waters that had been declared free of Japanese submarines. She went down with 399 men and left an-other 484 to perish from exposure and sharks as they clung to debris waiting for rescue.

The new *Indianapolis* dived to 800 feet.

Anderson felt a sense of excitement, exhilaration. The CIS came on:

INDIANAPOLIS REPORTS STRONGER SIGNALS. PRESUME
SUBMARINE. NO ID YET POSSIBLE.
 STAND BY.

He had opened a conference line to Washington, with the President and Bixby at the White House and Somer-ville and Combs at the Pentagon.

Mr. President," he told them, "we can't be sure what the *Indy* is tracking, but we must take every precaution. I'm launching all aircraft from the *Saratoga* to come to Captain White's aid. The Russians will pick up the launch. I suggest you let them know what we're doing."

"Fine," the President replied. "Fred, you get on that."

The Hot Line crackled with an urgent message to Mos-cow:

PREMIER ANDROPOV:

THE UNITED STATES NAVY REPORTS POSSIBLE CONTACT WITH THE USS JOHN HAY. WE ARE TAKING THE STRONGEST MEASURES TO DESTROY THIS RENEGADE. YOU WILL OBSERVE OUR OPERATIONS ON YOUR SATELLITE CAMERAS. OUR INTENTIONS TOWARD YOU ARE PEACEFUL.

The reply came back:

MR. PRESIDENT:

THE SOVIET UNION REGARDS ALL AMERICAN ACTION AS POTENTIALLY HOSTILE. WE ARE TAKING THE NECESSARY STEPS TO ENSURE OUR SAFETY.

CIS screens quickly reported that Soviet ships in the Atlantic were going to battle stations. Anderson ordered American aircraft to avoid flying near them. Then he made a decision that came straight from the gut. He decided to lead the *Saratoga*'s air group himself, to pilot a Viking in support of the *Indianapolis*. If the *John Hay* had to be sunk, it was his place to be there, to give the ultimate order. He went to the ready room and got into flight gear.

Indianapolis dived to 900 feet, her passive and active sonars probing the sea. The passive sonars listened for any sounds from the unidentified target. They heard nothing. The active sonars sent out pulses that struck the target and came back.

The pulses grew stronger, closer.

Gillespie knew. His sonar picked up the ship coming down from above. He knew by its sounds—its "signature"—that it was an attack sub of the Los Angeles class. Maybe it was the *Los Angeles* herself or the *Baton Rouge*. Or the *Indianapolis*.

He faced a fateful decision. He could remain silent and hope the attacker would lose him, or he could try to reach launch depth just below the surface and fire. He read the sonar signal, then read it again. The sub would not lose him. His decision was made. It might be suicide up near the surface, with the *Hay* pinpointed, but if missiles could be launched and nuclear war begun, it would be suicide with glory.

Gillespie ordered the engines started, the bow pointed up. He alerted his comrades to prepare for launch. Launch countdown commenced as the *John Hay* began its race to the surface. Gillespie knew he couldn't make it without fighting off the American sub.

The passive sonar aboard *Indianapolis* came to life. The *Hay*'s engines were clear, their signature unmistakable. The word went out to Anderson:

INDIANAPOLIS REPORTS CONTACT IDENTIFIED AS US SUBMARINE OF THE ETHAN ALLEN CLASS.

Anderson flashed the order back to White: "Sink her."

He climbed aboard the lead Viking on *Saratoga*'s flight deck, and moments later the plane bolted from the starboard catapult. Jet after jet followed in rapid, rhythmic order. Eighty-five planes flew off in a red Atlantic dawn as two American submarines prepared to fight it out under the sea.

24

White versus Gillespie. Both knew one had to die, along with his entire crew of more than 100 men.

The *Hay* kept rising. Gillespie turned her bow tubes toward the *Indianapolis*. He ordered two tubes loaded with Westinghouse Mk 48 Mod 2 antisubmarine torpedoes, the other two with Northrop submarine decoys.

He launched the decoys. They scurried around the deep, duplicating the sound patterns of full-sized submarines, their purpose being to confuse the *Indianapolis'* acoustic homing torpedoes.

Gillespie was ready.

So was White. His sonars showed a distance between the *Indianapolis* and the *Hay* of only 1,800 yards—too close to use nuclear warheads without destroying both ships, too close for SUBROC.

White's tubes were loaded with the same weapons as the *Hay*'s, and White now launched his decoys.

White came up to 400 feet, Gillespie to 300. White fired, and two torpedoes raced toward the *Hay,* their acoustic systems searching out the target. White immediately ordered the tubes reloaded. More decoys. More torpedoes.

The *Hay*'s sonar picked up the torpedoes coming at her, and Gillespie returned the fire. Now two torpedoes sped toward the *Indianapolis*.

Both captains maneuvered their ships violently in efforts to confound the sensors on the incoming weapons. Both fired more decoys, more torpedoes.

Streams of nervous sweat pouring down their faces,

White and Gillespie waited. The first torpedo from the *Indianapolis* homed in. It was 300 yards from the lurching *Hay*.

Two hundred. . . . One hundred. . . .

Then it suddenly veered to the left, hurtling past the sub and striking a decoy 130 yards away. The explosion rocked the *Hay,* but caused no damage.

Second torpedo, coming at the *Hay*. Strong. Straight. One hundred yards. . . . Fifty. . . .

It, too, swerved away, heading for another decoy, missing it, traveling harmlessly into the darkness.

Hay's torpedoes now shot toward the *Indianapolis*. The first came within eighty yards, then, inexplicably, blew up. The second slipped through the sea, but 110 yards from White's ship it veered off and struck a decoy in the distance.

The *Indianapolis*' next two torpedoes headed for their mark. The *Hay* was now 200 feet from the surface, and the launch countdown continued. Three missiles were armed and ready.

The third *Indianapolis* torpedo malfunctioned, missing by at least fifty yards. But the fourth was true. Gillespie watched it on his green sonarscope. It kept coming. It seemed unstoppable.

One hundred yards. . . . Fifty. . . . Twenty. . . .

Men in the control room clenched their teeth. A few prayed. Some wanted to scream.

Ten yards. . . .

Gillespie lurched his ship to port as the torpedo was upon him. It glanced off the hull, gyrated, continued another sixty yards in a spiraling downward dive, and exploded.

Captain White, stunned by failure, prepared to fire again, but the *Hay*'s next two torpedoes came at him. The first turned away, aiming for a decoy, tracking it, destroying it.

The second did not turn. It slipped through the chill Atlantic and struck the *Indianapolis* amidships.

Captain White and his men plunged to their deaths.

Anderson, flying the lead Viking, listened to battle reports relayed by Captain Ryan. Suddenly they stopped. Ryan had lost contact with the *Indianapolis*. Anderson waited, wondered. Four minutes later Ryan was back on the line. His message was terse: There had been a SECT alert.

The last time the Submarine Emergency Communications Transmitter had been used was when Richard Gillespie faked the sinking of the *Hay*. But Anderson knew this was no fake. He switched on his radio, connected by relay to Washington.

"Mr. President, are you there, sir?"

"I'm here," the President responded.

"Sir, the *Indianapolis* has been sunk."

"Oh, Jesus, no!"

"If the *Hay* has live missiles, she'll try to fire them now. We're going in."

Anderson was two minutes from the *John Hay*.

Gillespie's sonar picked up the dying *Indianapolis,* her shattered hulk fading into the deep. He resumed his missile countdown. The *Hay* was 100 feet under. Then fifty feet.

Forty seconds to launch. Target: New York City.

Anderson's planes fanned out. Sonobuoys were dropped into the sea and MAD detectors came on.

Thirty seconds to launch.

One Viking reported a contact. Other planes closed in.

Twenty seconds.

Strong contact. Sonobuoy. Definite submarine.

Ten seconds.

Gillespie watched his control panel.

Five seconds.

Launch.

The thump, then the tremendous *whoosh* as the Polaris left its tube. The shudder as thousands of gallons of sea water flooded the tube to equalize the pressure.

The missile lurched upward. Pilots above were stunned

to see it slice through the surface and ignite, a crackling flame trailing behind. It rose to 300 feet. Five hundred.

Two F-4 Phantoms broke formation, Lieutenant Wesley Reed of Spokane flying one, Lieutenant (jg) Sigmund Ellis of Chicago piloting the other. As they dived at the fast-rising Polaris, each fired two Sidewinder air-to-air missiles. The Sidewinders, trailing white smoke, converged on the Polaris like tiny ants attacking a lion. Sensors sought out the heat from its engine.

The first Sidewinder burst thirty feet from the rocket's tail. Shrapnel flew. The Polaris was punctured. It veered.

The second Sidewinder exploded fifteen feet away.

The Polaris spun out of control, its tail dropped off, and its fuel chamber blew up. It fell backward toward the sea.

As planes zipped in to sink the *Hay*, now clearly marked by sonobuoys and magnetic detectors, Gillespie prepared to launch again.

But the explosion of the Polaris had thrown the safety switches in its warhead, and as the rocket plunged downward, the warhead detonated.

A two-megaton nuclear fireball turned the ocean's surface to steam. It engulfed forty-six American planes, instantly turning them to molten metal and cremating their crews. It flipped a nearby Dutch freighter on end, sending it to the bottom without a trace.

In Washington the President of the United States watched his CIS screen in horror as the fireball erupted.

In the Soviet command center Gorshkov and Andropov also watched. Gorshkov turned slowly to Andropov, who was staring at his screen in numbed silence.

"Premier," he said, "they were telling the truth."

The explosion shook the sea below. The *John Hay*, still sufficiently protected by fifty feet of water to avoid direct destruction from the blast, spun into an uncontrolled dive. Crewmen flew around like paper clips. Some were killed as heads smashed against steel decks.

In his cabin Captain Lansing lunged at his guard,

ripped his pistol away, and shot him. Lansing then struggled down the reeling passageway toward the control room, joined by crewmen who had been liberated in the confusion.

Gillespie righted the ship and prepared a second launch.

Fifty seconds. . . .

Lansing burst into the control room, hit the deck, and took aim at Gillespie. He fired five times.

Gillespie stiffened, a questioning look in his eyes as blood spurted from his head and chest. He slumped to the deck, dead.

There was a furious, deafening exchange of gunfire as loyal members of the crew charged into the control room. Two were hit, but three of the five Crusade defenders were also hit. The last two, out of ammunition, finally surrendered.

Captain Lansing rushed to an instrument panel. He saw that the firing mechanism had been placed on AUTOMATIC and that the second Polaris was ready to launch. He flipped a red switch. The firing sequence stopped . . . at eight seconds.

Anderson survived the nuclear blast. His Viking, six miles away, had been flying at oblique angles to the Polaris, and though temporarily blinded by the flash, he recovered sufficiently to regroup his remaining thirty-nine planes.

The *Hay* was now a clear sonar target. *He* would sink her. He turned left fifty degrees for the final run in, 300 feet off the water, distance to target 4.3 miles. Then the radio crackled from Washington. It was Ryan.

"Admiral, we have a message from the *Hay!*"

Anderson continued his run as the *Hay*'s transmission was relayed. He heard:

"This is Captain Lansing of the USS *John Hay*. I have retaken command of the ship. I repeat. This is Captain Alan Lansing of the USS *John Hay*. . . ."

The President broke into Anderson's line. "Andy, you hear that?"

"Yes, sir!"

"We're okay!"

"No, sir!" He continued his run.

"What do you mean?"

"Sir," Anderson replied, almost shouting into his headset, "we have no way of knowing if that message is legitimate. We don't even know if Lansing is part of the plot."

"Well . . . what the hell do we do?"

"Sir, we must sink the ship!"

Somerville cut in from his Pentagon office. "You're going to kill those boys?"

"We have no choice," Anderson responded. "Mr. President, they can launch at any time, and we might not be able to stop the missile. We *must* make the sacrifice. We cannot take the chance!"

The President was momentarily confused, disoriented.

"Sir," Anderson asked, "may I fire?"

There was a tense pause.

"Yes."

The answer was faint and frightened.

Anderson's right hand reached for a trigger connected to an Mk 46 torpedo in his bomb bay. The warhead was nuclear. Anderson felt a sickness, a sense of revulsion, but a certainty that he was right.

Lansing gave the order to surface, and the *John Hay* rose to forty feet, then thirty. He kept sending his message: "I have retaken command. . . ."

Twenty-five feet.

Anderson slid in overhead. He squeezed the trigger.

The 512-pound torpedo dropped from the bomb bay, slapped the sea, and dived underwater. Anderson gunned his engines, pulling up sharply to avoid the coming blast. The Mk 46 raced toward the *Hay,* its sensors homing in on the sub's noises.

It struck.

The blast measured one kiloton—one-twentieth the size

of the explosion that destroyed Hiroshima. It erupted through the surface like a giant tidal wave.

The *John Hay* dissolved. Microscopic fragments and droplets of liquid melted into the deep.

25

The end of the crisis meant freedom for Julia Anderson and the other relatives of the CRITIC group. They had been told once before they were going home—when CRITIC believed the emergency had passed with the sinking of Soviet sub 343. At that time they had undergone a series of medical tests and debriefings, only to be detained again when Washington learned that the renegade sub was actually American. Now, after a final day of tests and debriefings, they were flown by helicopter to Andrews Air Force Base.

All but Julia went home. She was sped to the Pentagon, where she was met by a navy commander. He took her to the stage entrance of the auditorium.

She saw her husband sitting alone next to the podium, a single sheet of paper in his lap. He was being introduced by the Assistant Secretary of Defense for Public Affairs. He faced a room filled with reporters, glaring lights, and clicking cameras.

Anderson saw Julia enter. He smiled slightly, then turned again to the front, hoping she would understand.

The Assistant Secretary finished his introduction. Anderson rose, walked two steps to the left, and placed his paper on the podium. He looked around the room. It seemed only hours earlier that he had addressed the Women's Peace Alliance from this same spot. He cleared his throat and began reading:

"Several days ago the navy announced the loss of the USS *John Hay*. Now I must regretfully tell you that a second American submarine has gone down in the Atlantic.

The USS *Indianapolis* was lost after the inadvertent detonation of two nuclear warheads.

"In addition, a number of navy men have been killed in related incidents.

"These losses occurred during our recent worldwide alert. They were a direct result of operations that I planned, supervised, and helped execute. I take full responsibility for the tragic outcome.

"Under the circumstances, I believe the best interests of the navy would be served by my departure. This afternoon I handed to the President my resignation as chief of naval operations, effective immediately.

"I would like to thank all of you who have been so kind to me in your coverage of naval affairs. I wish you good luck."

Anderson turned and walked quietly off the stage. He swallowed hard. It had not been easy being the scapegoat.

He knew some details of the crisis would come out. That was inevitable since thousands of sailors and civilians had been involved. But he had taken the blame to protect the secret still held by a small group—that the United States Navy had lost control of a Polaris submarine. If that became known, Anderson realized, it would shatter confidence in the delicate system of deterrence that had prevented nuclear war for twenty-five years.

He reached Julia at the side of the stage. "It's all right," she told him. They shook hands with other officers, said a few brief farewells, then left the Pentagon.

Isaac Anderson had won his last victory as a naval officer.

He had defeated the North Star Crusade.